Becoming Hattie Mae

A Hardscrabble Life in an Appalachian Holler

CAROL GUTHRIE HEILMAN

Black Rose Writing | Texas

ISBN: 978-1-68513-668-0
LIBRARY OF CONGRESS CONTROL NUMBER: 2025936960
PUBLISHED BY BLACK ROSE WRITING
www.blackrosewriting.com

Printed in the United States of America
Suggested Retail Price (SRP) $22.95

Becoming Hattie Mae is printed in Book Antiqua

*As a planet-friendly publisher, Black Rose Writing does its best to eliminate unnecessary waste to reduce paper usage and energy costs, while never compromising the reading experience. As a result, the final word count vs. page count may not meet common expectations.

In honor of

Charles Ison Guthrie, my Daddy. 1918-2011

A gentle, hard-working Kentucky coal miner

He carried my first published stories around in his pockets and shared them with anyone willing to read them.

"As someone who fell in love with author Carol Heilman's character of Agnes Hopper, I am excited that she has created another enchanting tale of young Hattie Mae set in the backdrop of the Appalachian Mountains. The author's delightful gift of storytelling will keep you turning the pages as you follow this young girl's journey to *Becoming Hattie Mae*."
—**Andrea Merrell, freelance editor and author of *Praying for the Prodigal, Marriage: Make It or Break It*, and *Murder of a Manuscript***

"In coal mining Appalachia, books ignite big dreams for Hattie Mae Sizemore, a gutsy girl poised at the threshold of adulthood. Hattie's love of reading alarms her Pa. Her hardworking father fears losing everything he values if his children abandon the life that has sustained his people for generations. His attempt to squelch Hattie Mae's education draws us into a fractured family living in a mountain holler. Will Hattie leave the only home she has ever known to find her purpose in a whole new world? The word impossible whispers in her ear."
—**Mary Eaddy, author of *The Oaks of McCord***

"*Becoming Hattie Mae* delves into the lives of an Appalachian, coal-mining family in eastern Kentucky that is forced to confront the consequences of a secret assault. This compelling story unfolds with a mountain vernacular that makes the dialogue rich and satisfying."
–**Ann Brubaker Greenleaf Wirtz, author *Our Lives in Verse, Everyday Poetry*, as well as many newspaper articles**

ACKNOWLEDGMENTS

Thank You for the journey.

You
Listened to early, awful drafts.
Were kind with your critiques.
Encouraged and pushed me forward.
Opened my eyes to a better way.
Gave me the gift of your friendship.
I could have never dreamed of becoming a writer
Without you.

Your talents continue to amaze me.

From the Midlands of SC many years ago:
Carrie McGray, Carol Williams and Betsy Thorne.

To the NC Mountains: Cindy Sproles, director of Asheville
Christian Writers' Conference and award-wining author of
Appalachian novels. Eddie Jones, publisher, and Andrea
Merrell, editor, who saw potential in my first book, *Agnes
Hopper Shakes Up Sweetbriar.*

And in Hendersonville, NC: Ann Wirtz,
Leanna Sain, Karin Wooten, Sunny Lockwood and
Betsy Thorne.

Then to the SC Lowcountry: Jo Ana Finger, Tammy Jenkins,
Doug Freeman, Ginny Foard, Mary Eaddy, Vicki Bernie,
Susan Katz, Eliot Tuckerman, Nancy Blakeley and Rob Garzilli.

And thank you Ann Tatlock, a gifted author and editor who
believed in Hattie's story.

Finally, a **special thank you** to the readers who hopefully will enjoy my characters, both good and bad, almost as much as I loved writing about them.

I am eternally grateful and thank the Lord for each one of you.

Red Bird Mission, is a real place in the mountains of Bell County, Kentucky. It was established in 1921 by the Evangelical Church at the head-waters of the Red Bird River.

The river was named for Chief Red Bird of the Cherokee Indian Tribe. The land was made available by the Knuckles family of Beverly, Kentucky. Timber and labor for building were contributed by local citizens.

Beginning with teachers eager to educate unschooled children, Red Bird Mission has continued to respond to the needs of the community with resources, aid, and love.

Red Bird Mission's moto has always been: *"Enter to learn, leave to serve."*

Becoming Hattie Mae

CHAPTER ONE

The Gypsies

Ashworth Coal Camp, eastern Kentucky
Summertime 1929

Before the crack of dawn, Granny pressed a mug of chicory into my hands, the only coffee we had these days. It smelled like tobacco smoke and tasted bitter. I carried it to the back porch where Papa sat on a bench. He finished tightening his boot laces and looked up. His green eyes, the same color as mine, turned stone cold. He reached for the cup, his fingernails blackened from coal grime.

"It's time you come to grips with the facts. School's over for you and your sister. You're not goin' back come September. There ain't no need . . ."

Granny give me a sideways hug as she moved around me. She eased down the back steps, groaning from her stiffness, headed to the privy. I wanted to holler *Wait! Stay here beside me.*

Instead, I studied my feet and held my breath. Loetta didn't know yet. She always slept as long as possible, curled up in bed with our baby sister, Jewel.

Papa thumped his cup on the bench and stood. Overcome with a coughing fit, he turned away. It seemed his insides would come out as he spit into the wispy fog. He wiped his mouth across the back of his hand. "Get any notion of goin' back to the camp school outta your head. You got no need for more learning. Neither does Loetta. You girls gonna tend to things 'round here like you was meant to. Your Ma and your Granny needs both of ya. You know what I'm saying?" His sour breath hung in the air.

"Yes, Papa," I whispered to the damp porch floor.

He picked up his coffee and swallowed a gulp. "Look at me."

I lifted my head. Pushed my unruly hair out of my face. "Yes. I know." A lump grew in my throat, and I willed myself not to cry. Light shined from inside onto the scar across his nose, on a piece of his sickness caught in his beard.

"Go help your Ma. Pack my dinner bucket."

He was done talkin' to me. I turned toward the kitchen, opened the screen door and my stomach lurched at the scent of biscuits brownin' and fatback frying. I grabbed his miner's bucket, done what I was told. Mama looked up from stirrin' gravy, her pale face drawed in tight, but she never spoke.

When Papa set at the table, she smacked his plate down in front of him. He reached for her hand, but she jerked it away. He ate in a hurry. I'd filled the bucket's bottom part with fresh water. Biscuits, fatback and leftover sweet potatoes lay in the middle section and a lid held it all together. He lifted the handle. The bucket thumped against his leg as he moved to the stove. He stopped behind Mama, brushed her long, black hair aside and kissed her cheek. She caught her breath and watched him leave. "Oh, Isom Sizemore," she said as she touched her face.

Mama sighed and turned to me. Her normally milky-white face had flushed red and her dark eyes had filled to overflowing. "Hattie, you and Loetta ain't got no choice but to . . ."

I jumped up, rushed out the back door and headed to the privy. I always figured Mama would never stand up against Papa. Now I'd witnessed it for my own self. I passed Granny on the porch steps, but I never slowed down.

I knowed the day was comin' when our schoolin' would end, but not as sudden as a clap of thunder on a clear day. When I told my younger sister, she stomped off fuming mad. I feared she would only make things worse.

I couldn't abide thoughts of my life without school, without them books, especially story books. They never failed to reach out and take me along with 'em, to places beyond these hills, to places where folks surely lived in wondrous ways.

•   •   •

After breakfast, I always helped Granny get ready for her day. I never seen it as a chore, but a pleasure. Today, Papa's words on the back porch swirled in my head as I rushed into the front room, where Granny slept in a narrow bed pushed against the wall.

"I'll never hold a book in my hands again. For the rest of my born days," I mumbled as I thrashed Granny's quilt onto her bed. She cut her eyes at me, but she never said nothing.

She slipped her dress over her head and waited for me since them little buttons give her fits. I thumped her pillow into its place and went to her. My hands trembled, but at last every button was in its hole. I then stood behind Granny and brushed her long white hair. It felt as soft as a baby's. Mama called it angel hair.

"Papa's declared I'll never go to school again. Ever." I twisted her hair into a bun at the back of her neck.

"Not so tight, Hattie."

I eased up as she give me hair pins to hold her bun in place.

She turned around. Her cloudy blue eyes turned misty. She reached for my hands.

"Now ain't the time to stir your Pa up more'n he already is. Patience, child. Once he settles down, maybe he'll listen to me. If he don't, remember one thing—your life ain't gonna always be like it is now. You're comin' up on fifteen, near about grown up. Soon you can decide things for yourself."

I pulled away. "Mama said the same. What about Loetta? And what if me becoming growed-up makes no matter?"

Before she could answer, I left her and stomped into the kitchen, grabbed the empty coal bucket and headed out the back door. Mama picked beans in the hillside garden while nearby Loetta kept Jewel from toddlin' off somewheres she had no business going.

I thumped down the steps, searched through the pile of coal on the ground. Little pieces made starting a fire in the cookstove a sight easier, larger pieces kept the fire going. Satisfied I'd gathered plenty, I returned inside. Breakfast dishes waited for me. Mama said, "We'd talk later." No need. No need for Granny to speak up for me. Papa always had the last word.

•   •   •

When Saturday arrived, me and Granny headed to a rag sale. She had asked me to keep her company, but I knowed she weren't as spry as she used to be and might need my help. Loetta begged to come along. Mama said a bushel of beans waited for her on the back porch. It pleasured me to have Granny to myself.

We had moved beyond our yard gate and nearly out of his sight when he spied us.

"Hattie Mae Sizemore, you got no business going," Papa hollered from the front porch. "Our family don't cotton to charity." Silence. Then he added, "You'd best listen to me, girl." I never looked his way and played like I never heard him. Iffen Granny heard Papa, she never let on. We passed a clump of sweet-smellin' laurels, full of pink and white blooms and alive with bees.

We hastened our steps. I took Granny's arm and urged her to move faster. Even so, Papa's anger thumped on my back.

Before long, Granny stopped. She pulled out a pocket knife and a plug of tobacco and cut a small piece. She tucked it inside her cheek, sighed most powerfully and shooed me to go ahead.

I skittered down our mountain in the morning fog. I never stopped 'til in spittin' distance of the swinging bridge. Worry swelled up inside me. The best clothes would be claimed 'fore we reached Arjay's schoolhouse. What difference did it make anyhow? Papa said I'd not wear any store-bought, secondhand clothes. Would that be the end of it? Like the end of school? The end of books to hold in my hands? To read until the stories lived inside me?

Granny had her head set on going to this rag-sale. The Women's Missionary Union of Richmond, Kentucky had sent dresses, pants, shirts and coats. Arjay's teacher, Miss Mayes, had set her head on buying a new stovepipe, in spite of their coal company declarin' the old one good enough.

"Yes sir, she's one plucky woman," Granny had said. "Stood up to them company men and give 'em a piece of her mind. 'Old one's good enough.' Humph. Good for coughing up smoke and spewing cinder dust whenever a fire's lit. Oughtta be a law."

Plucky Miss Mayes hailed from clear over in Knoxville, Tennessee, and Granny had friended her right off. Papa called her a foreigner. He had no use for anyone whose people weren't from these hollers. I decided Granny knowed best.

Instead of runnin' across the swinging bridge high above the rushing creek, like I hankered to do, I peered up the trail I'd run down. Granny moved slowly down the footpath. I plopped onto a big rock and waited. The air had turned hot and smother-some. The birds hushed their morning chatter.

Noise from the other side of the creek rised up louder and louder. It pounded in my chest. I ran to the bridge and looked across to the dirt road runnin' through Ashworth. Metal struck against metal. Wood creaked and complained as something heavy inched closer. A goat bleated. A clangin' bell rang through the holler.

Sunlight poured into the clearing. A house on wheels tugged into sight, swaying over rocks, dipping in and out of holes. A passel of scruffy dogs charged out of the woods. Chickens squawked and scattered in all directions. Them dogs run in packs through the camps causin' trouble. The dogs left off chasing the chickens to snarl and nip at this strange contraption. Until skinny Willie Seabolt come walkin' along. He throwed rocks at the varmints and they yelped their way back to wherever they come from.

"Much obliged," a deep voice called out.

Willie threw his hand in the air. A gust of wind took his scruffy hat and tossed it down the road. Giggles flew from me as he chased it. He couldn't hear me, yet I clamped my hand over my mouth. He ran on and his hair, as dark as coal, lifted from his back. At last, he claimed his hat, dusted it off and stuck it back on his head. Then he sauntered on down the road like he had no care in this world. Willie had a cocky swagger worse than anybody I'd ever knowed. He also had buck teeth, but I never faulted him for something he couldn't do nothin' about. Like my wild hair the color of applesauce. Or the freckles coverin' my face. Wishing they'd disappear made no never mind.

Jim declared Willie was sweet on me. My brother liked nothing better than to tease me with foolish talk.

Willie was a runner for the moonshiners in these parts. He could fetch supplies, deliver messages, or serve as a lookout for the dreaded revenuers set on destroying ever moonshiner's still. Willie could slip over these mountains or into or out of our hollers same as a spirit. For certain he roamed abroad day or night and he'd not be seen or heard in all his travels. Unless he allowed it. Granny chuckled when I told her this, but she never denied it as truth.

The house on wheels pulled to a stop. Gypsies. I'd seen a whole passel of 'em when they passed through Ashworth coal camp last spring. Granny said they was headed to a gathering in West Virginia, gypsies from all over meetin' over there. They had looked ragged, dirty and beaten down.

This house looked mighty fine. Painted red and green and trimmed in gold with a curved roof and curtained windows, it could've rode off the pages of Cinderella's picture book. Only two mangy-looking mules pulled it instead of white horses. A scraggly goat tied to the back of the wagon hung its head. Its clanging bell slowed to a soft clinking.

With a flash of her ruffled skirt, a woman turned around on the wagon seat and slipped inside. A dark-skinned man with long black hair jumped down to the road. He wore a puffed-up shirt and he'd stuffed his britches into tall boots. Reminded me of a pirate I seen once in a book. He swept his wide-brimmed hat clear to the ground as he bowed to Sophie Tate sweeping her wretched dirt yard. Her white hair flew about her as she bent to her task. Even so, the gypsy man swung his arm toward the pots and pans strung along the sides of the wagon.

The old woman raised her head. She stiffened up like a fence post, shook her broom and fussed at him from her twisted mouth. The man nodded, squared his hat onto his head and climbed back up to his seat. A boy appeared in a window. I could hardly believe my eyes. He hugged a big book close to his chest. He looked up and waved. Someone jerked the curtains shut.

Sophie stood on her porch and watched them go as a naked baby tottered out of the house next door. A girl snatched it back inside. Not another solitary person appeared. Nearly two dozen pitiful camp houses had been strung along the creek bank years ago. Each one as run down and gray as the next. The only sign of life was smoke from a few chimneys and chickens peckin' in the dirt. A patch of ground fog settled where the sun had been.

Sophie turned and marched inside slamming her door like a rifle shot.

The man's deep voice rose in song as he rode away. His foreign words filled the tiny holler and echoed off the mountains. The sounds of his voice, the goat, the bell, his wares and his wagon soon disappeared.

Seemed the whole world held its breath along with me. No birdsong amongst the laurel. No creature moved about in the woods. Even the swift-running creek seemed quieter somehow. The gypsy man and the boy with his book had stolen the sun and the magic away from this place.

I didn't know nothin' about these people, seen as detestable outsiders by some folks including Papa. All of a sudden, I had a yearning like I'd never had before. It rose inside me as sure as sap rises in springtime. Sudden like, it knocked me off stride.

Where was they going takin' their house along? They'd see places I'd never see, maybe learn the ways of people who were not their own. Of all unimaginable things, they carried along books, or at least one book. I couldn't imagine the wonder of it all.

"Hattie. Come help."

Granny, clean out of breath, leaned all trembly on me. We swayed across the footbridge. I ignored the urge to jump and bounce along, makin' the old boards cry like a squeaky fiddle.

Once on the other side, I eased her down on a log.

"You certain you're up to this?" I asked. Sweat had run down her face and neck like she had chopped a garden full of weeds. I took off her bonnet and fanned her. Her white hair flew about as she grabbed her head covering.

"As certain as my name's Ethel Marie and your Momma slipped a nickel into your pocket." She pushed herself upright and latched onto my arm.

We continued on down the dirt road to Arjay coal camp. I hoped a flowered dress waited in a barrel of castoff clothes just for me. But if I come home with any dress, would Papa let me wear it?

•   •   •

We moseyed along. The sun beat upon our heads. Not a word had passed between us since I'd spied them gypsies. Granny hummed a tune of her own making. Something she did whenever she had right smart on her mind.

She stopped and turned to me resting her bony hands on my shoulders. "You're not to go with 'em if they should offer to take you away from here. These mountains has a powerful pull on us and you'd best pay attention. This here's our home and always will be." Her words, strong and steady, was like a commandment from the Bible.

"How did you . . ."

"I seen how you pined after them gypsies. They ain't our kind of people."

Granny and me had never been crossways with each other. I weren't about to start now.

"Yes'um," I mumbled dropping my head.

She lifted my chin. "You might have to leave us one day, but iffen you do, make certain you come to terms with what you're leaving behind. And you ain't no gypsy."

I nodded. She figured the matter had been settled, but I knowed better. Them gypsies had stirred something inside of me, a restless feeling I could not explain. Is this how my brother felt? Even though only fourteen, Jim had reasons to leave our holler. Leave before he had to work a vein of coal deep inside the earth for the rest of his life. He would strike out on his own one day. Iffen I was to walk out of these hills, I couldn't conjure up any way it could come to pass or where I might go.

I wouldn't speak of the gypsies again to my dear granny. I tucked the sight of 'em inside myself for safe keeping. I wouldn't forget 'em or the boy holdin' onto his book for dear life. I weren't no gypsy. But iffen some person, gypsy or no, was to offer me a way out of this holler I was bound tight to, would I, could I, take 'em up on it?

CHAPTER TWO

The Treasure Box

At long last we stopped at the wood's edge outside Arjay. A one-room schoolhouse, looking sad and worn out, sat in a clearing of tall pines. A strong wind could lift it up and carry it to kingdom come. Mostly women and children climbed its crooked steps while others left the schoolyard carrying armloads of clothes. One woman stopped and slipped her blue, rag-sale dress over her old one. She then plopped a red-feathered hat on her head and danced barefooted on the dusty road. A little girl wore a big wool coat on a day already hotter'n blazes.

"Ain't gonna be nothin' left for us" I said, feeling like a bag of grumps. "We've spent forever and a day getting here."

"The Lord knows what we have need of. Wait and see." Granny sputtered her words then spit a brown stream into a weed patch. She reached inside her dress, pulled out a hanky, and wiped her mouth. Her few teeth was as dark as the tobacco she chewed.

"How come I can't hurry up and see?"

Granny chuckled and shook her head. Our feet stirred the dust as I urged her on.

Once inside I had to swallow, "I done told you so." The only clothes left was ones not even a tramp would claim. A gray dress had no sleeves or buttons and a sash had been torn off. A brown dress had patches all over it. A stack of filthy men's pants stunk to the high heavens. Appeared we'd drag ourselves back home empty-handed.

"Lookie here." Granny pointed to a pile of hefty flour sacks stacked on the floor. She declared they had once carried flour to kitchens in hotels or in bakeries. I couldn't conjure up such places. I figured she'd make us a passel of kitchen towels or aprons and said so. "For certain," Granny said, "but not before sewing you a dress."

She shook out a sack of dancing girls twirling amongst a shower of red roses. I'd never seen anything so pretty. A picture and name of a flourmill was stamped on one side. Best Flour of Kansas. "That'll soon wash away and you'll see nothing but them flowers and dancin' girls," Granny promised.

We found other sacks, some with small flowers, others checkered, for my sisters. Granny bargained with Miss Mayes for my nickel. She then added a spool of thread when she seen we had no more money.

"Thank ye kindly," Granny said. She turned to me with a glint in her eyes. "This'll keep me busy and out of trouble for a while. Your Pa can't grouse about no brought-on dress. I'm fixin' to stitch it up my own self."

Maybe so, but for certain he'd not like me wearing naked girls all over my body. Granny informed me them ballerinas jumped and danced in tiny costumes for rich people. It seemed the world was full of wonderments.

Granny headed outside to rest on the schoolhouse steps. She said for me to fetch her a mess of quilting squares since the sign on the barrel said *Free*. I stirred up calico prints searching for the prettiest colors. Lo and behold, all my stirring uncovered a tiny book. I lifted it up and looked it over. "*The Treasure Box*," I whispered. It had a faded blue cover with black shadow figures marching up a hill. Each person carried a book and I wondered where they might be going. It had to be someplace magical. Tattered and taped together the book had hitched a ride from the Women's Missionary Union. I figured it weren't no accident and meant to be mine.

"I do declare," Granny said when I showed her. A grin spread over her face.

I carried my book home inside my flour sack, cradled in them quilting squares. It felt as dear as a baby bird, like a living thing to me. Would Papa let me keep it? I begged the Lord to make it so.

In the afternoon, after Granny rested a spell, she split my sack open and held it against me turning me every which way. She marked the cloth with a number two pencil stub. Then she spread it out on the kitchen table and snipped it into pieces—a skirt, a top with places marked for button holes in the front, short sleeves, and even a collar. She took everything to the porch, settled into the swing with her lap full of half-naked girls. I fetched her sewing basket.

She bent over her work. Her crooked fingers flew more like young, nimble ones. Mama sat in a straight-back chair nearby and commenced peeling taters. The strings of morning glories, with their end of the day tight blooms, danced in the breeze. Cooler air brought the sweet smell of honeysuckle from our fence.

Loetta plopped onto the steps. She turned her face to the clouds hurrying across the sky. Since she had turned thirteen, she had become even more of a pest. I counted a handful of freckles scattered across her nose while my entire face was covered with 'em. Loe said no boy would look at my freckled face twice and why didn't I take to wearin' a bonnet like Granny?

One day I answered her. "Humph. I'll have you know I like my freckles. Ever one. They is a sign of . . ."

"Of what?" Loe smirked with a toss of her long pigtails.

"Of gumption! That's what." That's all I could come up with at the time. I hated my freckles. Ever last one.

In the yard, squeals come from Jewel, nearly two years old and always on the go. Most likely she'd spotted a blue-tailed skink, her favorite, and had took out after it.

Granny sewed my straight-pinned dress with tiny stitches. She figured it'd take nearabout a week before she finished. She had dreamed of one of them fancy foot-pedal machines. More likely a blizzard would sweep into our holler on July fourth.

I opened my book and commenced reading to my family, except for Jim. He had gone off fishin' again, way up another holler. It seemed he stayed gone more than he hung around home these days. When he did appear, he nearly always brung us a string of fish.

Even though fourteen years old, he was small for his age. The perfect size for a *breaker* boy, Papa had said. Mama declared he weren't gonna have nothing to do with mining coal. Not ever.

Many a boy trudged to the mines every morning and drug themselves home every evening looking like stooped old men. The *breaker boys* would sit on wooden seats for ten hours a day hammering large chunks of coal into pieces. The worst part was picking out the slate or rock before sending the coal into "clean" coal bins. Boys would often leave work with their fingers cut or bleeding. Some even lost fingers or other body parts caught in gears or conveyor belts. I didn't know how Jim had escaped such work. But it pleasured me to no end he had.

•   •   •

I kept reading to my family gathered on the porch. Loe squeezed herself between me and Granny. She leaned over my arm and her lips moved as I read. It seemed all of us loved each and every poem and story. Even Jewel gave up chasing critters. She pressed her dark, curly head against Mama's side, sucked her thumb and took in every word. Soon as Mama put her knife aside, Jewel climbed onto her lap, but my baby sister kept her eyes fixed on my book.

After Papa come home from the mines and washed up on the back porch, we ate our supper of soup beans, cornbread, and fried taters. Me and Loe cleaned up the kitchen. Then everybody, except Papa, come out to the porch again. I took up my book to read where I'd left off. When Papa joined us, my insides quivered.

He leaned against the front door frame, a scowl writ across his face. He grumbled about them outsider's words coming into our holler, into our home, into our minds. Granny turned her sharp eyes on him. Mama reached up from her chair and laid her hand on his arm, but he wrenched free and stomped into the house. The front screen door banged behind him. The back screen door done the same.

A stormy tune rose from his harmonica, swept from the back porch clear though the house, quarrellin' with my reading voice.

"That'll do for now, Hattie," Mama said with a sigh. "Best put it away. Not much daylight left nohow."

Loetta flounced across the porch and down the steps. "Papa ain't nothin' but pure mean." My sister throwed open the yard gate and kept going down the mountain. She'd come back. She feared haints roamed about in the dark.

Granny put her sewing aside and pulled me close. Jewel fussed and whined until Mama started playin' pat-a-cake with her.

Loetta had spoken truth. Papa was mean, but there had to be a cause. He seen the book as our ruination, the same evil as any foreigner brung us. I never knowed why. For certain he never trusted anyone or anything turned different to our way of thinkin' or living. Outsiders. All lumped together in one pile. Them "do-gooders" sending us clothes or books or quilting squares was as hateful to him as them revenuers looking to destroy ever still tucked back in ever holler in the whole county. Or them big-time coal operators, most from up north somewhere. They had no misgivings about sending men or boys into the dark belly of the earth. They thought nothin' of fixin' the scales to their advantage when time came to weigh the tons of coal the miners dug. As long as they could squeeze out a profit for themselves, nothin' or nobody mattered.

I hugged my book close, stood to go inside, and eyed Mama then Granny. "How could stories and poems do nothin' but bring us pleasure? Why is it Papa's set against me havin' such a book? Didn't the Lord hisself tell us to be joyful?"

The only sounds come from the tree frogs and crickets. Mama's dark eyebrows raised up on her pale face. She shot Granny a look. They knowed why, and time had passed for one or the other to tell me.

After Papa turned in for the night, Granny lent me her pencil. I added my name to the Spring Hill Library card in the back of my book. Right below Mary Elizabeth Withers. Hattie Mae Sizemore, Ashworth, Kentucky, 1929. I erased Mary Elizabeth so you could hardly see her name at all, and I marked through the printed words of Spring Hill Library. Now the book truly belonged to me. I seen it as the first of hundreds of books.

I sat alone at the kitchen table, lost in my thoughts, the house quiet and dark. Then Loetta appeared. She stood by my side. "Whatcha gonna do, Hattie? About your book? About no more schooling? What can we do?"

"I ain't figured it out yet. Go on back to bed. I'm gonna talk to Granny."

Loe grumbled and stomped away. I feared she would stir the whole family, but Papa's snoring had settled into a rhythm. A screech owl called from the woods. I left the table, moved into a patch of moonlight and eased over to Granny's narrow bed where she slept in the corner of our front room. Jim's bed creaked from across the same room. He turned in his sleep and sighed.

Granny raised her hand to mine. "I figured you'd come. I was waiting." She patted her bed and scooted over. I sat down, comforted by the scent of her lavender dusting powder. She slipped her arms around my waist. I leaned to her ear.

"I got to know why Papa is dead set against us goin' back to school, not allowin' me or Loe the pleasure of even one book. I see why he hates them revenuers and them coal company operators, but a story book ain't gonna do nobody no harm."

Granny touched my face. "It ain't easy to tell you or easy to understand, but I'll try my level best. Your Papa's scared."

I shook my head. "No he ain't. Papa ain't scared of nothing."

Granny stroked my head. "Ahh . . . Books can change folks. Make 'em look at things like they never done before. Might even turn a person against the family, against their birthin' place. Cause 'em to yearn for things beyond these hills. Books can do that. Gypsies can do that. Your Papa's trying to protect you, keep you girls the same as you've always been, safe, in this holler."

"He's wrong. He can't keep me here iffen I ain't willing. And I ain't no child."

"Right or wrong he's gonna try. His own Ma walked away, left a good husband and six children. Your Pa, the oldest, only nine years old. By the time he was ten his Pa had died. Some said he grieved hisself to death. That's when your Pa become a miner to put food on the table. Back when the family lived near Harlan."

"How come I never knowed this?"

Some cats commenced fighting underneath the house. Their hollering and hissing hushed our talk until one of 'em was run off.

"How come nobody told me?" I asked again.

Granny shifted in her bed. The night air had turned damp and cool, and I pulled the covers over her arms. "Most likely you would've knowed iffen we'd stayed up in Harlen with our kin, but we come up to Ashworth, your Pa lookin' for work. And well, your Ma and me decided no need to burden any child with such sorrow. So we kept it to ourselves."

"I ain't no child now. I'm near about grown."

"For shore. Hard to believe you'll soon turn fifteen, standing on the edge of being a woman, and a mighty comely one at that."

I could hardly take in her words about a granny I never knowed. What did her leavin' her husband and all her young'uns have to do with me? "Tell me why she left," I whispered, wanting to know, but fearing to hear. Granny made room for me. I turned, stretched out beside her and snuggled close, her warm breath on my back.

"A feller come into them hollers from Washington. Government man, educated, sent to teach 'ignorant' folks the right way to live. Brung stacks of books, including science ones filled with lies. Said we come from monkeys instead of us being the good Lord's young'uns. This man caused an uproar I can tell you. He spoke in the churches and the schools until one day he up and disappeared. Talk was some of the men either run him off or killed him. Not long after, she left. Right or wrong the foreigner, and the books he brung with him, got the blame. I expect his way with words turned her head. Nobody's certain."

Papa hated books, as well as foreigners, but knowing why didn't help. Granny's words hung in the dark like a haint. I lay still and quiet beside her, but my thoughts tied themselves into knots.

Granny's breathing turned heavy with sleep. I eased from her bed, stood and tucked the worn quilt around her. A screech owl cried out again. Our two hounds settled into their places underneath the house as the sound of katydids growed louder. I tiptoed to my room, climbed into bed beside my sisters. I slipped my book underneath my pillow. Before long words from *The Treasure Box* danced in my head—one poem in particular.

A little shiny box am I,
And treasures, vast and rare,
I hold beneath my lid for one,
Whose name is written there.

And that meant me. Hattie Mae Sizemore.

My heart pined for a book to call my own. I couldn't abide Papa's fractious ways much longer. But could I, would I, find a way to leave my own kin and these hills I loved? The idea burned in my chest. It also whispered in my ear. *Impossible*.

CHAPTER THREE

My Ruination

Days drug by until June slipped into July. As the sun dropped behind the ridgeline, Papa huffed his way up the back steps. He clunked his empty dinner pail by the kitchen door and flopped into a straight-back chair. Before comin' home, he'd scrubbed hisself good at our camp's bathhouse. He wore his clean, threadbare pants and shirt on a Wednesday, commonplace only at the end of his workweek. Mama never questioned him. I didn't ask why he weren't headed to the mines come morning.

Papa could never shed the black underneath his fingernails or the coal dust in his neck and eye creases. I studied him, and laid my hand on *The Treasure Box*, open on the bench beside me.

Jim eased into the house without a string of fish, not even one small brim. His mop of red hair fell forward as he set a bucket of kindling by the cookstove. Then he propped his banjo into a corner. He'd fashioned it out of a cigar box two years ago and he had taught hisself to coax a decent tune out of it. "Granny's gone to the privy. Said she'll be a spell and not to wait on her."

I turned to Jewel and recollected a story from my book. I knowed better. I reckon playing like the wee woman talking to the king had took over.

"Hattie," Papa hollered, making me jump to my feet. My book slapped the floor. "I'm gonna feed your damn book to the stove one of these days. Learn you to tend to things you was meant to." He struck the table with his fist.

Loe's fork flew into her lap. She didn't move. Mama stopped slicing tomatoes and turned, her dark eyes looking. She laid down her knife, reached for a plate of cornbread and clunked it onto the table. Jim passed by me and picked up my book. He slid it beside the flour sifter and shut the cabinet door. I hurried to Mama's side. She handed me a big bowl of soup beans. Brimming full, I set it down careful like and slid back onto the bench seat. My insides quivered.

Granny stumbled as she come inside, but she caught herself. Jim helped her sit at the table. "You alright?" Mama asked. She nodded, but her face had drained of any color.

We eat our supper with little talking, though Jewel babbled on as always. Even Jim weren't his usual self. His blue eyes never danced with stories about a wondrous waterfall he'd come across, or giant ferns as tall as he was. Only later I'd learn of a graveyard he'd seen without nary a name of those buried there, piles of rocks as markers. He'd stopped there to pick his banjo awhile.

• • •

Long about sundown, Papa whistled for Colonel and Neverblue. He went off into the woods — to hunt and to tend to his sour mash. Smoke would be harder to spot in the dark for some revenuer sneakin' around. Any kind of liquor, store bought or moonshine, had been outlawed in our country. Government agents had swarmed into our mountains, sometimes as thick as them locust in the Bible. Talk was if them revenuers had their way, white lightning would flood our creeks all the way to the

Kentucky river. According to the old men playing checkers on the commissary porch, Prohibition was out to ruin 'em all.

"Talk don't make it so," Papa said.

He declared whiskey as his cash crop and mining coal could wait. The foreman always took him back. I wondered how Papa managed to get away with workin' whenever it suited him. One night, after he'd been gone nearly a week, I reckon I got pure careless.

Mama, with Jewel on her lap, sat on the back porch steps where she liked to watch the sun slip behind Wilson's ridge. She softly sang tunes from her church going days. Loetta plopped down beside her and joined in. My sister's voice rised up strong with a sharp edge to it, but Mama didn't hush her. Granny, feeling poorly, had turned in early. It had become her habit more often than not.

I carried my book to the front porch steps to wait for Jim. He'd left with his banjo and his cane pole, the only things he claimed as his. He said pickin' a tune and fishing was almost better than Mama's vinegar pie. He'd most likely come running up the steps directly with a string of sun grammies or small catfish, my favorite. The thoughts of 'em frying in hot grease made my mouth water. I could see Jim sitting at the table, eyes shining from his mess of red curls, a grin spread across his face. He was always proud when he could help provide for us. Even so, Papa never cut him no slack.

Once in the quiet of night, too hot to sleep, Mama and Papa's voices carried from the front porch. Their argument settled over me clear as day.

"It's past time Jim pulls his weight around here. If he refuses to be a breaker boy, he can swing a pick like the rest of us miners. You've got to leave off coddling him."

"Jim has a flair for music. The Lord has gifted him. A sin iffen he wasted it in the mines. He don't belong there." Mama said.

"Pickin' a tune ain't never gonna put food on the table. His head's filled with foolish dreams."

Mama dropped her voice, but I could feel her anger.

I'd laid awake worrying about my brother. Foolish dreams. Me and Jim.

*   *   *

Recollecting that night filled my head as I dropped biscuit pieces between the steps for a stray cat. The pitiful creature appeared whenever he took a notion. Mama declared him ugly as sin, but I figured him to be a sign. Granny always said to pay attention to signs. I hadn't decided what kind of a sign, but I wouldn't let Mama run him off. Skinny, coal black fur with white hind feet, a stub tail and a notch out of one ear, I named him Scrapper.

The Treasure Box lay open in my lap. I recalled one of the stories and spoke it to the wretched cat like Miss Baker at Ashworth's camp school. A mighty fine storyteller, but she walloped anyone whose mind or eyes wandered. Which mine did, more often than not. I'd find myself taking up my own tale from the spark she give us.

"Answer me true or false, Scrapper. The wicked giant could blow the moon and the stars away, turning the earth darker than inside the drift mouth where Jim don't want to go."

A quivery "Meow" answered.

I don't rightly know why I didn't hear Papa movin' through the woods, coming closer and closer. Nor did I know when he stopped and stood in the deepening shadows. My bones whispered someone was there. I raised my head.

Scrapper zipped underneath the house. Papa coughed, ragged and phlegmy. I disrememberd a time when he never coughed. Tonight it seemed worse.

"You sitting there talking to yourself? You touched in the head, girl?"

"No, Papa. I ain't touched." I scooted up a step.

Colonel and Neverblue sprang out of the woods prancing and yipping. They crowded under the steps sniffing. I leaned over, and stuffed my book down my dress. I'd worn my new dress with the dancing ballerinas for three days without fail. I jumped to the ground, pressed my book to my chest and tore what was left of the biscuit in half.

"Come here, Colonel. Come on, Neverblue."

They rushed to me wagging all over theirselves. Our hounds gobbled the biscuit, licking my hands with their thick tongues. I squatted and rubbed 'em behind their ears.

Papa stood over me, his boots covered with dark splatters. "Quit babying them hounds. Ain't going to be no use for hunting. Quit it, I say." His words pecked like an ornery crow.

I jumped up, and nearly choked on the stink of his clothes, his sour hair and his liquored breath. Three rabbits, hanging from his belt, dripped blood.

I touched their soft fur. "I'll take 'em to Mama."

My book slipped, fell at my feet. Papa's red streaked eyes narrowed and his eyebrows bunched together. I held my breath. His scowl darkened. He picked up my book and shook it in my face. "People is ruint by such as this. Including that dress Granny stitched up. They is both sinful. You hear me?"

I reached for *The Treasure Box* and for a short spell we both held it. He jerked it loose. My book sailed into the woods, pages flying every which way. We watched them float in the air. I wanted to run, gather the stories and poems to me, but I stood there and did nothing. Nothing.

Papa righted his tattered hat and turned back to me. He fixed his eyes on the ground and sighed. "I reckon it's for the best. Go help your Ma." He held out the rabbits. "Tell her to fix some gravy, too. I'm wore out and near starved."

I willed my feet to move. He grabbed my arm. Seems he weren't finished. "Find yourself something else to wear. One of your Ma's old dresses ought to do. I don't want to lay eyes on that'n again."

My insides felt like a laurel leaf curled against winter's icy wind. He had ruint my book. Besides that, I could no longer wear the most comely dress I'd ever had in my entire life.

I runned around the house to the chestnut stump where Mama cleaned fish and small game. Drops of blood splattered onto my dress like the dancin' girls' tears. I'd leave them there, a reminder of Papa's spiteful ways. Them angry thoughts, and more, filled my head like great thunderclouds. I couldn't push them away any more than I could change my applesauce-colored hair, which I hated nearly as much as my freckles.

Mama's long black hair shined after she washed it on the back porch and dried it in the sun. I was stuck with mine, sticking ever which way no matter how much I brushed it or slicked it down with spit. Stuck with hair the same color as Papa's. Like his. Even my eyes the same brown or green as his. Always changing color from one to the other as they pleased.

If I got enough gumption to leave home, I'd be leaving him. I'd read stacks of books all day long and into the night if I chose. And I'd wear a different sinful dress ever day of the week, even Sundays. But no matter what I done or what I wore I'd always have hair and eyes like his. Loetta said, except for being covered with freckles, I was the spitting image of Papa. I didn't favor him. Not one bit. No siree.

I dropped the rabbits onto the stump. Mama appeared at the back door with Jewel in her arms. Loe stood beside her. A knife flashed in Mama's hand. "If them's bruised, they won't be fit to eat." She come down the steps. "I can manage here. You girls run out yonder and catch some lightning bugs."

"Mama, my book…"

"I know. I'll fix it later. Now go."

Glad to be shut of Papa, we took our baby sister and headed to the edge of the woods. Dozens of golden lights flickered. Jewel squealed and throwed her hands in the air. I ached to be like her, not near growed up, not thinkin' of leavin' the only home I'd ever known my whole life.

"Things ain't ever gonna change," Loe said. She kept on grumbling under her breath.

"Hattie," Mama called softly. I stopped and turned. She looked like a dark shadow figure against the inside light. "Your Pa…he…he ain't a well man. Remember that."

"Yes ma'am." My insides burned hot as a fire in a slag heap. When slag burned, no one could put it out, not even rain sent from heaven.

Loetta grabbed my arm. "What are we gonna do? We got to do something."

I had no answer.

Mama always told me the good Lord can take a bad thing in your life and turn it into something good, beyond anything hoped for or imagined. Maybe so. What if He chooses not to do such a thing. Who am I to question?

•   •   •

Jim never come home for days. Later he told me he'd sauntered up the footpath toward home, carrying a string of sunfish, at the same time Papa pitched my book into the dark woods. Jim took off to the top of Black Mountain, cooked his fish by wrapping 'em in cornhusks and laying 'em on hot coals. Then he stretched out afterwards to count the stars. It seemed to me Jim disappeared whenever such an idea took hold. I feared change was coming. In the past, Papa had ignored him more often than not, unless the whiskey took hold and Jim got a whipping for doing nothin' I could see. Now he was bound to become a miner. Even so, I wished I could be him. Or Jewel. Anyone but Hattie Mae Sizemore.

Mama stood by my bed for the longest time before she lifted my dress from its peg, laid it over her arm. I sat straight up. "No." She held up one hand. "I'll tuck it away for a while. Maybe Granny can stitch you another one day."

I turned my face to the wall and beat my feather pillow. "I will not cry. I will not." Yet hot tears escaped onto my pillow. Loe mumbled in her sleep and thrashed about.

A whippoorwill called from the woods, again and again. A sign somebody would surely die. Maybe *somebody* was me. I was already dyin' inside myself.

CHAPTER FOUR

Camp Livin' Rules

Mama kept her word, and patched my book best she could. Dew had caused the pages to curl, and we never found the poem about Mrs. Moodle's poodle. When no one was around, I slid *The Treasure Box* underneath the mattress I shared with my sisters.

Granny never argued with Papa about my schooling, my book, or my dress. Not like her a'tall. Seems she had no spunk these days to do much of anything. She tried fitting a threadbare dress of Mama's to my frame, but her heart weren't in it. I took to wearing some of Jim's old clothes, and discovered they suited me just fine, even though the pants landed above my ankles.

Near about two weeks slipped by before Papa returned to the mines. Unknown to us, things there had changed. We hadn't made a trip to the camp's commissary or we would've heard the latest news. And no one had climbed our footpath to come calling.

We lived in a four-room, wood-plank house, two bedrooms, a front room and a kitchen. Outside the kitchen, our back porch had a railing with a wide board nailed on top. Here's where we washed up before dinner or supper in an old dishpan. A piece of lye soap and a rag lay nearby. A washtub hung on the back of the house for our bath if Mama determined we needed one.

The front porch was my favorite place. It ran across the whole front of our house. Our wooden swing creaked and jerked on its chains when we swung high in it. In spring and summer, strings of morning glories along the edge of the porch give us much comfort.

Our house was perched halfway up a mountain across from the camp. We sat alone in the woods. Nearly hidden by thick laurel bushes, our house looked as gray as the trees' bark around us. No whitewash had ever touched it. Black soot had settled in ever crack and crevice. It crept inside too, touched our bed covers, our plank floors and our dishes. We could taste coal dust on our tongues.

Mr. Harper had cut the miners' workdays down to three a week. Said the demand for coal had slacked off and he had no choice. Maybe so, but he also cut the hourly wages. Ashworth, a small mining operation, had no union to speak up for the miners. Mr. Harper did as he pleased. Nobody mentioned Jim becoming a breaker boy.

•   •   •

Papa said the vein of coal he worked had near about run out anyhow. When it did, he and a handful of miners would rob their tunnel. They would knock down the columns of coal holding up parts of the ceiling, starting at the ones deepest inside the earth and winding their way toward the mouth. As they went along, they'd have to shovel any fallen coal into small rail cars before moving to the next column. 'Robbing the mine' was as good a name as any for their dangerous work. If the ceiling started caving in, they'd have to run like the devil chased 'em. They could be buried alive. No thought for the pitiful mule they'd most likely leave behind.

When their job was done, would the mines close? The miners and their families could no longer live in their coal company houses strung close together along the creek bank, each one as shoddy as the one next door. Their outhouses stunk to the high heavens and rats run all through the camp unless one of the big cats snatched one. Even so, the camp houses was all these folks knowed. They'd have to pack up and leave, search for work elsewhere. The end of Ashworth coal camp. A handful of families like ours had settled on these mountains and turned to coal mining in order to survive. Our house belonged to us — not to the coal company. Papa declared this to be true.

If the mines closed, we had other means. Mama said it best.

"No matter what happens up at the mines, we'll make do." She stood at the back door, fixed her eyes on the garden. She twisted her hair into a knot on top of her head and stuck a hair pin through it. "Time'll come for plantin' turnips and such before the days turn too short and the nights too cold. First thing come morning Jim can break up more ground."

I groaned. Granny shot me her look and shook her head. Everyone had to pull his weight. I dreaded lugging rocks into the woods or chopping out roots for days on end before we could sprinkle a few seeds into the dirt. "It seems these hills grow rocks overnight," I grumbled underneath my breath.

"Folks'll always needin' a drink of whiskey, for sure and certain. Even more so since the government has declared Prohibition against store bought or moonshine. Don't matter which. They's out to get us all." Papa said as he bent to his whitling. "Yes, sir, folks'll be knockin' on our door day or night. Travel from counties near and far. Iffen their money is lacking, we can barter. Eggs, fresh killed deer, or a bushel of corn might fit the bill."

Mama and Granny left to see about their supply of seeds. Seems my family was determined to beat the hard times. I fretted, but never spoke my worries. Hard times was coming. I could feel it as sure as the knot in my stomach.

Like Mr. Harper's word, the mines started operating three days a week. We fell into expecting the routine to last. Papa figured the rumors about closing the mines was nothin' but idle gossip.

When payday rolled around, Mama sent me to the commissary with Papa. We had run clear out of cornmeal and dried beans. At the bottom of our mountain, we crossed the railroad tracks and the creek's swinging bridge. We then followed the dirt road past a dozen camp houses, each one as wretched as the other. Little children chased each other around the houses. A dirty baby with a sagging diaper stood on a porch and watched us pass. A big, ugly dog bared its teeth and growled. A woman carried two buckets of water from the creek. She slipped in the mud and fell. Water sloshed over her.

"Papa, can we . . ."

"No. We ain't stopping."

I clinched my teeth together until my whole face hurt. I knowed not to look back or say a word.

•   •   •

We walked past Ashworth's schoolhouse, lookin' sad and deserted for the summer. The windows had been boarded over. Cobwebs hung in the corners of the shut door. Weeds growed up between the steps.

Next, we come to the commissary and it was a welcomed sight. As big as a barn and whitewashed ever spring, it set in a clearing beside an old apple orchard. Up the hillside behind the commissary Silk Stocking Row looked mighty fine. Five whitewashed houses had been built for Ashworth's rich folks, such as Mr. Harper, the mine foreman, and the camp doctor.

We climbed the steps and entered the store. The smell of oiled wood floors was nearly overcome by the sharp smell of coal. Miners shuffled in a line grumbling about their cut in pay. When they shook out the measly amount from their envelopes into their grimy hands, there was more scrip than ever. It had to be spent at the commissary, where everything cost twice what it ought to.

"I've a mind to spend what little money I got somewheres else," a young miner said in a loud voice. His fellow workers give him hard looks and moved away from him.

An old man took him aside. "Don't you know nothing? Smitty's wife made the mistake of buying some yard-goods in a store up near Crockett. Saved her money to make their little girl a church dress. Word traveled back to Mr. Harper. Not only did Smitty lose his job, he had to take his family and move elsewhere." He shot a brown stream into a spittoon making it dance. "Maybe before your time here," he added.

The young miner ducked his head and said no more.

•   •   •

At supper we gathered around the table for pinto beans, cornbread and fried green tomatoes. A heavy weight pressed upon me.

"It ain't fair," I said looking over at Papa. My voice come out louder than I meant. "The coal company saying where we got to spend our money."

"Smitty knowed the rules," Papa said around a mouthful of cornbread.

"Could such a thing happen to us? What if there's some rule we don't know nothing about until it's too late? Could Mr. Harper make us move? He don't own our house. Right?"

"Eat your supper," he said. "You worry too much."

Maybe so. My fried tomatoes had growed cold. Loe scraped 'em onto her plate. I couldn't get the fear of losing our home out of my head.

"If the mines shut down, the commissary would close and our scrip would be worthless. If we saved a little money, how far could we stretch it before it would be gone too?" My words hung in the air.

No one answered. Papa give me a hard look. When he finished eating, he pushed back from the table. He stood and walked out the back door carrying his rifle. Colonel and Neverblue yipped with excitement.

Papa come home later that night empty-handed.

•   •   •

On Wednesday of the next week Mama carried ever piece of scrip to the store. She come home with extra staples, flour, corn meal, salt, dried beans, and fatback, things such as that. "We'll not be caught unawares," she said. Eventually our lives settled into commonplace routine.

•   •   •

Papa sat on the front porch playin' a mournful tune. A jar of his whiskey sat by his feet. I sat on the steps snapping the last of our half runners. He hadn't hollered at us for days and I figured him workin' a three-day week had eased his aching bones as well as some of his crotchety ways. He slipped his harmonica into a shirt pocket and took up his whittling.

I didn't want to get him stirred up, besides bringing on one of his coughing fits, but there was something I wanted to know. I took a deep breath, blowed it out, and turned to face him. "Tell me 'bout the little canary bird some of the men take into the mines. I seen one in the commissary. As yellow as the jar of lemon drops sitting on the counter. I always wanted to have one of them birds my own self. I got a birthday coming up 'fore long and . . ."

He looked up from his whittling. "Humph. Them birds ain't for hankerin' after like a pretty. Get it outta ya head. They's for one purpose only. Iffen a miner wants one of 'em, he's got to buy it from the commissary. The cage too. And they ain't cheap. A canary bird can save a man or even the whole lot of us iffen it keels over from the gas. Considering we run fast enough." He shook his head, clinched his jaw and the wood chips flew faster. He never mentioned my birthday.

Iffen a miner had a little yellow bird would he have time to run for his life? Or maybe a spark from someone's pick would blow everything to kingdom come, bird or not. Dangers underneath the earth was a plenty. Did Papa look up when them timbers, shoring up the roof, groaned and creaked? If the columns of stacked coal shifted, did he notice? Did he pray to the Lord down in the dark, damp hole? I'd heard tales of rats stealing your food unless you put a good size rock on top of your lunch pail.

Two weeks later, on a Monday, Papa took off hunting. He declared he'd make another run of moonshine as soon as the time was right. I wondered if Willie had spotted some revenuers snooping around.

We bent to our washday chores. Jim carried more buckets of water from the creek to finish what he'd toted up the hill on Sunday afternoon. He added 'em to two big iron pots. Then he built a fire under the one used for washing.

Soon as he was done, he picked up his fishing pole and his banjo laying across a tree stump. I walked over to him. "There's something I got to know."

He grinned at me. "And what might that be?"

"Papa says since we own our house, Mr. Harper could never force us out. Is it true?"

His smile disappeared as he sat down on the stump and looked up at me. "Well, Sis, it's like this . . . It's true we own our house, but not the land it's sitting on. The mineral rights was bought by Ashworth Coal Company years before we come here. And iffen there's a rich vein of coal underneath this mountain, ain't nothing gonna stop 'em. For certain not us. We ain't got no rights."

I moved closer to Jim and poked him in his arm. "How come you never told me all this?"

"What good would it do? Look how you're getting' all riled up over something you can't do nothing about." He stood, gathered his pole and banjo. He moved into the woods. With a flash of his red hair, he disappeared.

•   •   •

I hurried past Loe who played with Jewel so our little sister wouldn't wander too close to the flames. Back to my chores, I threw a piece of lye soap into the wash water and set a long stick nearby. Mama would pound the clothes.

With Granny's washboard stuck in a bucket of water, I scrubbed on a pair of Jewel's soiled bloomers. I hoped it weren't long 'fore she'd get to the privy in time. This was Granny's usual chore, but I had left her resting on the front porch. She was deep into sleep, her chin dropped onto her chest. I'd turned away, opened the screen door and walked through the house.

I dropped the bloomers into the wash pot. "Seems Granny sleeps a lot these days."

"She's past seventy. Sleep is good." Mama said.

"She'll be spry as ever after her nap," I added.

We worked for a while in silence, but things on my mind wouldn't let me be. I looked up from scrubbing Papa's shirt collar and caught Mama's eye. She turned back, but I figured she was listening. "How come nobody told me about the coal company owning the mineral rights on this mountain? What good is it to live in a house that's sitting on land we can't never lay claim to?"

Mama lifted Jewel's dress on the end of her stick and dropped it into the pot of rinse water. "We never knowed such a thing when we moved here. Now we know, but what good is it? We got nowhere else to go. We got to look to the good Lord to take care of us. And one way or the other, He will."

I couldn't see any way He could do such, but I never voiced my doubts. "I wish Papa'd never took up with mining coal. His lungs is failin' and when he has a coughin' spell he's left with no strength a'tall. Ain't you noticed? He thinks Jim's gonna take his place one day, but Jim ain't built for mining coal. He's skinny as his fishing pole he totes around. The rest of us ain't all bony like him. And his hair. As red as a fiery sky when your hair's black as coal and mine . . ."

"Seems you got a belly full of questions this morning." Mama pressed her hands into the small of her back and stared at me all misty eyed. "Some of your questions ain't got no easy answers. Them mines ain't a fit place for boy or man. They've left your Pa a broken man, but he ain't ready to give it up." She bent over the steaming pot and swished the clothes around. She raised up again, turned toward me and pushed her hair out of her face. Her dark eyes locked onto mine. "Jim? He's got his sights on a better life. Far from this holler."

"What are you saying? Leavin' us? Does Papa know?"

Her quick glare sent my way told me enough. He didn't know. Mama throwed a pair of Papa's work pants into the wash water and beat 'em with her stick. His clothes was last. We'd soon be done.

"Why would Jim do such?" I twisted my toe in the dirt and squinted toward Mama but she never looked up. "This here's our home, even if the land beneath us ain't ours," I added, near the edge of tears. I couldn't tell her my own dark thoughts of leavin' these hills soon as I figured a way. Maybe Jim wouldn't always be here to look after our family. Iffen he was to leave, how could I?

She dropped Papa's work pants into the rinse water. "Throw dirt on the fire and make sure it's out." She lifted a cranky Jewel to her hip, turned and walked inside with Loe following close behind.

I grumbled and bent to rinsing Papa's clothes. All of a sudden, I stopped what I was doing and fixed my eyes into the hills. I'd been counting the days since I'd asked Papa about the canary. Today was September fourth. My birthday. Not only Papa, but none of my family had spoken of it. Not even Mama. I'd turned fifteen and no one said a word. I grabbed the long stick from the wash pot and pounded the work pants in the rinse water until pain shot through my arms. I tossed the dripping pants across the clothes line. Then I threw dirt onto the fire and huffed toward the house.

•   •   •

My birthday and Jim was in fact leavin' us. Mama seemed glad of such. Papa was sure to find out. I tried to think where my brother might go, what he might do, but I couldn't picture it in my mind. The sun was well past midday and I was soaking wet, wore out and hungry besides feeling like a grump.

I stomped up the steps. I wished Mama had never told me 'bout Jim. His secret felt as heavy as Papa's dripping-wet clothes thrown over the clothesline. As hard as the earth, we could never lay claim to, beneath my feet.

If my brother was to leave 'fore I found a way, Papa would hold on to me tighter than ever. The thought stole my breath. Maybe the whippoorwill I'd heard called for my death right here, in this place. Not a sudden death, but in little bits until I was empty inside myself. Empty. Dark. As dead as winter leaves trampled underfoot.

•   •   •

Soon as I stepped inside the kitchen, I smelled fish frying. Then I seen a bundle on the table. It was wrapped in newspaper and tied with twine. Mama and Granny, my sisters and Jim hollered "Surprise!"

They had not forgot me. My present turned out to be better than any yellow bird in the commissary. I unwrapped a double wedding ring quilt stitched by Mama and Granny whenever I weren't around or asleep. The beauty of its soft colors looped around each other and stole my breath. "But I an't fixin' to get married," was all I managed to say.

"I predict it won't be long," Granny said. She grinned all over herself.

Mama hugged me tight. "Whenever the time comes, you'll decide if you're ready."

Loe put in her two cents. "I seen how Willie eyes Hattie when she ain't lookin'. Love struck is what he is. She ain't givin' him the time of day."

Everyone laughed. Especially Jim. Heat rised up my neck and my ears burned like fire.

It was the best birthday I'd ever had. Ever. Jim had even managed to snag a dozen little catfish, my favorite.

CHAPTER FIVE

Crossing Over

We had a spell of unusual hot and smother-some days for October. Made Scrapper and our hounds plum skittish, myself included. One such morning, after Papa left for the mines, I chased after Jewel through falling leaves before she could escape our yard again. Her favorite trick since she had learned to unlatch our gate. I scooped her up in the nick of time, held her above my head. She squealed like a piglet.

"Look what I got, Granny," I hollered. A gust of air moved the porch swing. Granny never answered or looked up.

My eyes fixed on her slumped form. Her sunbonnet tilted askew, a lock of white hair fluttered and settled onto her calico dress. I knew what I didn't want to know.

I raced up the steps with a squalling Jewel and plopped her inside.

"Mama, come quick!"

Granny had done crossed over Jordan. Her hands lay limp in a dishpan of half-peeled apples, the paring knife fallen loose. Her hands gone idle before their chore was done. Her eyes not seeing, her voice never to speak or lift in song again on this earth.

A sob caught in my throat. I stroked her cold cheek and righted her bonnet.

•   •   •

Even though Loe fussed, she took Jewel to play underneath the giant hemlock near the bathhouse. Me and Mama had work to do. It would be a sight easier without a toddler underfoot.

We lifted Granny from the swing, carried her inside, and laid her gentle-like on our heart-pine table. Thoughts of us gathering there to eat her cat-head biscuits or to grind hog parts into sausage under her exacting eye brought tears. They spilled onto her still form. We would go on eating biscuits, grinding sausage, and a dozen more things around our table. My life, however, would never be the same without the one person who always said, "Follow your dreams, Hattie. Don't go off halfcocked. You got to be sensible. Have a plan."

Although she called me out when she thought I done wrong—like pining after them gypsies—when push came to shove, she stood unflinching between Papa and me. Said when the time was right, she aimed to find a way to change his mind about my schooling. The time must've never been right.

"You reckon she knowed how much I loved her?"

Mama reached over, pulled me close and stroked my head. "For certain. She knowed." I rested on Mama's soft bosom. Her dress was tear-soaked before we returned to our task.

•   •   •

We washed ever inch of Granny, even lifted her little breasts and washed underneath. Then I dusted her with lavender bath-powder until clouds rose into the air. After I returned her puff to the powder-box, I pushed down the lid and set it aside. Something of hers to keep.

We slipped her navy-blue dress over her head, her Sunday best with the crocheted collar. Mama brushed her long white hair, loose now from her tight bun. We slipped her clear glass beads around her neck. I covered her eyelids with two shiny pennies. Then I tucked a rose bud behind one ear. She loved them climbers better than anything. I'd found one still livin' on mostly shrived up vines.

•   •   •

Mama opened her tobacco tin and give me two dimes. "Tell Mr. Caywood we have need of his best right away. There's always some boys hanging around his hardware store who can carry it to us."

The commissary had gracious plenty coffins in their basement, reserved for miners in case of a mishap. It seemed to me they was ready and waiting for such a thing to happen one day.

The coffins Mr. Caywood built and stacked on his store's porch weren't much better than the miners' coffins. There was no need of saying such to Mama. I took off running down our mountain and followed the railroad tracks into a small settlement, Five Mile Creek.

•   •   •

Mr. Caywood took one dime from my outstretched hand, but wouldn't take the other. "Tell your Mama I'm powerful sorry to hear she's passed."

He pointed to two scruffy boys playing a game of mumbly-peg in the dusty dirt. "You and you. Carry this coffin to the Sizemores. No lollygagging neither and you might earn a nickel when you return."

The boys snapped their knives shut. They rushed over and lifted the coffin.

Mr. Caywood stopped us before we took our leave, and told them boys to sit the pine box onto the ground. He opened the lid and laid a length of calico inside. "Wished I had better'n this."

Now her resting place would look like a field of flowers. My eyes filled up and overflowed. "We're beholden to ya. Exactly what she would have wanted."

Mr. Caywood nodded. He pulled a bandana from a shirt pocket. He blew his nose, turned and climbed the steps to his store.

The two boys was not from around here, but from a place west of our mountains called Corbin. Papa always said, "Them city boys ain't nothin' but trouble."

For certain they didn't know my Granny. They soon commenced grousing about their heavy load. We followed the narrow dirt road to our holler, stopping whenever someone spied us. They wanted to know who had died and wanted all the particulars. Little children thought such a sight called for singing and skipping along beside us. When they tired of their game, they dropped away.

At last, we neared our footpath. The boys set the pine box down by the miners' bathhouse. "We ain't going no further," the taller one said with a smirk. "Unless you give us the dime in your pocket. If you ain't so inclined we aim to take it." He took out his knife, opened it, and pressed his thumb against the tip.

"Yeah," the other one said as he tossed his long hair and leaned against a tree. "And you've something else we might help ourselves to while we're in a taking mood. You might find out you like it." The boys laughed. Like Papa said, they was nothin' but trouble.

I faced the hooligans and crossed my arms. "My Pa makes the best whiskey there is in these parts. But since you ain't from around here, I reckon you ain't heard tell of Sizemore's moonshine."

They moved closer and studied me. "Exactly what are you sayin'?" the tall one said as he pointed his knife at me.

"I might be inclined to give you some, iffen you don't lay one hand on me."

They looked at each other. The knife disappeared into a pocket. The boys hefted the coffin to their shoulders. They scrambled around the giant hemlock and headed up toward our house.

Turned out, I didn't have to give them nothing. Colonel and Neverblue bounded out of the woods raising a ruckus. Papa appeared 'bout the same time with his rifle slung over his shoulder. He stepped forward and raised his gun.

"Holy ...," one of 'em hollered. They dropped the coffin like it was on fire and took off. Our hound dogs nipped at their heels. Granny would've loved seein' it.

·   ·   ·

Papa helped me and Mama settle Granny into her coffin before her body growed stiff. I eased her hands across her chest. Mama remembered she hadn't covered our only mirror, hanging by the back door. She rushed to Granny's bed, pulled out a box from underneath. After rummaging around she pulled out a folded black cloth.

With the mirror covered, Mama sank into a kitchen chair as she quietly wept. She turned toward Granny. "What am I goin' to do without you beside me?"

I had no answer when her question was my own.

·   ·   ·

Word about Granny's passing had traveled to Widow Baker, our doctor woman in these hollers. On her way to us, she stopped at the hemlock tree and brung Loe and Jewel home. She also brought along a pot of turnip greens and cornbread. My sisters eased over to Granny. They patted her hands easy like and asked dozens of questions.

Jim run up the back porch steps and hurried to the coffin. He fell to his knees, bowed his head and stayed there for the longest time.

After Jim gathered hisself, we scooted our straight-back chairs to each side of the coffin. We'd stay with Granny through the night. Jewel climbed into Mama's lap. Papa pulled out his harmonica and played *The Old Rugged Cross*, one of her favorites.

No air stirred. Not even a candle flame flickered. I could hardly abide the smell of death.

• • •

The next morning, Mama brung me the dress Granny'd made for me. I wore them sinful dancin' girls to her funeralizing. Papa gave me a black look, but he never said nothing.

It seemed the whole of Ashworth camp climbed the mountain to put Granny to rest. It fell on a Sunday, which was a good thing since the miners didn't have to work.

The preaching drug on and on, not about my dear Granny but about sinful people needing to repent before they was sent straight to hell. I stood on one foot and then the other. Sweat ran down my back.

At last, the preacher closed his Bible. The dirt throwed over Granny growed higher and fell softer until the earth claimed her. Her spirit had done flown to heaven from our porch swing days before. It weren't her down in any hole. She was having a good time in heaven. Didn't the preacher say no more sorrow, no more pain, no more tears? Yes. Even so a sob flew from deep inside me and burst forth. Willie sidled up close and took my hand in his. His touch was a mighty comfort.

Jim broke out in Amazing Grace with his clear voice and everyone joined along. Some voices was deep like Papa's, some sweet and quivery like Mama's. Other coal camp voices swelled around ours. The red, yellow and orange-colored mountains seemed to quiver with our singing. Granny was in heaven. Yet I could hear her voice rise and fall amongst us.

A cloud of butterflies swarmed around us before lifting up into the sky. I watched 'em until they was gone. Somehow, a peace come over me, like a sign from Granny herself.

When the singing was over, folks milled about. They mostly talked to Mama about Granny and the good things she'd done for 'em. Then the Ashworth's camp school teacher, Miss Smith, pulled me aside. She was a hefty woman with pink skin and dark hair streaked with gray piled on top of her head. Outside the classroom, she didn't look as fierce as I remembered.

She touched my arm. "I'm sorry your granny's passed. She was a wise woman."

I nodded. It was all I could manage.

"I've missed all you Sizemores in school. Loetta's mind jumps from first one thing and then another. Some strong discipline might tame her. Jim's got a head for figures and a heart for music, a mighty combination. You're a thinker full of questions and you always added a spark to the lessons."

"I done that?" I mumbled.

"Your granny wouldn't want any of you to give up schooling. Talk to your parents. Tell them what I said. Find a way to come back."

Miss Smith give me a strong hug and turned away to join the others heading down the mountain. She lived in a small room attached to the school house, except for the summers when she moved in with her sister near Pikeville.

My heart was broken for Granny, but also for Loetta, Jim and myself. Papa would never let us return to school although it seemed I was the only one who truly cared. Even though Loe complained, she seemed happy playin' with Jewel and keepin' an eye on her. And a schoolroom would smother the life out of Jim, much like diggin' coal in a dark tunnel.

Miss Smith meant well, but she didn't understand Papa's ways. He was watchin' when she was talkin' to me. He never come over to ask me about it, but he give me a black look. That was enough.

·   ·   ·

A wind picked up and brung the smell of rain. Mama lifted her face to the darkening sky. "Storm's a coming."

Thunder grumbled across the distant mountains. The preacher hugged his Bible against his black coat. He lit out to lay hands on his mule's harness before the animal bolted and ran off to no telling where. Others hurried behind him mumbling and anxious. Our family, even Papa, stayed. We stacked heavy pine branches and rocks over the fresh mound of dirt so the rains wouldn't wash her grave clear down the mountain.

Jim and me was the last ones to leave. Fat raindrops splattered onto our heads. Once home, I hung my dress on its peg to dry and changed into some of Jim's old clothes.

·   ·   ·

Come morning, I folded the dancing girls and eased my dress into a gunnysack. Then I added my birthday quilt and Granny's box of lavender dusting powder. I thought of my book underneath the mattress, pulled it out and added it. Then I pushed the things most dear to me clear out of sight. Iffen, no when, the time come for me to leave, I'd be ready.

CHAPTER SIX

A Little Man Ridin' a Big Horse

Loe, tugging a squalling Jewel behind her, busted inside the house. "Some man's a coming! On a . . . a giant horse! And it's white as snow!"

I stopped sweeping the kitchen floor and leaned on the broom. "You're funnin' us. Only a Billy goat could make it up our path."

My sister was always claiming things was true when they wasn't. She was like the boy who yelled wolf too many times. We knew better than to get all worked up.

Mama rinsed the last canning jar and set it aside. A half-dozen waited for the green tomatoes we'd picked and wrapped and stored in the cellar weeks ago. Our garden's last pickings. She dried her hands and eyed her middle daughter. "The Lord don't cotton to any child telling whoppers."

Loe folded her arms across her scrawny chest. "I ain't telling nothin' but truth." She stomped her foot and her face turned as red as a rooster's comb. "Ain't that right Jewel?"

Our little sister hid herself in Mama's dress tail. If Loe was fixin' to get in trouble, she wanted no part of it.

"Tell us what you know for certain," Mama said. "Take a big breath, and start from the beginning." We gathered around her to listen.

"Well . . . me and Jewel was playing underneath the hemlock next to the bathhouse, like we always done, when we heard a horse clomp, clomp, clomping closer and closer. I hushed Jewel for she was fixin' to cry. We peeked out from the branches. A scrawny little man who looked worse than one of them hobos was riding a big ol' horse and they was headed our way. That's when we took off for home."

Strangers who come to our out-of-the way house was scarce. Papa taught us to be suspicious of any such person showing up where he had no business being in the first place.

Loe and me and Mama, with Jewel on her hip, moved outside to have a look-see for our own selves. The heavy air pressed upon us. No breeze stirred the dried-up morning glories. It was the middle of October, but we'd had a string of unusual hot days.

All of a sudden, we heard sounds like creaky gates opening. We peered into the woods. Mama laughed. "A mocking bird's got a nest out yonder."

"I knowed that," Loe said as she moved closer to Mama. Sweat trickled down my back. Jewel wiggled down to the porch. She pranced around and fanned her dress so her belly shined.

A raggedy little man appeared a few feet from our yard gate. He struggled to climb one step more. He toted bulging saddlebags over his shoulders. He slid his burdens down to the ground.

"Where's his horse?" I whispered in Loe's ear.

"How do I know? Must've tied it up somewheres."

He looked up to the porch. We hadn't moved or spoke a word of greeting.

"Howdy," the man hollered waving his ragged hat. He swiped his wet face against his shirt sleeve. "Could you spare a dipper of water? I'd be powerful obliged for your kindness. I come a long way." He fanned hisself with his hat while sweat fell from his scraggly nose.

"State your business first," Mama said sounding as stern as a lawman. Jewel whimpered. Mama lifted her up and she buried her face.

"I brung you folks some books to read. You can keep 'em for nigh on to three weeks until I return. Then you can swap 'em for some others. This here's a traveling library."

"I never heard tell of such a thing. You say you're up here with books?" Mama's curiosity had took hold. She leaned to me. "Get a bucket of water and a dipper before he keels over."

He drank his fill in loud gulps while we waited. I eyed his saddlebags and couldn't keep my heart from nearly thumping out of my chest. Had he for a fact brung us books? Why would he?

He pulled a dirty rag out of a pants pocket and wiped his face and neck. Then he looked me square in the eye like he'd heard my questions.

"President Roosevelt's woman's worried about folks living up in these hollers with no idea what they're missing in this world. She says reading books, magazines, and newspapers will open the minds of the isolated and ignorant. The Kentucky library system has put her thinking into action. Now do you want to see what I brung?"

Us young'uns jumped up and down. We clapped our hands and hollered.

"Come on up to the porch," Mama said. "Show us what you got in them saddlebags."

And so he did. By the time the little man left, each of us had a book. Jewel chose *Mother Goose*, Loe claimed *The Boxcar Children* right off, and I picked *The Adventures of Tom Sawyer*. I wanted to get one for Jim, but the man said I'd have to share my book. He would only lend to a person he could lay his eyes on. "Ain't right," I grumbled. Did he think my brother weren't a real person?

Mama latched onto a *Good Housekeeping* magazine. We had three whole weeks before the library man's return. No one mentioned what would happen if Papa learned what we'd done. After a few more days he'd return from making his liquor. This was the first run he'd been able to manage in a while.

A worrisome fright rose up in my throat. It nearly choked me.

Mama left her magazine on the kitchen table and returned to canning tomatoes. Loe and Jewel looked at the pictures in Mother Goose. I took Tom Sawyer and slipped him underneath my pillow. Safe. Just in case . . .

Mama said not to worry.

·   ·   ·

Later, before nightfall, we piled in the middle of Mama's bed and shared our riches. Jim paced the floor beside us and listened. He was more excited over Tom Sawyer than me. He stayed up in the kitchen reading long after we turned in.

Come morning, we learned of Mama's plan. We'd carry our books to Widow Baker's, the doctor woman in these parts, where we could walk to her house and read 'em anytime we stole a chance. She lived by herself in the woods past the Ashworth camp houses.

Considering Papa didn't find out. For sure he'd never darken her door. He declared she was a witch who cast spells on any person who crossed her.

She was a tiny woman, more the size of a child who could fit underneath my chin. Her black hair was streaked with white. It hung in a long braid down her back. Her face and hands was as wrinkled as a dried up walnut and as brown as a plug of tobacco. I figured she must be part Indian or maybe full-blooded.

•   •   •

Me and Loe carried our books in a tow sack down the railroad tracks. Then we followed a tiny footpath into deep, dark woods. Reminded me of Hansel and Gretel, but I never said so. We clomped up her front steps where a patch of sunlight fell upon plants in lard buckets of dirt "Come in," she hollered. "Been expecting you."

She was busy in her kitchen. We stood and watched as she reached for one clump of weed after another hanging in a window. She mashed bits together in a wooden bowl. Then she poured from one bottle and another until the mess stunk to the high heavens.

Mama said she weren't no witch, but was gifted with healing by the good Lord. I chose to believe Mama knowed what she was talking about.

We lined up in front of her table. One at a time we held up our books. "My, my," she said. "Excellent choices! We'll have us a good time with 'em."

We tucked our books inside a blanket chest at the foot of her bed. Except for Mama's magazine. She asked us to leave it on a kitchen chair.

Then we said our goodbyes and headed home.

Mama was teaching us to lie about having books. I figured the Lord knowed the reasons we had to keep 'em secret, and he wouldn't hold us accountable.

"In three weeks, we'll meet the little man at Widow Baker's," Mama said as she met us at the front door. "Before he left us, I laid out the directions to her place. He said he'd be most grateful not to have to climb our footpath again."

I thought the plan was as grand as could be and nothing could turn it upside down.

•　　•　　•

The night before the library man was due to come again, I was too excited to give into sleep. Papa was tending to his whiskey making, so the timing seemed perfect for us to exchange our books.

All of a sudden, someone's voice whispered outside my bedroom window. "Psst. Hattie. You asleep? Psst."

"What? Willie?" My voice rose as I jerked myself straight up and peered toward his shadow. I crawled over Loe and Jewel sprawled out like dead bodies.

"Meet me out near the privy. It's important." He was known to roam these hills day or night delivering messages, or maybe sugar or corn to the moonshiners. Things such as was needed. But what had brought him here?

I felt my way through the dark house. Mama slept light as a butterfly and I prayed she didn't wake. I eased outside the squeaky screen door and down the back steps. No moonlight shone on the path. Our nights had turned cold, the ground frosty some mornings. I shivered. My teeth chattered.

Close to the privy, Willie reached out and grabbed my arm.

"Yikes!" I nearly jumped out of my skin.

"Shhh. I gotta make this quick. The little man you told me about bringing them books? Have you took 'em to Widow Baker's?"

"Certainly. No one knows our plan 'cept you. What's happening?" I couldn't stop shaking.

Willie grabbed my shoulders. "The library man ain't coming no more. Not to any of these hollers near Ashworth. I suspect no one else will neither. He's been run off and word of it will spread. Your Pa was leaving the commissary yesterday with a sack of sugar when the man was passing out some books to some young'uns."

Willie dropped his hands and stepped away. He rubbed the back of his neck. "The short of it is the little man jumped up on his horse and took off. Might not've stopped yet."

"How do you know all this?"

"I've learned to keep myself near invisible and my ears sharp. I had gone into the woods to . . . to take care of my business when your Pa started hollering. He threatened to shoot the man iffen he was spotted anywhere in these parts. I toted sugar clear to his still and neither of us spoke of what had happened."

"You reckon Papa'll find out what we've done?"

Willie shrugged. "He'll not hear it from me. Keep on reading what's at Widow Bakers. There'll not be no more books. That's the end of it."

"What he's done is wrong! Just plain wrong!" I shouted to the clouds moving across the moon. I disremembered picking up a rock until it struck the outhouse. A screech owl lifted from a nearby tree and swooped over our heads. Other disturbed creatures added to the racket.

Until . . . silence.

All of a sudden Willie wrapped his arms around me and pulled me close to his warm chest. He smelled of wood smoke and the outdoors. "Don't give up hope. Don't." His breath tickled my ear.

Then his lips brushed my cheek before he turned and slipped away. My eyes followed him into the dark woods, and I gazed at the place where he'd disappeared for a long while. A sudden breeze lifted my hair off my back. Chilled me clear through. A screech owl hollered. Maybe the same one we'd roused from its roosting place. I hurried inside and crawled into bed, but sleep would not come. Willie had been my friend forever so long. More like a brother. Wasn't he? If he had become more, he'd caught me unaware.

Papa had found out about the man bringing books. My mind set to whirling. Why had the library man come a day early? Why had he tied his horse up at the commissary fer all to see? Didn't he know there'd be folks, like Papa, who wouldn't want him here? Had he forgot we'd told him we'd meet him at Widow Baker's?

Papa had put a stop to reading any more books other than the few we had. Hate festered inside me like a pus-filled boil. When I figured my life was about to get better, things had got worse.

We had as good as stole them books and hid them where Papa hopefully would never lay eyes on 'em. Would the library man send others to lay claim on them three books and a magazine? What would President Roosevelt's lady think of us ignorant thieves?

CHAPTER SEVEN

Unsettled

The days drug along, cold and dull and gray with no books to comfort us. Mama said to stay away from Widow Baker's for a while. Jewel kept jabbering about the old woman who lived in a shoe. We feared Papa might start paying attention and ask us questions.

Neither did we have Granny to add spark to our lives. My heart ached to hear her rise from her creaky bed in the early morning dark, pad through the kitchen, and head out to the privy. Her wispy singing often floated on the foggy-damp air through my open window. *I Come to the Garden Alone* or *Barbara Allen* was her favorites.

Besides pining for Tom Sawyer and for Granny, there was the uncertainty of my standin' with Willie. I'd scarce laid eyes on him since he'd let me know the library man weren't comin' no more. Since he'd pulled me towards him in the woods.

Papa said Willie'd been sticking close to home lately 'cause his Ma was ailing. Truth or an excuse to stay away? I could, even yet, feel the brush of his lips across my face, his warm breath on my ear. He'd whispered. 'Hope. You can't give up hope.' How could I give up something I couldn't conjure up in the first place? Where could I get it? I didn't even know what to hope for.

Even November's crisp air and applesauce bubbling on the stove didn't help my sour thoughts.

Now it seemed the moonshine business claimed Willie's time. "He's the best runner I've ever had," Papa declared at the supper table. "Traipses all over these hills toting messages or supplies. Near invisible. Makin' nary a sound. More like a spirit."

Would he ever come around again? To see me? What would I do if he didn't?

After a couple of weeks, me and my sisters slipped away to Widow Bakers once again. Papa was either mining coal or tending to his still. Mama mostly stayed at home. Said it was more important for us young'uns to get some learning. We took turns readin' aloud 'til Tom Sawyer, Mother Goose, and the courage of the boxcar children lived inside all of us.

One afternoon Mama made a trip to the commissary, and on her way back home she stopped by. We girls was sprawled out on the floor with our books. I looked up. "Head home directly," Mama said. "Chores a'waiting."

As she turned to leave, she eyed the *Good Housekeeping* laying on a chair. She hugged it to her chest. "I've read it cover to cover," Widow Baker said. "Might be time it brings you some pleasure."

Mama looked at her friend, then her magazine before she returned it to the chair. I squirmed. Was she gonna leave it? I had stopped reading out loud. Jewel pulled on my arm and whined. "Shhh," I said. "Quiet."

Mama picked up the magazine again and slipped it into her basket. She covered *Good Housekeeping* with a bandana, a sack of dried beans and a small greasy package of fatback. I sucked in my breath, and prayed Papa never discovered it. If he learned about our stolen books, he'd burn ever last word.

"I'll make certain they leave here in twenty minutes," our neighbor said from the kitchen table where she pounded bloodroot. Her tonic was much in demand.

•   •   •

The miners continued working three days a week. On his days off, Papa tended to his whiskey. The liquor kept us in enough money to get by. We didn't go hungry, but my shoes had pinched my feet for ever so long. I had no choice but to wear 'em for winter was upon us. I had growed taller and skinier. Jim's pants rested higher up on my legs.

My brother tried to stay clear of Papa best he could. Other times, their voices would rise up in anger. Papa called Jim 'a good-for-nothing lazy bum,' among other things.

"Mr. Harper says it don't matter if the mines is operating on a cut schedule. He needs another breaker boy, since the last one up and quit," Papa said one morning after breakfast. He laced up his work boots as he cast his eyes on Jim.

Since my brother was small for his age, he'd easily fit on the wooden seat perched over the moving coal. If he was to lose his balance and topple over, he'd be done for. I feared for my brother's life. He was prone to daydreams, and I seen him falling. He'd end up in a coal car on the tracks below, broken and buried.

Jim ducked his head. He sat on his shaking hands and clinched his jaw. The quiet fell upon us and sucked the air out of our kitchen. Papa stood. His chair crashed onto the floor. He turned, grabbed his lunch bucket and stomped outside. He thumped down the back steps as the door slammed behind him.

Mama reached over and laid her hand on Jim's arm. "We'll find a way," she said.

I couldn't see no way. What on earth did she mean?

Jim looked at her like he was thinking the same as me. He stood and left his nearly full plate. He slipped into his threadbare jacket, gathered his fishing pole and his banjo. He disappeared out the front door.

I grabbed the broom and swept the entire house in no time. If Mama had anything to do with it, one day soon my brother would leave us. I refused to pray the Lord would help her make a way. My heart would grieve over losing Jim.

Maybe, just maybe, he'd take me with him. Would he? Where would we go? Thoughts of such a thing happening set my heart to poundin' faster and louder in my ears. It almost seemed possible.

CHAPTER EIGHT

Not Even Samson

Early December and not a cloud in the clear blue sky. The afternoon air carried a sharp chill. Me and my sisters put on ever stitch of clothes we could find and paid it no mind. We held hands and skipped around and around near our hillside garden. When we fell down laughing and dizzy, the mountains spun around us.

Mama had shooed us outside while she canned a few quarts of beets. We had saved nearly a half bushel from the garden. Before morning, Jim had headed up another holler to Hidden Pond. Talk was good-size bass was plentiful there. He planned to snag a string of 'em.

All of a sudden, the quittin' whistle blasted three long times. We cast our eyes towards the mine. The sound rolled off the mountains, filled my chest, stole my breath. A disaster had surely fallen upon the miners, upon us. Jewel latched onto my legs and squalled.

Mama flew out of the house. Before long, women and children from the camp houses tromped amongst us. Nary a soul cried or spoke—in all the mess of people.

Feet thumped against the earth. Pebbles rained down the mountain behind us. Some folks left the crowded footpath and scattered out in the woods. When a tree branch swung out and struck, a sharp cry or a curse rose up. We kept on running up the mountain. My heart pounded in my ears. Faster. Louder.

We stopped in front of the mine's drift-mouth. The dark hole belched black smoke like an angry beast. The smell of sulfur hung in the air. The crowd huddled together. All we could do was wait. Wait for news from inside the earth.

A woman wrung her hands and wept. Another lifted her face and her hands to the sky. "Lord, have mercy!" she hollered in a trembly voice. "Bring our men home! Alive, Lord. Alive." She crumbled into a heap with bowed head. Her shoulders shook. A small boy and girl knelt beside her.

The nearby tipple creaked and groaned as its gray wood settled. No coal tumbled down the long chutes, spewing clouds of coal dust. No coal fell into one L&N car after another on the rails below. Water dripped from somewhere inside the mine. Loud in the unnatural silence. Nary a bird chirped or fluttered in the nearby woods.

Then a distant rumble. From somewhere deep inside the mine. The noise grew louder, moved closer. The ground beneath my feet trembled. A mule bellowed as it busted out of the earth. Eyes wild with fright, it scattered us like chickens. Two men grabbed its reins, but the animal drug them along like they was nothing. They howled and cussed. The beast brayed and screeched and kept on going clear down the mountain. The three of 'em raised an awful racket. Another day, another time people would've laughed 'til they cried at the sight. Today, all our faces was drawn in tight.

"That mule'll never be fit for mining again," someone said. "Might as well shoot the critter."

Willie stepped out of the woods and rushed to my side. I was weak-kneed with relief. I threw my arms around his neck nearly knocking him sideways. He hugged me tight and patted my back. Then he loosened my grip and eased me away. "Any word?" he whispered as he searched my face. I shook my head.

He never reached out to draw me close once again, to offer more comfort. I fought the urge to shake him good. Did he not see my tears spilling over?

Jewel wiggled out of Loe's arms, run over to us and tugged on Willie's shirttail. He turned from me and lifted her up. I stomped away. Me and Loe found Mama and huddled close to her. We prayed for the miners buried inside the earth.

•   •   •

Mr. Harper paced back and forth, chewed on a fat cigar and checked his gold pocket-watch. His scrunched-up face was wrinkled with worry. Was it for the men or for the coal not dug this moment? Minutes could drag into hours or days. Or forever.

Finally, a few men commenced straggling out. They looked like they'd been fighting bobcats and lost. Yelps and squeals went up. Women and children claimed one and then another. Papa weren't amongst 'em. Mama's beet-stained hands pressed against her white face as her eyes searched for him.

Two miners led Mr. Luellen, the foreman, over to a pile of rocks and set him down. He stared off into the distance. Mrs. Seabolt wrapped a blanket around his shoulders. She spied Willie and motioned him over. "His wife ain't here where she ought to be. Maybe you can go fetch her."

He shook his head. "Not home. Seen her leave early this morning."

"Humph," a woman said. "I expect she's took their child and gone shopping clear to Foggy Mountain. Again."

Other voices grumbled in agreement.

Their family could trade anywhere they pleased, no need for one piece of scrip. Even so, Papa had once told me Mr. Luellen worked alongside the miners when he weren't required to do such. "He ain't a bad sort. For a foreigner."

"Where're they from?" I asked him.

"Don't matter. He ain't from around here."

Doc Evans, our camp doctor, tended to one injury and then another. He tied a man's arm against his chest and passed him and Mr. Luellen a whiskey flask before gulping some hisself.

I caught bits and pieces of miners talking as they huddled together.

"The big 'ol kettle bottom give out. Rotted timber couldn't hold it up no more. Bound to happen. I told 'em . . ."

"So did I. What did they expect? Nothing could shore up Number Nine."

"Not to worry, according to Mr. Harper. He had sworn them timbers was as strong as Sampson."

"We run when we heard the first crack, seen the kettle bottom shift. I ain't going back in no hell hole."

Seemed even Samson couldn't hold up Number Nine.

• • •

They carried Papa out on a stretcher. Mama sucked in her breath. "Isom, oh Isom," she cried out. She hurried over to where they eased him onto the ground. He never moved, never opened his eyes and the blood. So much blood...

Doc Evans ripped Papa's pant leg open. A shiny bone stuck out of his flesh. Mama knelt beside his head, her long hair on the ground. She commenced whispering in his ear and wiped his face with her apron. A pitiful groan come from deep inside him. One of the camp women, Mrs. Gilbert, pressed a flask into Mama's hand. She drizzled some whiskey into Papa's mouth. He sputtered and coughed. When he settled down, she done it again. Willie handed Jewel to me. Then he knelt behind Papa and pressed his arms and shoulders down as the doctor started to work.

I turned away and tried to comfort a squalling Jewel. "Shhh. Hush, now." Papa screamed, Jewel cut loose with one of her own, and I near about dropped her. Loe leaned into my side and sobbed. A trickle of blood inched across the ground coming closer.

The whole world seemed a madhouse. "Loe! Get hold of yourself!" I tried to shake her loose, but she clung tighter.

Mrs. Gilbert gathered us to her soft bosom. "Take these young'uns and get home. Iffen you stay here any longer you're borrowing trouble. Your Mama's got enough on her right now. They'll carry your Papa there directly. Go."

I stumbled away, but stopped and looked back. Willie raised his white face and nodded a good-bye. I threw my hand in the air. Doc Evans' shirt looked like a butcher's. "Hold him down Willie," he barked. "Where's that laudanum?" Heat rushed through my body yet I shivered and couldn't stop. Jewel whimpered and squirmed. I tightened my grip. Loe stumbled behind us and hitched her breath in great gulps.

•   •   •

Swirling air spit snow as I held the screen door open. Willie helped Mama up the steps. They made way for the two men who carried Papa inside on a stretcher. His right leg had been stitched together, wrapped tight and latched between two boards. I wondered if his bone would find its rightful place. His eyes stayed closed in his soot-black face. "Is he dead?" I asked. "No," Willie said. "But he's hurt bad."

His arms flopped about when the men lifted him from the stretcher onto the bed. He moaned, but never opened his eyes. "Doc give him a gracious plenty of laudanum," Mama said. "He ought to sleep for a spell."

Willie touched my back. "Got to go. A miner's trapped inside."

"Who?"

"Don't know yet."

I fought the urge to beg him to stay as he headed out the door. "Don't you dare go inside them mines," I said. "Don't you dare."

A sour taste rose in my throat as I hurried to the kitchen. My sisters had plopped together onto a kitchen chair. Not only had Loe come to her senses, she rocked Jewel in her lap and crooned some old hymns like Granny used to. I returned to Mama with a dipper of water. She drank first and left me some. Then she pulled me to her and we held on to each other for a long spell.

"What if Papa can't work no more?"

Mama leaned over him with a wet rag and bathed his face. "We'll have to wait and see how he gets along. Doc Evans will be the one who decides when or if he's fit. But able or not, we don't live in no coal company house. Nobody can tell us to leave."

I hoped Mama knowed what she was saying. What if Ashworth coal company claimed the mineral rights to whatever lay underneath our house? Jim declared they had been sold to 'em long before our time of moving here. Owning our house would make no never mind. It had happened to the Morgan family. Would the same happen to us? My fears hung in the air.

I rung out another rag over the dishpan and handed it to Mama. "Willie says there's a miner trapped inside. Couldn't put a name to him yet."

"Lord, have mercy." She wiped Papa's face and neck, but the coal soot hardly budged. "Get me a piece of lye soap. I'll bathe him best I can."

I returned and give her the soap. "Anyone else hurt as bad as Papa?"

She nodded. "Worse. Young Billy Jones. His back's broke. Doc says he'll not walk another step the rest of his days. Good thing his older brother is strong. Unless he gives up mining."

I had no words for my sorrow and returned to the kitchen. We'd not had a bite to eat since early morning. I built a fire in the cookstove, and pushed Granny's skillet onto the eye.

"I'm needin' more coal. Little pieces," I hollered to Loe and Jewel playing now in our bedroom.

I stirred up some corncakes, but instead of Loe, Jim appeared with a bucketful of kindling. He thumped it down by the stove. "I heard the whistle clear over at Hidden Pond. Got here as fast as I could. Where's Papa?"

"He's here. Hurt bad."

He hurried to the bedroom. I felt much relieved.

I mixed the cornbread and dropped spoonfulls into the hot grease. After the corncakes bubbled and browned around the edges, I flipped them over. The smell of 'em as they sizzled made my mouth water. When they was done, I fried some more. Thankfully, we had leftover sweet potatoes and cooked beets.

Jim would have no choice, but to become a miner now. How else could our family get by? It looked like Papa wouldn't draw a paycheck no more. And likely he'd not be fit enough to make whiskey. Jim couldn't leave home. He was stuck. Same as me.

Willie rushed into the kitchen. My sisters joined us at the stove. "We is all starving," Loe announced.

"Wash up and have a seat," I said. Willie wouldn't look my way and I knowed he didn't have good news. I no longer felt spiteful toward him, but only regret for my selfish thoughts earlier. I fussed at myself. What kind of man would he be if he didn't comfort a little child? I fixed three plates and set them on the table.

"Mama, you coming?" I hollered.

"Not now. Maybe later."

Jim carried a dishpan of black water through the kitchen and tossed it out the back door. He returned with an armful of wood, and got a good fire going in the living room fireplace. "Save me some of them corncakes," he said with a grin as he carried the dishpan and a bucket of water back to the bedroom.

By the time I sat down at the table, my sisters played in front of the fireplace and their plates was empty. Willie hadn't touched his food. My hunger had also disappeared. I scooted my chair closer to him. "What about the trapped miner? Did he get out?"

He looked over at me. His face had lost all its color. "George." His lips quivered. "George Gallaway's buried in the mountain. Buried deep. It's his grave for sure and certain. No proper funeralizing. His Ellie and their five young'uns'll pack up before week's end. Head back to Virginia where they come from." He struck the table with his fist.

I leaned over and rested my hand on his arm. Anger burned in my chest. "How can Mr. Harper send a sickly widow and her children away without so much as a fare-thee-well? It ain't right."

Willie sighed and shook his head. "No it ain't. But that's one of the rules of camp livin'. Iffen a family has no miner, be he dead or alive, they have to move out. Make room for an able-bodied man who can dig for coal."

I'd never seen Willie so disheartened. I couldn't tell him to never give up hope when it seemed there was none.

"You got to eat," I said at last. "We need you around here. I need you."

He nodded and picked up his fork. I carried a plate to Mama and Jim, told them the latest news. By the time I returned to the kitchen Willie had gone. I hardly knowed who to pray for first. I jumped into the middle of it all and counted on the Lord to straighten it out.

Papa was hurt. And hurt bad. Jim and me had no choice but to help our family any way we could. We'd have to make the best of what had fallen our way.

CHAPTER NINE

Mending

For three days and nights Mama never left Papa's side. Whenever he fretted the least bit, oftentimes calling out, "Clara. Clara," she'd give him laudanum drops mixed with a swallow of whiskey. On the fourth day, the medicine was gone. When Mama unwrapped his leg, the wound had turned an angry red. He had come down with a fever. He moaned and hollered, thrashed about and talked out of his head.

Mama sent me to fetch Widow Baker. She weren't truly a widow, but Mama promised one day she'd tell me her story. She was known to mix up peculiar potions she declared would cure most any ailment known to man. Her doctoring sometimes took hold and sometimes it didn't. Talk was some had died by her hand in screaming fits.

"Pay no mind to such tales. She has powers from the Lord," Mama said.

•   •   •

Me and Widow Baker was back climbing our footpath in no time. She might be scrawny and old, but she was as surefooted as a nanny goat. I huffed and puffed keepin' up with her.

After she cleaned Pap's leg, she smeared her medicine over it. Then she wrapped it with a clean cloth and secured his leg to the boards. Papa never roused up enough to know who was working on him.

When she was finished, Mama urged her to rest a spell with a taste of Papa's liquor. She declared one of the camp women was about to bust open like an overripe melon. She had promised to help with the birthing. In an instant she was padding down our front steps and vanished out of sight.

The next day Papa's fever was near about gone and he was more at hisself. Doc Evans come by a day later. He questioned Mama about what she'd done to make him better so quick like. And what was that gosh awful smell? "I doctored him best I knowed how, but it was the Lord's doings," she said. She puffed up a pillow and raised his leg. I busied myself with cookin' our supper of boiled cabbage, sweet potatoes, cornbread and more beets.

For certain we'd not let on Widow Baker had darkened our door. Folks, such as the Doc and Papa, feared she'd cast a spell on ya if she took a notion.

Doc Evans left shaking his head. "Beats all I ever seen."

•　•　•

Even so, Papa's mending took its good time. For weeks he'd have a good day followed by a string of bad ones. Caring for him took over our lives. One night Mama opened the family Bible and read from the book of Luke. Christmas had come and caught us unaware.

I grabbed our hatchet from its nail by the back door and flew outside. In no time I returned with a scrawny, little pine wet with snow. Loe thought of an old pot of dirt on the porch. Mama would plant a flower in it come spring. We had no presents, no decorations, but we had a tree stuck in a pot of dirt. We moped up the dripping water. Jim added a log to the fire and we gathered around. He strummed his banjo and we sang ever carol we could think of.

Papa roused up. "What in tarnation is all that racket?

We girls giggled. Mama smiled. After she settled Papa down, we sung some more only softer. Papa sighed and closed his eyes.

I wished for a visit from Willie or Widow Baker, but an ice storm come the next day. Walkin' anywhere become impossible.

I never pulled my book from underneath my bed. When Scrapper meowed at the back door, I'd slip him some scraps from my plate. Jim stayed close to home. Sometimes he'd appear in the kitchen with some grouse or a squirrel or two.

Loe and me tiptoed around the house, spoke in whispers, but I don't think thousands of angels blowing their trumpets could've woke Papa when sleep overtook him. Not from laudanum, but drops from a little brown bottle Mama kept in her apron pocket. Papa never knowed she added Widow Baker's magic to his bowl of beans or soup or whatever she was feeding him. And she made certain he ate every bite.

Most days his bed covers stayed twisted ever which way like he'd been running from some awful nightmares. Maybe that's what he done. Sometimes he stretched out and slept on his back. He snored loud as thunder, his bushy beard rising and falling on his chest. A near-empty jar sat on the floor beside his bed. Home brew, white mule—no longer set aside for Saturday night. I wondered what he'd do when there was no more.

One afternoon in February, springlike weather come and teased us. Mama raised the windows and opened the doors. The air seemed to bring us a spark of life. Papa managed to push himself upright. He commenced grousing. "These covers need a fixing. I'm powerful thirsty and my jar's near empty. Where is everybody?" His hollering filled our house and sent us scurrying.

Mama straightened his bed covers and wiped his face with a wet rag before handing Loe his chamber pot. She left with a scrunched-up face. I poured whiskey into his pint jar from a jug kept in the kitchen cupboard and carried it to him.

He took a long swig, wiped his mouth on the back of his hand and screwed the lid on tight. He tucked the jar beside him. Then he nodded to a tall pair of laurel poles in the corner. They had leather-covered crosspieces across their tops and smaller crosspieces down lower for griping ahold of.

"Set 'em where I can reach 'em iffen I should take a notion," he said. His voice sounded stronger, but his face was pasty white. He blew his breath out and shut his eyes as a coughing spell overtook him.

The foreman, Mr.Luellen, had brung the crutches by one day. "Always keep a pair on hand," he had said.

"Much obliged," Mama said as she took 'em. "Isom'll be needin' 'em 'fore long." Their wood was worn smooth by many a hurt miner before Papa.

I propped the crutches against the bedpost before easing out of the room.

Mama and Loe met me in the kitchen. "Your Pa's on the mend for certain and since a warming spell has melted the ice, we're off to the commissary. Weather's been fickle and it's liable to bring us another snow 'fore long."

After they left, Jewel tugged at my shirt-tail, her eyes heavy. I pulled Mama's rocker to a place in the center of the house where I could tend to Papa iffen he should need me. I picked up my sister. She plugged her thumb into her mouth and we started rocking.

Papa dozed sitting up with his head throwed back against some pillows. I patted Jewel and recollected the last story in my book. Soon the words fell in soft whispers from my lips. "Once upon a time, when the moon was young and the stars talked together, a wee woman, walking by herself on the king's highway, spied a little box all catawampus in a ditch. Do you know what she done?"

I looked down. Jewel's eyes had shut before story telling had got goin' good. Her thumb slipped from her mouth. As sleep took over, she jerked in my arms. I carried her to our bed. She looked like an angel-baby, her dark curls around her face, her mouth round and red.

I pulled the bedroom door shut, and walked towards the kitchen for a dipper of water. Colonel and Neverblue commenced cutting a ruckus out front. Someone had come calling. Someone they didn't cotton to.

"Grab my rifle," Papa said. "See who's out there."

CHAPTER TEN

Knocked Off Stride

I done what Papa said, walked to the front porch. I leaned the gun against the house and watched as red-faced Mr. Harper puffed his way up our muddy footpath. He stopped and fanned hisself with his fancy, brown hat. The sun shined off his bald head. Our dogs danced around and carried on like they'd eat him up if they could get to him.

Papa hollered for me, and I went back inside. He'd throwed the covers off and scooted to the edge of the bed where he dangled his feet and swayed. I rushed to his side in case he keeled over. He looked like a shrunken old man, thin and pale. He reached for his crutches.

"Who's out yonder?" His words was pinched up tight.

"Mr. Harper."

"Humph. See what he wants." He slipped the crutches underneath his arms.

I left him and went back outside.

Mr. Harper had stopped at our yard gate. "Call your mutts off," he said.

Out of a leather pouch hanging over his shoulder he fished out a pure white handkerchief and swiped at mud splattered on his trousers. He groused underneath his breath and crammed his dirty handkerchief into a pocket.

I squatted between our dogs, laid my hands on their heads. "Hush, now. Hush I say." They whined and whimpered, but at last stood still, their tails hanging down, necks stretched out. Colonel growled deep in his throat.

"Where's your father? I need to have a word with him."

"Papa's feeling right poorly." I stepped back and pulled the dogs along. I finally managed to shoo them underneath the house.

Mr. Harper moved closer, and hung his soft-looking hands over our gate. His diamond ring sent sparkles into the air as pretty as fairy dust. I never knowed a miner to have a ring nor to have fingernails without a speck of black grime. His eyes run over me, landed on Jim's shirt stretched tight across my chest. A crooked grin spread across his face. I hugged myself and turned away.

The screen door banged shut. Papa pulled his body along the porch with them laurel sticks. Thump, drag…thump, drag. My heart pounded louder with each thud. He managed the steps and made his way to the gate. I was afraid he was fixing to lay into Mr. Harper.

The owner of Ashworth Coal Company reached over with his right hand and Papa took it. One crutch fell to the ground. "I know you're not mended enough to return to the mines. Might never be, but that's not why I'm here. We're short of help since the accident, five men short. I've managed to round up an able-bodied crew from nearby camps willing to clear out a portion of number nine. We had to seal off the back tunnel where a miner'll have to stay buried. A shame to pass up a rich vein of coal. But another cave-in could shut the whole operation down. Too risky."

I clenched my fists as heat rose inside me. "George. George Galloway was his name. And his widow is Ella. Ella Anne."

Mr. Harper glanced my way, but paid me no mind. He straightened his jacket and leaned toward Papa. "The more pressing problem has occurred up at the tipple. We need us a little man, someone young, too, limber and sure on his feet. Someone to manage the breaker boys. The Collett boy was good, but he's up and left us. Run off to Cincinnati, I understand. Just like that. Put us in a bind too, I tell you."

Papa cleared his throat. "Jim's fourteen, though you'd never know it to look at him. Stringy and light on his feet. He could be a hard worker, too, if he puts his mind to it. He'll be there first thing come morning. I'll see to it."

Mr. Harper squared his hat on his head and gave it a tap. "He'll have to pull his weight. You know I don't allow slackers. I let you get away with working whenever you took a notion only because your whiskey is the best there is in these parts."

Papa nodded. "Fair enough."

"Don't suppose you've got any to spare."

"Last batch was ruint 'cause I coundn't tend to it on schedule, but if a paltry bit would suit ya . . ."

"It will do. For now."

Papa turned to me. "Fetch Mr. Harper a pint."

•   •   •

I handed the moonshine to the man sporting a diamond ring. He held the clear liquor up to sunlight streaming through the trees and shook it. Large bubbles formed and then quickly disappeared. He grinned all over hisself as he tightened the lid and stuffed the jar into his leather pouch. He glanced at Papa and then nodded to me. "Your oldest girl has grown up. You might need to keep an eye on that one." He chuckled to hisself.

"Humph," Papa said. His face turned fire red as he glared at me. "Get in the house." I was glad to do as he said. It seemed he was blamin' the wrong person for me growing up.

I peeked out the front room window as Mr. Harper turned, eased on down the footpath slick with mud. He was soon swallowed by thick brush. He had never paid me any mind until today. I vowed to stay out of his way from now on.

•   •   •

Jewel whimpered from the bedroom door. I scooped her up and returned to the window.

Papa settled into a straight chair on the porch where a patch of sunlight had fallen. He opened and closed his pocketknife, scowling towards where he'd stood with Mr. Harper. Snap…click…snap…click. He kept his knife sharp in case he wanted to whittle or challenge someone to mumbly-peg. Today, I weren't sure he knowed he held a knife.

I kept Jewel inside the house and played Eye Winker, but after a while she growed tired of ever game I could think up. We crawled around on the floor together, giggling at nothing. We ended up underneath our bed, my book in the tow sack. I wanted to slip it out from its hiding place to read to Jewel.

Instead, I told her a story the best I could and she did a right good job of listening. I played like I was the prissy Mrs. Moodle trying to make her poodle behave.

When we heard Mama and Loe talking and laughing, climbing the footpath, we scooted outside. The packages they carried held flour, meal, and fatback plus Mama held a bucket of lard. Loe danced around clutching a small poke. Me and Jewel begged her to open it and at last she did. Peppermint sticks.

One for each girl and Jim. We grabbed ours, hugged Mama and jumped into the swing. I felt like Christmas had come after all.

"How did ya pay fer all this?" Papa asked.

"Mr. Emmett give me credit. It was the only way."

They looked at each other for a long moment. Both of 'em had tight set mouths. At last Papa spoke. "Jim's got to step up. Do his part."

She untied her shoes, left them on the porch to dry and gathered the packages. Then she padded inside without any more words passing between them.

As the sun disappeared behind our mountain, the air turned chilly and the sky a dark gray. An owl hooted. We went inside and shut all the windows as Jim climbed the back steps with a string of fish. He was whistling like he didn't have a care in this world as he laid a fire in the front room's fireplace.

Mama fixed a fine supper of fried catfish, cooked cabbage and cornbread. Not to mention them beets we had wrapped and saved. I was beginning to wish we'd never pulled 'em out of the ground.

I'd not said a word about Mr. Harper coming to our house or Papa promising Jim to tipple work. No need. Mama knowed trouble had come calling.

Papa come inside and eased hisself into a straight-back chair close to the fire. Mama filled his plate and carried it to him.

After a spell, Mama called, "Jim, come here please." Her voice rose high and quivery.

He grabbed the last piece of cornbread. He flashed his crooked grin at me. He sauntered into the front room, his red hair swinging, like he owned the world. I feared he'd never wiggle out of becoming a breaker boy.

I tried to eat, but couldn't swallow more'n a bite or two. Loe pinched my arm. "What's happening?" she asked, her eyes so wide and scary I never offered to pinch her back.

"Jim's got to work up at the tipple. Starting tomorrow."

"Why?" Loe asked.

Jewel banged her spoon on the table.

"Shhh," I said.

"Ain't there no other way?" Mama cried out.

Papa's voice—low and soothing—like the time when I weren't much more than a knee-baby. He'd lifted me up from a yard chicken pecking my toes. When had he turned cantankerous and downright spiteful? I couldn't recollect exactly when.

Heavy footsteps thumped out the front door and Mama's voice cut into the gloom gathering around me. "Where you going?"

"Don't matter," Jim said. "Can't tolerate being shut up tonight."

I set a plate of leftovers on the back of the stove. I didn't know if he'd be back 'fore morning or if he'd left us for good. Papa fought with a coughing spell. Mama hurried to the kitchen. She mixed some whiskey, honey and hot water in a cup and carried it to him. After a while, he settled down.

Jim had rushed out in such a hurry, I worried he might freeze out in the woods. I opened the back door with scraps for Colonel and Neverblue. The air had turned colder and was spittin' snow. I searched the shadowy darkness for Scrapper, but never seen him. I went back inside.

While Loe pulled out our chamber pot and sat Jewel on it, I stacked our supper plates. My hands shook. One slipped. It landed on the floor, but thankfully didn't break.

"Hattie Mae," Mama called from the front room, "we ain't got no spare plates."

"Yes ma'am."

I took a deep breath and tried to quiet my trembles. It was no use. Worry for Jim pressed down on me.

CHAPTER ELEVEN

Jim's Fate

Mama started a pot of chicory and turned from the cook stove. Her stringy hair hung about her white face.

I finished drying our iron skillet and set it aside. "You're worried about Jim too, ain'tcha?"

"I'm certain the Lord's watchin' over him. I predict we'll see him 'fore morning." She sighed. "I reckon I'm worried all the same." She reached out and pulled me to her. "We got to keep praying. Don't give up on God."

"Yes. I will. I won't."

Me and Mama set the kitchen in order, but she was far from finished. She looked 'ragged around the edges,' but I knowed by the spark in her eyes she meant business. She planted her hands on her hips. "Loetta, fetch the washtub off the porch. Hattie, round up the lye soap, a washrag and a towel. Then scoot a chair close to the tub. He'll need to prop up his leg. Your Papa's gettin' a bath."

Whenever things got bad, Mama set about scrubbing something. This time it was Papa. At long last the washtub was ready. We had filled it with rainwater caught in a barrel and then warmed in buckets we'd set on the stove. When everything was fixed to her liking, Mama went into the front room. She said something to Papa as she handed him a cup of coffee.

At last, he come into the kitchen.

Thump…drag…thump…drag…He groaned, let himself down on a kitchen chair and glared at Mama. Then he stared at the floor. She told him to unbutton his shirt. He snorted and said something under his breath. After her sharp glare, he pressed his lips together and said nary a word.

He fumbled with a button. His hands shook until he give it up altogether. Mama walked over and stood in front of him. She unbuttoned his shirt. He reached up, pulled her closer and rested his head against her belly. Her hands got lost in his thick hair.

"Go play," she said, when she saw me watching. She took her hands away from Papa and shooed us girls. "Go. In your bedroom."

It was long past our bedtime, but I wasn't about to tell her so. With a quilt pulled from Jim's bed, we made us a tent—between two straight chairs. We hunkered under there, quiet as lightning bugs, except for Jewel who sucked her thumb. When we was settled, I told some stories I remembered Mama telling—though I couldn't tell them near as good.

After a while, I made up some of my own. "Once upon a time a fair lady with shiny black hair traveled across her mountain to a land where no one laughed or smiled. There was no stories and there was no songs. This made the lady sad. I have nary a thing to give 'em, she thought.

Then she remembered the rose bushes she'd planted along her yard fence."

"The next day, she come dragging a tow sack with the biggest rose bush she could dig up. Well sir, she planted it in the middle of the town square and everybody come to see what she was doing. The lady hummed as she worked. Soon the little children started humming. An old man asked what in tarnation she was doing and she said, "My great-great-granny gave her oldest daughter a rose bush as a wedding gift. She gave a piece of it to her daughter and so on until the rose bush was passed to me. I figured these here roses would make this a happy land."

"Humph," the old man said. But his mouth commenced to twitching. In spite of hisself, he not only smiled, he laughed out loud. The roses had worked their magic. The lady commenced singing the tune she'd been humming. Soon all the people was singing and laughing and dancing. They asked the lady to tell 'em more stories. And so she did."

Loetta and Jewel clapped and clapped. Loe whispered, "The lady could've been Mama."

I nodded. Granny Guthrie had give Mama a rose bush when she left home. Mama had always said she would do the same for us girls when we growed up. We had red roses climbing up the side of our privy, clear up past the roof like they was reaching for the sky. And Mama had started little rose bushes everywhere she could find a sunny spot.

"Tell another. Tell another," Loe begged.

"...and the fierce giant had a great bushy beard and he walked with a stiff leg and he throwed storybooks into the woods. Stay clear of his reach or he'll grab ya and..." I raised my arms and growled like a bear. My sisters screamed and hollered.

"Hattie Mae," Mama said, pulling the quilt up into the air, "what are you telling?"

Loe, always the tattle, said, "Hattie said..."

"Tell us one of your stories, Mama," I said. "Please..."

She bent over and lifted Jewel into her arms. "Not tonight, girls. I couldn't recollect no story if the Lord hisself asked me. It's past time we all get to bed."

Mama fixed her dark eyes on me. "Keep your words sweet. One day you may have to eat 'em."

After everyone had gone to bed, I sat in the kitchen and tried to pray for Jim. My thoughts soon strayed to my own worries.

What was Mama talking about tonight? Why would I ever eat my words about the giant, about Papa, when they was bitter as a persimmon? Don't she see me livin' under his roof ain't never gonna be sweet?

"Hattie," Jim whispered as he slipped in the back door.

I jumped up.

"Shhh. It's me."

"Mama said you'd come home tonight. Are you frozen?"

"Pretty near." He shivered and moved close to the stove. "There's no way around what I got to do. I'd as soon get on with it."

"You want some supper? I saved you some."

"Couldn't abide nothing in my stomach." He rubbed his hands together and held them over the stove.

Hattie?" Mama called in a half-asleep voice. "You and Jim best be getting' to bed."

"Yes ma'am."

Jim come over and stood in front of me. He didn't seem like my little brother no more. He griped my shoulders. "We got to look at things the way they are, not like we wished they was. We ain't got no choice."

I never argued with him, but his words turned sour in my stomach.

He turned away and eased inside the front room. His bed creaked and then all was quiet.

•   •   •

Before daylight the next morning, I tiptoed into the front room. His bed was empty. I opened the front door and looked outside. Jim stood on the front porch, gazing towards the mountain where the tipple waited. The air was cold and foggy, but no more snow had fallen.

Mama insisted Jim eat two biscuits stuffed with fatback. He ate in a hurry, gulped his coffee and picked up Papa's dinner bucket we'd packed for him. We headed outside to see him off. I passed by the bedroom where Papa lay, his face turned to the wall. He squirmed around and coughed, but he never got out of bed. Me and my sisters and Mama, wrapped in quilts, watched from the porch 'til Jim was gone from sight.

Mama wasted no time. She twirled around, snapping orders. We set about cleaning. We washed walls, shined ever window, scrubbed floors, drug the front room rug to the clothes line and beat it to death. Papa stayed out of our way, mostly sitting near the fireplace whittling. I figured we had the cleanest house in all of Ashworth camp. In wintertime no less.

    •   •   •

Weeks drug by until two months had passed. One morning, Papa managed to limp off into the woods with one crutch. He headed to his still, to see what he'd need to get it up and running again. Seems our family would lean on his whiskey makin' now more than ever. Papa weren't a miner no more, and Jim's pay turned out to be a miserly amount. According to Mr. Harper, if Jim didn't shape up, he'd have no choice but to let him go. Seems Jim spent more time daydreaming instead of tending to the breaker boys, just like I feared.

Hard times was knockin' at our door. I wished my brother would walk away from the mines and never look back, away from our holler, away from us. His leaving would wrench my heart clear out of my chest, but I didn't see no other way. If he stayed, we'd lose him just the same. Had Mama forgot she'd said he'd leave one day, she had better plans for him other than working a vein of coal his entire life?

Right then and there I figured I'd best look after myself. Jim had enough of his own troubles. He could never take on any of mine.

The next day, after I finished making the beds, I went to Mama sitting in our rocker in the front room. She was sewing a patch on Jim's pants. She stopped her mending and looked up.

"I plan on earning some of my own money. I ain't decided how yet, but I'm gonna do it. Could I have one of your canning jars to put it in? And could this money be my own? To do with as I please? After I give you part of it, for certain."

Mama studied me. "Forever more," she whispered. "Appears you've growed up in front of my eyes. I'll set you a jar out. 'Spect you're bound to leave home one of these days. Can't keep you or Jim here forever. Just promise you won't go too far. Got to be close enough so I can rest my eyes on you most ever day. Promise?"

I never looked her in the eye. I picked at a scab on my arm. "Uh, surely, Mama. I ain't planning to go far." I was glad Papa weren't around the house today. He would know I had plans to leave and would try to stop me. Did Mama know I might be telling a black story? I might have to go a far piece one day?

I turned to Mama. "I expect Jim's gonna up and leave us soon, money or no since Papa's leg's mendin'."

She stood, laid the pants aside and pressed her hands to the small of her back. "Reckon it's time I let you know. I've sent word to some kin livin' near Louisville. Told 'em to expect Jim by mid-July, if not before."

"You did?" A sharp nod was enough. "Does Papa . . ."

A flash of her eyes was enough. Me and Mama had us a secret. Jim was leavin' us.

The tension amongst our family grew thick as year-old molasses. Papa must've learned Jim was leaving. Would he stop him?

Mama and Papa kept acting quar. At the supper table, she'd say, "Hattie, ask your Papa iffen he's gonna sit there like a lump or iffen he's gonna eat." Or Papa'd say, "Hattie, tell your Mama I'm going over to the commissary," when she was standing right there. Made me addled in the head. I found myself wishing for the day Jim would be gone from us. Then I'd beg the Lord for forgiveness.

My cannin' jar stayed empty. I couldn't conjure up any way to earn any money to drop into it. *Impossible,* whispered in my ear.

CHAPTER TWELVE

Words of hope

Sunday's dawn brought the promise of springtime. I awoke before my sisters and watched the sky turn from a gray-white into a soft pink. No hard work allowed this day. From the lowest sinner to the Bible thumping preacher, everyone knowed the Lord had declared this a day of rest. Even the scrawny mules rested from hauling coal out of the mines.

We didn't go to the Freewill Baptist Church no more. Mama never said why, but I figured she finally give in to Papa's fussing. He declared 'them church folks ain't nothing but a bunch of hypocrites and them preachers is worse'n that.' For sure he was dead set against us going and his rantin' and ravin' must've wore her down. She read from our family Bible ever day though, without fail. He never spoke against her doing so.

I missed going to church, especially the singing, but today stretched out in front of me to do as I pleased. The possibilities felt as delicious as Mrs. Wilson's apple stack cake. I hoped the Lord understood. As always, the Sunday quiet surprised me. Fingers of fog drifted into our bedroom. The whole world seemed to be holding its breath. The tipple didn't rumble and shake. No coal flew down its chute into the waiting cars on the rails below. No coal filled one gondola after another. The train cars didn't slam into each other, coupling to pull coal out of Ashworth.

No clouds of soot choked the breaker boys or rained onto the camp. In my mind I seen the old gray tipple sigh as it leaned against the mountain, thankful for a day of leisure.

No need for a nine-year-old boy, Sam Collett, to climb the footpath leading to the mine. He wouldn't spend his waking hours hunched over, hammering the coal, throwing out slate or worthless rocks. He looked like a little old man when he stumbled home.

•   •   •

Now I could hear sounds I'd missed on workdays. Me and Granny used to tell what we'd heard in the Sunday morning stillness. As days, weeks and then months without Granny slipped by, I missed her more. Did she know, like the Lord knowed, ever troublesome thing falling upon our family? Upon me and Jim?

A dog's yelping broke into my wondering. Other dogs joined in until their noises grew faint, probably on the trail of a bobcat or coon. It seemed quar neither Colonel or Neverblue had stirred. A cow's bell clinked and clanged, then another answered from somewheres far off. Dew dripped from the trees. A wren announced the morning. Before many more days, the bees would work the honeysuckle outside our bedroom window, their humming a comforting sound.

My stomach growled something fierce. I remembered the leftover corncakes on the back of the stove. I tiptoed through the front room. The covers was throwed back on Jim's bed in the far corner. Gone. Most likely off fishin' and lingering as long as he could. He'd trudge to his breaker job come Monday.

Papa's rifle-gun was missing from its place by the back door. He was either hunting or tending to his sour mash, our dogs trailing along. Maybe they'd not return for days.

I felt like skippin' through the house shoutin' and singing. I'd take my book from its hiding place, climb to the ridge-top and read for hours. Maybe even read one story a dozen times or more. I danced ghost-like, my hands in the air to music only I could hear.

I grabbed the last corncake and flew to the privy. I needed to get on with what was bound to be a glorious day.

My business there took longer than I had planned, but if it hadn't . . . I would've never read the newspaper laying nearby. We saved 'em to cover all the privy's cracks before the next winter. The words in an ad jumped out at me. I couldn't believe I hadn't knowed about this before. Plans to spend this day reading *The Treasure Box* flew away as easy as a hawk glides through the sky.

I studied the newspaper again. This was how I was bound to make some money. Money for the day, the someday day, when I left home for good.

After tearing the paper around the words, I hurried back to the house, stopped at the back door, eased inside and to my bedroom.

Just as my hand touched Jim's old clothes I'd claimed as mine, Loe whispered, "Where you going?"

I nearly jumped into the wall. "Shhh. Go back to sleep."

"Better not be sneaking out on your work. I'll tell Mama." Her voice rose loud and tetchy.

"This is Sunday. Keep your drawers on," I slipped into Jim's pants and grabbed his shirt. "I'll be back directly."

Jewel fretted. I hurried away before the whole house stirred.

With the newspaper scrap in my pocket plus holdin' an empty coal bucket with a tow sack inside, I was fixing to run down the front porch steps. I spied Mama wrapped in a quilt and rocking. How long had she been there? Had Papa left in the middle of the night and she'd come out here then? Her dark eyes bore into mine.

I knew I had to make this good. I could see she weren't in no mood for foolishness. "We need coal. If I get to the tracks early, before the swarm of young'uns from camp, I won't have no trouble filling my bucket and be back here before you miss me. If I wait 'til later, why there won't be no coal left, and you won't have enough to cook our hen for supper."

Mama shivered, pulled the quilt closer. "I do declare. Do you reckon you can stop hopping around? You're making me dizzy."

"Yes ma'am." I stood on one foot like a bird.

"Jim took off 'fore daylight. It was time," Mama said in a raspy voice.

"He always says the best fishin' comes early. What do you reckon he'll catch?"

"He ain't comin' back." Her words flew from her pinched-up face and hit me square in my chest. I could not catch my breath. Gone? For good? Would I ever lay eyes on my brother again?

"He never told me he was going. He never said good-bye." The only things I could think to say. I flopped onto the porch steps. I refused to swallow her words as truth.

Mama walked over and plunked herself beside me with a loud sigh. She drew me into her quilt. A sob caught in my throat, but I willed myself not to cry. What good would it do? Jim was gone. He'd never have to be a breaker boy or check the tunnels for gas or mine coal deep inside the earth, which was bound to come next. He'd never been suited for such. In my heart I knowed I ought to be happy for him. Now he was no longer around to tease me about Willie or strum his banjo or sing a nonsense, made up tune. And besides all that, now his wages, pitiful as they were, would never be placed in Mama's tobacco can. Where did this leave me? Responsible for more than myself. I never wanted such.

Mama pulled me tight against her breast and her heart thumped against my ear.

"Does Papa know?"

"Not yet. Soon as he left to tend to his still, Jim slipped away."

My heart froze and I couldn't breathe. "But what . . ."

"Don't you fret none. Your Pa knowed Jim couldn't stay, same as me. He just ain't admitted such yet. He'll come around."

I wanted to holler no, no he won't. Papa won't stand for it. He'll send someone after Jim and drag him home. What was Mama thinking?

We sat for a bit without talking, but my mind was in a whirl. Mama had flat out gone against Papa.

I pushed away from Mama and sat up straight. "I give Jim what I'd been puttin' back for awhile now," she continued. "We'll make do somehow. And as soon as Jim gets hisself a job, he'll send us some money. You'll see."

Mama hadn't set aside any money for me. Jim had took all we had. She seen his need more urgent than mine. Maybe so, but his leavin' put our whole family in a bind. I knew enough of the world to know I couldn't leave without a dime in my pocket. I'd have to find a way 'cause there weren't gonna be no money to spare.

Mama opened the quilt and stood. "You know I like those little pieces and no slate. I was thinking about fixing some dumplings, and since you love them so, you might try your hand at it. Be off now. The sooner you get gone, the sooner you'll be back." It seemed she had put Jim aside and turned to a matter at hand. How could she? Then she reached down and touched my head. Her hand trembled. I looked up. Her pale face carried worry wrinkles. For Jim. And for Papa. She sighed and turned to go inside.

Our lives would have to go on without Jim amongst us. The ache he left behind, just like Granny's, would grow bigger the longer he was gone.

· · ·

The excitement I'd felt earlier huffed into thin air. I jumped into the middle of half-awake hens pecking in the smooth dirt. They squawked and scattered in all directions. "I ain't givin' up! No sireee. I ain't."

Jim wouldn't want me to and neither would Granny. And Mama? She'd like to keep me close and for sure she needed my help with my sisters and the never-ending chores. I counted on her to not stop me from leavin' when the time came. I weren't certain of what she might do.

Running down the footpath my eye caught a swirl of black in the woods. "Scrapper? Come on, Scrapper. We're going hunting." He meowed and pranced to my side leaving a ring-neck pheasant scurrying under some briers.

All week long a train had rumbled and huffed out of Ashworth spilling coal along the tracks. Whatever fell belonged to the first person who claimed it. In wintertime, we scrambled for the pieces — sometimes even while they fell. We used the coal in warm-morning stoves as well as cook stoves and fireplaces. But in spring and summer there was always plenty of coal scattered around. Mama knowed that. Just when I think I got her figured, she surprised me. I was glad she never asked me the real reason. She would have said certainly not and that would've been the end of that.

Snakes. I come for snakes.

I set the coal bucket on the tracks and found a forked stick. Just the thing to pin a snake behind its head and fling it into my sack. I crept into the ditches and lifted the ends of blackberry bushes and briers and stirred some tall weeds. All I roused up was chiggers in abundance. "Reckon I'll have to come back on a scorching hot day to find them snakes." Scrapper tipped his head at me and settled on his haunches. He licked his paws and washed his face.

I wouldn't give up, my eyeballs nearly coming out of my head with looking, but didn't find one single solitary snake. Not even an old black...Scrapper skittered up the bank and into the woods.

In the distance, Rachel Elizabeth walked towards me. She balanced herself on a rail, her arms outstretched, a shoe in each hand. Her yellow hair shined white in the sun—like it had a light of its own. I set down to watch. Rae lived on the other side of Turkey Creek in Silk Stocking Row. In summer, her whitewashed house had purple petunias spilling out of window boxes and a yard full of green grass.

Her Pa, Mr. Luellen, was the mine foreman. He'd brung his family here from Ohio and they talked fast and had some quar ideas. Even so, he worked alongside the miners ever day even though he could've told 'em what to do and go sit in the sunshine—well, maybe check up on things now and again. His job was to see the miners done their work and report it to Mr. Harper. I didn't understand the need because the evidence was in the tons of coal dug.

Rae was bent to acting uppity. Mama said Mrs. Luellen was born with a silver spoon in her mouth and she couldn't help but pass it on to her only daughter. I was glad I weren't born with such if it made a person behave sideways.

She plopped down beside me, her hair yellow now instead of white. I looked her over. "Ain't you gonna get dirty? Bet your Mama's looking for you. Bet she don't know you come across the creek."

"Mother's dressing for church." She bent over, pulled pure white socks over her blackened feet and slipped on her shiny black shoes with buckles. "I thought it was you over here. I came to tell you something."

Rae was always wanting to "tell me something." She always had "secrets," but they never amounted to nothing. This time I had something to tell. I hadn't decided if I was going to or not. I watched her buckle her shoes. A red ribbon, tied in a bow, fell down the back of her long curls.

"I bet you got ribbons of every color there is. How many you figure you got?"

She stood, dusted her pleated navy dress. "I'll give you this ribbon if you'll show me your cat. You told me ages ago you had…Snapper? I think you made him up."

When Mama had sent me to the commissary for a wee bit of snuff, she allowed herself ever now and again, Rae was there buying a bag of chocolate drops. I told her about Scrapper showing up one day, makin' hisself at home.

I jumped up and threw some coal into the bucket. "Scrapper ain't about to come 'round unless you believe he's real."

"Who cares if you have a cat. I came over here to warn you, and if you're not going to listen…well, I have to go anyway. I'm surprised Jim hasn't told you." I wasn't about to tell her Jim had left us. Her pa, as well as Mr. Harper, would find out come Monday morning. No reason for them to know sooner.

She walked away slow, knowing I'd follow. "Well? What?" I was ashamed, but I begged. "Please. What is it?"

She faced me and looked me up and down. "How come you're dressed like a boy? Don't you have any decent clothes?"

"I didn't hanker getting my best dress all dirty. My brother give me these." I'd told no lie and she seemed satisfied.

Rae moved closer. She commenced talking so fast my ears could hardly keep up. "An old man came walking into camp yesterday and asked Father if he could stay in the bath house for a few days. And do you know what? He told him he could until

Monday morning. Mother and I think he should tell him to keep on moving. After all, Father is foreman."

I'd just come past the bathhouse on my way down to the tracks and hadn't seen or heard a thing out of the ordinary. I shivered to think maybe a stranger had been inside all along. "He could be in the bathhouse right this minute? The miners won't like this. Don't your Pa know that?"

Rae talked faster. "…and he wears a patch over one eye and he walks like a hunchback and he has a beard dragging the ground."

"I've got better things to do with my time than worry about who might be in the bathhouse," I said as I fumbled in my pocket for the newspaper scrap. I pulled it out and handed it to her.

She unfolded it. Her eyes, the color of morning glories, growed bigger and bigger. She shivered and threw the paper back at me. "Snakes? Why do you want snakes?"

"The church wants 'em. The Pentecostal Holliness. It says Preacher Sam Smith will pay top dollar for live, healthy ones. Don't say what kind, but I hear tell they like the ones with lots of poison."

Rae swallowed hard and whispered, "Why?"

I threw some more coal into the bucket. "I don't know, but I've heard if a body gets bit and don't die, it's a sure sign he's right with the Lord. Wanna help me look for a rattler or a copperhead?"

She looked around her feet and commenced backing up. "I…I have to go. Nobody takes snakes to church. Do they?"

"You're afraid, ain't you?" She shook her head. "Prove it," I said. "Meet me at the church tonight."

She shook her head again. "I have to squeeze lemons."

"Lemons?"

"The missionary society's coming over. You know how much lemonade ladies who talk too much can drink?"

I tried to imagine a tall glass of lemonade, all sweet and sour at the same time. "Whatcha doing after supper?"

She played-like she didn't hear. "Mother says their president called a meeting to talk about the old man in the bathhouse. Decide if they want to help him before he's sent on his way."

"What if he don't want no help?"

"Doesn't matter. If they vote to do something, they'll do it come hell or high water. That's what Father says."

Rae's mother called, "Ra-cha-el E-liz-a-beth!" She stood on their porch, waving her big, feathered hat like a bird takin' flight. Rae took off running, her shoes sending cinders flying, no time for balancing on the rails.

I hollered, "I'll be at the church tonight if you can sneak off."

She waved her hand as she ran and I knew she'd heard me. Then something soft as a laurel bloom floated down to the tracks. I ran and picked up a red ribbon.

Walking slow back to my bucket, I pulled the soft silk through my fingers. Then I folded it careful like and put it in my pocket beside the snake paper. "Rae's got plenty more," I said to no one in particular.

The ribbon floating off Rae's yellow hair, laying there just waiting for me to pick it up, maybe it was a sign. I wished I could ask Granny.

A pokeberry bush quivered and Scrapper appeared. He come straight to me, rubbed against my legs. I hadn't called him, didn't have no food to feed him neither. Seemed like another sign. I squatted and rubbed behind his ears.

I had to hold myself back from grabbing him up in my arms and twirling him around and around.

I turned back to gatherin' coal. I hadn't seen one solitary snake this morning. Maybe Jim could help me, maybe he'd know a better place to look. Jim. I'd disremembered. He'd not be comin' around no more. He'd left us. I'd not have a chance to ask him nothing.

I threw more coal into the bucket and yanked it up with both hands. Pieces of coal tumbled out. Catching snakes was a dumb idea anyhow, I grumbled to myself.

CHAPTER THIRTEEN

Birdman

Sweat stung my eyes and Jim's shirt stuck to my back as the sun broke through the fog. Unusual hot for early spring. I set the bucket down, rolled up the shirt sleeves and tied up my hair with Rae's ribbon.

From the railroad tracks, I followed the path to the bathhouse. In front of the big sagging door the earth had been trampled smooth by miners' boots. Miners gathered here after the end of their workweek. If me and my sisters played underneath the nearby hemlock, we'd watch 'em share a chew of tobacco, roll a cigarette or sip some homebrew.

Beyond the bathhouse lay a hint of a footpath, the one leading to our house. It disappeared into the giant hemlock where branches drooped to the ground. The tree reminded me of a lady's skirt when she curtsied before a king, like I'd seen in a storybook. Before Papa said I'd had enough schooling and was needed at home.

The path took up again on the other side of the tree, pretty near invisible. Since mostly our family was all who walked it, Papa said he wanted it to stay that way.

I'd passed the bathhouse coming down the mountain a short time ago with no thought of anyone being inside. If I took what

Rae said as truth, a man was there who didn't belong. An outsider. When Papa learned of him, he'd run him off.

If Mr. Luellen had paid attention to our ways, he would've knowed the miners seen the bathhouse as the nearest thing to a church. Mama said that's where the miners tried their best to leave their worries behind, along with their work-clothes.

I edged towards the hemlock while keeping an eye on the bathhouse door. I'd snuck in there one Sunday morning because I knew no one would be inside, to see what it looked like. Shadowy darkness swallowed the feeble light comin' through a row of small, dirty windows near the ceiling. The sharp smell of coal overtook the smells of lye soap and wetness.

When I eyed the miners' work clothes pulled up to the ceiling, they looked like rows of hanged men. A powerful fright then and recollecting it struck me afresh.

•   •   •

Relieved to leave the bathhouse behind, the familiar path beyond the hemlock was a comfort. Thick with dead leaves, moss and turkey's foot the path was as soft as a feather pillow. I hurried up the mountain. Never stopped to catch my breath or to hush the pain in my side. The bucket slipped and some coal tumbled out. Scrapper run after a covey of quail, scattered by the falling coal.

Loe sat on the top porch step, her legs stretched out in front of her. Her face turned up to the sun. Jim loved to sit in the same spot, exactly the same way, on his day off. The memory of him squeezed my heart.

She raised up and glared like I'd committed a mortal sin. "You sounded as loud as a wash tub rolling up the hill. Who's chasing you?"

I leaned over and sucked in some air. "If you thought something was after me, why didn't ya…"

Loe stretched her neck out like a chicken. "What in tarnation did you steal?"

I'd forgot the ribbon. I snatched it from my hair and stuffed it in my pocket. "Found it and plan on keepin' it."

She settled back again to drink in the sun. "Don't reckon I care if you burn in hell. Why ain't you told me 'bout Jim leavin' us? Most likely you knowed all about it. Papa know or did you and Mama keep it from him, too?"

I never answered her.

"Mama come out on the porch a dozen times hollering for you," she continued. "Ain't you heard her?"

Loe was up to her exaggerating again. "I ain't heard nothing but my own self coming up the mountain." I stopped, looked down on my sister. "Did ya know you got freckles spreadin' from your nose clear underneath your eyes? Soon you gonna be . . ."

She squinted up at me and frowned. "That's Rae's ribbon. Nobody else in camp has ribbons but her."

"I found it." I huffed back at her.

She twisted her behind and smoothed her dress tail. "You stole it. Wait 'til I tell Mama."

Loe smiled and closed her eyes. I felt like jerking one of her pigtails. Quick as a flash, she jumped up and hollered for Mama. I chased her inside. The screen door slammed behind us.

I rushed into the kitchen under Mama's frown while Loe flew out the back door. Most likely she'd wet her drawers before she reached the privy. She was always waitin' too long.

I scrubbed my hands on the back porch. Water flew out of the old dishpan. It danced on the railing.

Loe was mad 'cause I hadn't I shared about Jim. We used to tell each other everything. She could use Rae's ribbon to get back at me. My sister could be a pure irritation, like a prickly thistle.

The dishpan flew off the porch. I chased it down the hillside, glad it was already beat up. As I climbed back to the house with the runaway pan, my head weren't filled with Loe, or the red ribbon, but with someone called Birdman.

• • •

I'd missed plucking the feathers off the hen after it'd been dunked in scalding water. The worst smelly job in the whole world and it turned my stomach upside down to think of it. Chicken broth bubbled on the stove. Mama dropped dumplings into the big iron pot. I was sorry I'd not been here to help like I'd intended. Mama never fussed at me. Made me feel worse.

Our chicken and dumplings that Sunday seemed more delicious than any I could think of havin' before. Mama filled my bowl twice and said we had plenty more. While we ate, I thought of asking her about Birdman, but decided to wait. Lou would want to know all the particulars when I didn't know them my own self.

After dinner, Mama said to put the dishes in the pan to soak and we'd tend to 'em later. Squeals and claps from Loe and then Jewel. "Come on," Mama said as she untied her apron and spread it over the bowl of leftovers. "Mrs. Wilson's giving us a basket of paw paws she'd been saving and we're takin' her some pickled beets." More squeals. We dearly loved the fruit and were sorely tired of more beets. I had right smart on my mind and never made a sound as we headed out.

Loe run ahead, her pigtails flying, teasing Jewel to follow. Me and Mama lagged behind. She said, "Ain't nothing wrong with an old man talking to a bird. He's not from around these parts, but it don't mean he's gonna put a hex on the mines or on anyone. Yesterday, after supper, I took Widow Baker some soup beans and stopped to see him for my own self. I figured this morning you was off to see him too, when you was anxious to gather coal we didn't need. But you never seen him?"

I shook my head.

"Well, I allow Loe can manage the dishes later and you can take him some chicken and dumplings. Hard times has a grip on him and won't let go, although he ain't said such. One thing's for certain. He's bound and determined to get back to his kin on Newman's Ridge in Tennessee. They is Melungeons and he's one of 'em. For certain he ain't had any decent food in no telling when."

"Melungeons?" I'd never heard of such. "Where're they from?"

"Not sure. Some say they're from a lost tribe of long ago."

"Indians? How did they get lost?"

"Birdman says he's mostly Portuguese, which I never heard tell of. Widow Baker says they're part gypsy and part Indian. They bury their dead above ground and build a little house over the body."

"What does Birdman look like?"

"His hair is pure black, his skin is darker than ours and his cheek bones set up high. He ain't much taller than you."

Tennessee? When would he go? How far is it? Would he allow me to follow along? These thoughts never took voice. "Impossible, anyhow," I mumbled under my breath.

Mama had gone to the bathhouse and learned for herself. More than Rae or Mr. Luellen or anybody. How come she weren't afraid of this Birdman? Maybe I wouldn't be neither.

$$\bullet \quad \bullet \quad \bullet$$

I squatted under the hemlock with a quart jar of chicken and dumplings between my feet. Scrapper meowed and rubbed his skinny self against my legs. Finally, I opened the jar, lifted a dumpling out and let Scrapper have a feast. He licked my hand, his pink tongue running tickles up my arm. His stub tail twitched and he purred as loud as a beehive.

When I come out from under the tree, I walked to the bathhouse, sucked in my breath, and banged on the door. Maybe he'd moved on, though it grieved me not to see the bird. Something shuffled around inside.

I commenced backing up. Scrapper shot off into the woods. The bottom of the door drug against the floor because the hinges was coming loose. Whoever was on the other side tugged it open a little at a time.

Birdman shaded the sun from his eyes with one hand and his other gripped a walking stick. He wore a red bandana around his head. His face was darker than Widow Baker's and I heard tell she was the nearest thing to being a full-blooded Indian.

He didn't look nothing like Rae said he did. He had a scraggly beard and it barely reached his waist. And where was the bird?

He spit like he had a bad taste in his mouth. "Well, missy, you got your eyeballs full?" His voice gurgled like he needed to spit again.

I held the jar out. "Uh…my Mama says you ain't had any decent food in a good long spell."

"That's a fact if ever there was one."

He took his hand down and I couldn't help but stare. One eye was as blue as the sky while the other was as brown as Neverblue's. His blue one looked straight ahead and never blinked.

He swung the walking stick under his arm. The head of a bird had been carved on top It was like the stick growed from the bird's throat. He stepped closer and took the jar. He smelled sour.

He turned to go. "Wait right here."

When he returned, he had pulled the red bandana over the blue eye and his brown eye seemed as soft as a kindhearted woman's.

He reached out, took my hand and put something smooth and hard in it. I never paid attention 'cause a black bird swooped from inside the bathhouse and sat on his shoulder. Sat there watchin' me.

Wonder of wonders, the bird said, "Hello," plain as the freckles running across Loe's nose. "Hello, hello, hello," it said again, bobbing its head of blue and then black and then blue again.

"Ain't you gonna speak?" Birdman asked. "This here's Maggie. Like all women you can't trust her worth a damn."

"Hello," I whispered, the sound caught in my throat. "Pleased to make your acquaintance."

I looked at what I held in my hand. It was a bird carved from a dark wood. It looked like a wren with its tail feathers sticking up.

"That's for your Mama. She's treated me kindly."

Her favorite songbird. How did he know? He must be an Indian because he knew things about people, like Widow Baker.

"Open your other hand." I done as he said, and he placed a shiny gold button in my palm. "Keep it open, now."

Maggie swooped down and picked up the button, as light as a butterfly's kiss. Birdman laughed, showing a gold tooth and I wondered if Maggie ever tried to take it. The bird sat on his shoulder again, the shiny button in its beak.

"She takes things sometimes. Brought me the prettiest ruby ring you ever did see. Three women claimed it was theirs. Now she's old like me, and don't wander off like she used to, getting both of us into a heap of trouble."

"Here in Ashworth you gonna be in a heap of trouble if you don't head out 'fore morning."

"Don't Mr. Lulellen run this camp?"

"He come here from Ohio and don't know much."

"That a fact. Tell your Mama I'm much obliged for them vittles. I'll leave her canning jar under the big hemlock yonder.

I'll be on my way 'fore sundown. I know what folks sometimes conjure up."

"Where you headed?" Suddenly I was sorry he had to leave.

"Some traveling preacher passed me by, up on the ridge. Calls hisself a 'Pentecostal bathed in fire' and he wears a long black coat and a black hat and rides a sway-back mule. You ever hear tell of him?"

"That'd be Preacher Sam Smith. Are you sure you seen him? He's a snake handler and always on the move."

"Missy, I can see more with this one good eye than most can see with two. And there's worse things than snake handling."

"Oh I ain't faulting that. I think it might be mighty fine. You figuring on picking up one of them snakes your own self?"

"I'll stick to me Maggie. This preacher asked me to help him build a brush arbor up around Red Bird Mission. Reckon that's as good a place as any to stop awhile. Besides, he says he's always had a hankering to preach the word in Tennessee. Says he'll come along with me once we put Red Bird behind us. I'll be close enough to smell home."

"You can smell it?"

"The breeze from my Tennessee holler's sweeter than honeysuckle."

I figured he was funning me. All I could smell where we lived was Papa's sour mash when it was cookin', Jewel's milk breath or her diaper's stink, the rotten egg smell of our water, or the sharp coal stench always in the air. The only savin' grace was Mama's roses. Since they grew next to the outhouse, the only way you could drink in their sweetness was when she fixed 'em in a canning jar on the kitchen table. As long as they bloomed, we had roses in the house. As soon as the flowers commenced going back, Mama saved the petals. She sprinkled 'em in our blanket chest. I vowed to do the same…

"Ain't the Holliness church around here somewheres?" Birdman asked as my scattered thoughts left me. Maggie danced on his shoulder. "Preacher said he'd be there tonight."

"I hear tell they handle snakes up there."

"Tarnation and thunder. All you got in your head is snakes? Best stick to the stub-tail cat of yourn and tying ribbons in your hair. Little girls ain't got no business messing with snakes."

Maggie chattered like she agreed.

"Name's Hattie. Hattie Mae Sizemore. And I'm near growed up."

"Well can ye tell me, Miss Sizemore, where the church be?"

"Follow the railroad tracks two mile up yonder," I pointed. "You'll see an old graveyard with nary a marker, 'cept for a few rocks piled around. There's one little grave, a baby-child's, that's got rocks lined up clear around it. It's always got flowers sitting there in a lard bucket. Go around the graveyard, turn left and in a clearing of tall pines is the church."

"Tell your Ma I'm obliged for the food. Watch out for them copperheads. Ye can hear the rattler shaking its bones but the copperhead lays quiet like, waiting for a hand or foot to sink its fangs into. When it does, it won't let go. I seed a big man die with a snake still hanging on. Ye step careful like. Shame if your Ma has to bury her oldest girl-child."

He turned and left me. How did he know about Scrapper, about me looking for snakes, about the ribbon in my hair? Maybe he'd been watching me while I was down on the tracks. But how did he know I was the oldest? Maybe he was kin to them gypsies who everybody knows has magical powers.

Could be I'd see him again. At the church tonight. Could I go with this strange man clear to Tennessee? I'd never gone far away from home in my entire life. Would he let me? Would I go with him and his bird iffen he did? Granny would say he weren't no better'n a gypsy. But since she weren't here to stop me . . .

CHAPTER FOURTEEN

Snake Handlers

Sorry to leave Birdman and his Maggie, but anxious to show Mama the bird, I skedaddled home.

Soon as the screen door slammed behind me, I hollered. "Mama, come look. Look what I got."

She dried her hands on her apron and took the bird gentle like and stroked its head. "I declare," was all she managed. "Well, I do declare."

Loe and Jewel jumped up and down. She bent over, give 'em a good look-see and let 'em take turns holdin' it. "Now girls, this here bird's gonna rest in my apron pocket and as long as you don't tell a single living soul it's in there, we'll take it out and have us a story come bedtime." She smiled and slipped the wren out of sight.

Mama weren't foolin' me. She didn't want Papa to know Birdman give her a pretty. I come near giving up the Holiness Church after supper. By the time I returned, storytelling would be done for this night. No matter. Could be my only chance to talk to Birdman. And If Rae showed up and I didn't, she'd figure me a coward. I knew better than to care one whit about what she thought of me, but I couldn't help myself.

Mama was surprised when I asked, but she agreed to let me go to the evening service. "It'll be dark when you head home, but Widow Baker's always there. Make certain you walk with her or one of the ladies from Camp."

"Yes ma'am. I figured I'd take some of them wild iris along. I seen some behind the bathhouse this morning. They'd look mighty nice on a little grave up near the church."

She studied me for a moment. "My, my. One day I'll tell you the story 'bout that grave."

•   •   •

Scrapper's eyes shined in the dusky dark. A swarm of lightning bugs blinked and swayed until they hooked together and meandered through the air like a long string of fairy necklaces. They danced through the old graveyard while the tree frogs and katydids tuned up.

Rocks, stacked in piles, was the only grave markers. These folks had no names or dates of birth and death. No fine marble tall and straight like I'd seen in Foggy Mountain's Cemetery with words like *Dearly Beloved* or *Heaven Bound*. And for certain there was no angel statues keeping watch.

Nobody seemed to care who had been laid to rest here, except for Widow Baker. One time I seen her kneeling there, Queen Ann's lace in her arms. She never raised her head, and I eased away into the woods. I headed to the place where black walnuts waited for the gathering.

Aunt Sue, Mama's sister, said the little grave was dug for one reason and one reason only—God's punishment. She shushed when she saw I was listening. Mama said to always remember a broken heart didn't need no burning coals heaped upon it.

I stuck the iris into the lard bucket spilling over with sweet pea vines. Most time when I come up here, I'd sing *She'll be Coming Around the Mountain,* Jewel's favorite. Tonight, I had a stronger urge to hurry toward the singing coming from beyond the pines.

"Wait for me, Scrapper," I said. I give him a good rubbing behind his ears. "I'll be back directly."

When I stopped and looked back, he was sitting beside the lard bucket, his eyes like two shining jewels. I waved before going on and my heart filled up and spilled over for my stub-tailed cat.

•   •   •

In the churchyard, a handful of men squatted on their haunches. They was mostly miners who never darkened the church door, unless the preacher sent some of their kinfolk to drag 'em inside. They was called out-and-out sinners or backsliders. They had a chance to make it into heaven iffen they was to repent in front of the whole congregation with shameful tears.

The men stopped their jawin' and eyed me as I moved past 'em. Their talk soon took up again. My ears perked up.

"My bones don't lie. Something bad's gonna happen…"

"Should've taken care of the good fer nothin' before he left …"

"Where in thunder is he?"

"It's like he disappeared into thin air. Him and his bird. It ain't natural. For certain he ain't from 'round here."

"It ain't fitten to do nothing."

"Well, we shore can't lynch him iffen he ain't here."

They was waitin' for Birdman. Surely he knowed enough to stay away. Maybe he'd caught the smell of Tennessee and I'd never lay eyes on him again.

My troublesome thoughts lifted as I climbed the steps and was pulled into a place like it weren't of this earth. Flickering lamplight cast shadow figures on the walls. They took on lives of their own. The people stood clapping, singing, swaying and toe-tapping with a scattering of shouts. "Hallelujah!" "Yes, Lord!" "Amen, brothers and sisters!"

Soon I was singing along...*On the banks of the Jordan I stand, ready to cross into the promised land*...clapping my hands and doing a little jig step. A woman cried out like she was in great pain. A shiver skittered clear down to my toes and my heart thumped about wildly. No one rushed over to see about the woman or paid her any mind. She soon settled down.

Preacher Sam, dressed in black, walked to the front of the church in long strides. A hush fell over us. "Let us pray," he said in a booming voice like thunder.

His coat raised up with his long arms. He lifted his face.

"Dear Lord, forgive these sinners, for they are your children. Send a revival upon this land. It's shorely ripe for the harvesting..."

After a look-see around the room for Birdman, I was satisfied he weren't there. Granny would say it was a sure sign the Lord kept him away for his own good and maybe for mine. Rae weren't around nowhere, which didn't surprise me none. If they took up snakes tonight, coming here would be worth the trouble.

Someone's eyes burned into me as a bony hand tugged on my hair. I jerked away, a cry in my throat. Elsie Lampert. I don't know why I didn't smell her before she got up next to me. Her cloudy blue eyes searched for someone or something besides me.

Elsie hadn't been right for years, but she was a harmless old woman. She roamed the mountains wearing a brown coat, held together with a latch pin, and a man's black felt hat, no matter what the weather. She was toothless and smelled like a molded mush-melon. She never bothered nobody, and everybody fed her if she showed up at their back door. Somehow, she always knew when a revival was fixing to take place, from Arjay to Crockett and she'd be there. Whenever she'd had enough religion, she'd run out the door and disappear into the woods.

I held my nose against her putrid smell. When she plopped down on the bench, she took up rocking and humming. I moved close to an open window.

Preacher Sam stopped praying, his arms moving high in the air like Moses on the mountaintop. "Brothers and sisters, the Lord told me to prepare for revival. A revival so big this church won't hold all the people hungry for the word. Are we to build a bigger church?"

Feet shuffled about, a man coughed, but no one answered.

"No," the preacher continued. "The Lord says to build a brush arbor and people will come from miles around. If folks won't darken a church door, they'll climb up a mountain to see such a sight. And all God's children gonna meet the Lord under the stars. Can't you see it?"

There was a few scattered "Amens" and "That's right, Brother Smith."

"Each one of us must pray for revival. Do it, brothers and sisters. The Lord has spoken to me as surely he spoke to Noah to build the ark."

The people catched hold of the Holy Spirit and fell on their knees, adding their prayers to the preacher's. Before long weeping and wailing and praying was all jumbled up together, swelling and falling like a living thing. I hoped the Lord could straighten the mess out.

Little by little the people fell off praying, even the preacher, 'til only a few was left. The sound was like a buzzing in the air. One woman's voice rised up, her gibberish known only to God hisself. Taking up snakes was bound to be next.

I was right. Preacher Sam lifted a long wooden box from the floor and set it on a bucket-bench. He raised the lid and reached in without looking. He lifted out two of the fattest snakes I'd ever seen in all my born days. Lumpy, like they'd feasted on mice. Patterns of gold and brown and black was twisted together like a woman's braid. They hung still, draped over the preacher's big hands as if dead. A hush fell over us. The hair on my arms tingled. A cool breeze blew in the windows smelling of a far-off rain.

A woman hollered like she was in terrible pain. Everyone turned toward the sound. Widow Baker. Her long braid swayed back and forth across the back of her flowered dress as she made a beeline towards the preacher.

She looked like even more of a wee woman since Preacher Sam was a giant of a man. She stared at them snakes as she bunched her apron into her hands. Tears streaked down her face.

She reached her hands out, stepped closer and a calm washed over her. The snakes commenced moving, tongues flicking, but their rattles was quiet. I held my breath. The lamplight shined on them creatures with a pure golden light and I wished Rae could see it. Yes sir, such a sight was worth coming tonight, Birdman or no.

Widow Baker stroked one of them snakes with her finger. Then smooth as ribbons, the snakes moved. First one, then the other slid from Preacher Sam to Widow Baker just like it was what she'd told 'em to do.

One traveled up to her neck, slipped underneath her long hair and come around like a pretty necklace. The other hung over her hands and she brought it close to her breasts, cuddled it like a baby. The snake nosed under a bulge between two buttons on her dress and everyone gasped. Widow Baker shut her eyes while the snake pulled its head back and lay still. She mumbled something and smiled.

The Preacher's face shined with sweat. He lifted the snake from her neck and returned it to its box. When he reached for the other one, it must've not been ready to go. It struck, caught the preacher on his thumb. His face turned white as chalk, even his lips in the midst of his black beard. He stumbled back. Widow Baker laid the snake in the box and shut the lid. Church service had ended.

Quicker then a blink, Widow Baker drew a knife from her lace-up shoes. She grabbed the preacher's thumb, made two cuts and sucked his wound. She spit onto the floor and sucked again and again, doing the same. The preacher sank onto a chair pushed to the back of his legs. Mr. Simpson, a miner from camp, rushed to the front of the church with a pint of whiskey and give it to Widow Baker. She rinsed out her mouth and spit three times. Then she poured some whiskey over the preacher's thumb.

"I need some chaw," she hollered. An old woman ran to her, reached inside her mouth and held out a wet glob. Widow Baker pressed the tobacco onto his thumb and wrapped her hanky around it, while the miner tied a piece of rope around the preacher's upper arm.

Women clustered around the preacher, saying since he was a mighty man of God, having such faith as could move mountains, this varmint's poison weren't gonna bother him much more than bee sting. No siree, the preacher had been bit many a time before. The Lord seen him through ever time and this time weren't no different. A test of faith, that's what it was. And the Lord didn't give no man any more than he could bear. Ain't that right, preacher?

His eyes shut and his lips moved beneath his beard. No sound come out of his pale face now dripping with sweat. He might've been praying, but Widow Baker must've figured it weren't gonna be enough. "Not nairy a one of you is gonna deny this man the doctoring he needs. Pray if you've a mind to, but I'll tend to him. Help me get him to his mule. He's coming with me."

Men from the churchyard loaded Preacher Sam onto his swayback mule. His face had changed from white to a sickly yellow and his eyes was half open. His head wobbled about. Widow Baker lifted the reigns and off they went. He was looking more than a little puny. She was the best doctor woman in these parts, but she lived at least two miles from here. It didn't appear to me the preacher would make it.

The church turned dark as the door was pulled shut. The people lost no time hurrying away. I passed by the graveyard to see if Scrapper was around. I wished the moon would show itself for it was pitch black dark

I called for him and he come pouncing to my feet. I stooped to his twitching ears and poured praises into him before scooping him into my arms. "Birdman's gone. Ain't no need for the miners to get riled. He ain't around no more. Don't reckon I'll ever lay eyes on Tennessee. Too far from home anyhow." Scrapper meowed and squirmed and I let him go.

I hurried down the railroad tracks and caught up with Widow Baker and the preacher. His head had slumped down on his chest.

"You reckon he's gonna die?" I twisted around to scratch a chigger bite on my back.

"Iffen he does, either he weren't fit to be a preacher in the first place — and I ain't the one to be the judge of that — or his time to live on this earth is finished, and there ain't nothing nobody can do to change it."

"You gonna doctor him?" I stumbled on a rock but righted myself.

"What kind of fool question is that? Appears to me you need some doctoring your own self. I've got some fresh ointment mixed up that'll take care of them pesky bites. You remind me in case I forget."

"Yes ma'am."

The moon slipped clear of the clouds, spilling light across the sky and the train rails shimmered like gold. Our shadows jumped ahead of us as if urging us on. We picked up our steps and the mule clomped faster. A terrible moan fell from the preacher.

After a bit, Widow Baker said, "Hattie, you got legs like a young filly. Run ahead yonder to your house. I'd be much obliged if your Mama'd allow you to stay the night. It's bound to be a long one, and I could use your help. Iffen you should get to my place before us, build a fire in the cook-stove and draw some water. We oughta be there directly." I took off running, Scrapper at my heels.

Preacher Sam might die. Birdman was gone. I had to give up all foolish thoughts of goin' anywhere. *Impossible* shouted in my ear, thumped in my chest. I'd never leave these mountains. I'd always loved 'em, but this night they was hemming me in. The mountains pressed down on me. They stole my breath.

CHAPTER FIFTEEN

The Preacher and
the Doctor Woman

Mama popped up from the swing. Its chains jerked and creaked behind her. "Pray tell where you've been, young lady? Preachin' bound to be long over."

Before she could lay into me good, I jumped ahead to save us a world of time. "Preacher Sam's done got hisself bit by a rattler and he's near death's door and Widow Baker figures he needs more than praying over and she's taking him home with her and she said she'd be obliged for my help." I took a deep breath and blowed it out. "Said she needed my help powerful bad or he'd die for shore and certain."

Mama left off studying me and rushed inside. I followed her. She stood at the stove wrapping fried apple pies in a cloth. She gathered biscuits and stuffed 'em with pieces of leftover fatback and packed everything in a lard bucket. After tapping the lid shut, she handed it to me.

"Iffen it's his time to go, he'll die no matter what doctoring she done. But iffen the Lord wills it, he could live with her help. Loetta can take up the slack 'til you return."

I hugged Mama quick and hard, the yellow and blue pail thumping about wildly. She took our lantern off its nail by the back door and put two matches in my hand. "Light it only iffen the moon ain't enough," she said. "Kerosene's got to last a spell."

"Yes, ma'am."

Mama's dark eyes shined as she touched my cheek and tucked a lock of hair behind my ear. Then she turned back to the stove making an awful racket.

Me and Scrapper ran past the old chestnut stump and moved into the darkness near the garden. The back screen door squeaked open. "Hattie Mae," Mama called. "iffen you're fixing to go down that a way… You ain't got no business doing such…Your Pa'll tan your hide iffen he finds out. Hattie?"

She waited. I never made a sound. The screen door slammed and I continued in the direction of Papa's whiskey-making operation, the shortest way to Widow Baker's. Besides, he weren't tendin' to his sour mash tonight. He'd gone huntin' with Colonel and Neverblue. Even cripped up like he was, he was determined to go.

The woods thickened. Not one speck of moonlight. The dark was as black as coal. I squatted next to a tree. I struck a match against the bark, lifted the lantern's chimney, lit the wick and turned it down low.

Papa had made certain there weren't no footpath to follow in these woods. I'd have to pick my way with light no brighter'n a lightning bug.

A panther screamed sounding like a woman. I took off running until I was clean out of breath. I stopped and leaned against a tall pine. Paws pounced on my feet. A holler flew out of my throat.

Scrapper rubbed against my legs. I bent down and gathered him under my chin. "I knowed it was you. I knowed it was you all along." I held my breath wondering if Papa had heard me, was behind a tree waiting till I come by.

"Oh Lordy sakes alive, Scrapper, we got to get down this here mountain. We got to go help Widow Baker like she asked."

I set him down and off he took, moving through the underbrush. A hoot owl called. Or maybe it weren't no owl a'tall, but Papa's warning to whoever was where he weren't supposed to be. I took off, making a racket, running down and down and down.

I swore on Granny's grave I'd stay away from this side of the mountain for the rest of my borned days. All of a sudden, moonlight fell on Widow Baker's tin roof. I had made it. No light showed in her windows. A shot whizzed in the thickets behind me, then another.

I blew the lantern out and flew like my feet'd sprouted wings. I never stopped 'til I ran into her kitchen table with clang of pail and lantern. I felt about, set 'em down on the smooth wood, my wits returning. I found her stove, struck my last match, spotted a lamp and lighted it. Thankfully, a box of matches laid on a shelf. I got busy laying a fire.

After the fire caught, I picked up a bucket to pump some water. A basket of little June apples was on the table and beside it was a small wooden bowl with something like a potato masher only smaller. There was a little bit of fine yellow powder in the bowl and a dozen or more brown bottles, their stoppers in a pile, sat to one side.

I loved her kitchen. Especially the bunches of plants hanging from the ceiling, some fresh picked, some dried and drawed up. Clumps of gray, white, brown, blue and yellow. Like an upside-down flower garden. The smell was better than stretching out in fresh hay. Then I remember my chore and rushed outside to the yard pump.

Back inside, no sooner had I filled two large pots and set 'em on the stove . . . a commotion out front drawed me outside in a hurry.

The old swayback mule snorted and heaved for air. I'd have to tend to the pitiful thing later as I tied it to a hitching post. Preacher Sam slid to the ground. Me and Widow Baker got underneath his arms, drug him inside and dropped him onto her bed. She rushed off to mix her snakebite medicine, instructing me to keep a wet rag on his head. "And pull his boots off," she hollered back. The first part was easy, the bucket of water I'd pumped still cold. Preacher Sam had big feet and his legs was as heavy as tree trunks and he weren't no help a'tall. I wiggled and tugged one dusty boot off and then the other.

Widow Baker returned and helped me pull him up higher in the bed. We propped his feet on the footboard. When I changed the cloth on his forehead, he opened his eyes, but they rolled back in his head. I wondered if he died would I help get his body ready for burying, like Mama and me had done with Granny? An ordinary coffin, stacked on the porch of Caywood's Hardware, wouldn't be long enough. It'd have to be special made.

"Hold his head still, Hattie. He ain't wanting to take this."

He struggled to get away from the spoon of thick liquid, black as molasses. It smelled like rat guts ought to smell. I climbed up in the bed behind him and kept his head from thrashing about. When Widow Baker was satisfied she'd gotten enough down him, she sent me after soap, hot water, and a slop bucket. I welcomed the chance to escape the smell spreading throughout the room.

When I returned, the worst was yet to come. "Get here quick," she hollered.

She held his head over the side of the bed. "Here it comes."

The bucket caught thick, yellow liquid spewing from his mouth. The smell of the medicine weren't nothing compared to the stink pouring out of him. My stomach heaved and I felt weak-kneed. Time after time he puked. I feared his insides would come out. Finally, he fell back on the bed looking like death itself. I sat the bucket down and run to the front porch, leaned over the railing and emptied my own stomach. How could I go back?

Widow Baker hollered my name.

"We got to do it again! You fit enough?"

I nodded, pushing my hair out of my face.

"Wet a rag and lay it on the back of your neck. Move!"

This time the preacher was too weak to fight the medicine. The foul mess come out of him again and again 'til he tried to puke but couldn't. When he fell back, Widow Baker said, "We're done for now. We'll see how he gets along."

She wiped her hands on her apron, turned to me and looked me over. "In all our doings I clean forgot. Bring me the brown jar sittin' on my dresser."

She smeared a cool cream all over my chigger bites. Then she handed me the jar and said for me to go in the next room and spread it wherever else I itched. I never argued, though in tendin' to the preacher I'd forgot to scratch.

Widow Baker washed him while I stood near an opened window and watched. My skin felt like I'd been bathed in mint and the cream had dried into chalky white patches. "Look," I said, holding my arms out. "I'm a leper. Like in the Bible."

She glanced up. "Smear some more salve on them arms. They ain't white enough, yet. Don't be skimpy with it and don't you be washing it off neither for nigh on two days."

I felt a bit crotchety over her bossiness. Then I noticed she weren't doing nothing to the preacher's thumb. "Ain't you gonna suck the poison out again?"

"I'll take care of his thumb when the time's right. Not before." She went about unbuttoning his shirt.

"Of a certain, though," I added, "you got the power of healing. Not me. No siree. I don't know nothing about such. 'Cept for maybe a burn from grease or a sting from a honeybee. Granny always…"

"You could learn if you've a mind to. Folks is always in need of a doctor woman and it won't be long 'fore I'll be too old to traipse all over these hills."

"Who learned you?"

"An old Cherokee woman mostly. Named Goingback. Hadn't thought of her in years. She's bound to be dead by now. The rest I learned as I went along, I reckon. Folks talk about Red Bird Mission being the place to get such learning these days. I fancy the old ways myself.

We raised the preacher up and took his shirt off. I sucked in my breath. He was covered with thick black hair. It spilled over the top of his undershirt. Afraid to touch him there, I run my hand over his fuzzy arm.

She sent me to throw the dirty water out the back door and get some fresh. By the time I returned, the preacher's pants laid across a straight-back chair and a quilt had been throwed over him. I wondered how she managed when she weren't bigger than a minute, as Mama would say.

Widow Baker smeared a yellow salve over his thumb. The smell was sharp and burned my nose. He stirred and opened his eyes. He looked fierce, like a wild animal. Was death standing outside the door…waiting…biding its time?

•   •   •

We stood over him for hours, wiped his face and neck with a wet rag. I held him still when Widow Baker gave him more medicine. I held the bucket when he puked. In between all our doings, Widow Baker told me about her remedies for this and that.

A bleeding wound called for spider webs. If a person had tired blood, she'd beat lady's slipper to a powder and mix it with a little water. Burns required castor oil and egg whites bound to the wound with a clean cloth, but if a person had never seen his pa in his entire life, he could draw the fire out of a burn just by blowing on it.

White whiskey, which she declared Isom Sizemore made the best in these parts, was the main ingredient in many a cure, from snakebites to pneumonia. There was a few I weren't too sure about. Such as if a person had a fever, all he had to do was cut his toenails, gather the pieces in a cloth, tie 'em to a live eel, put the creature back in the water and it'd carry the fever away. A fried rat cured whooping cough if all else failed. And if you had cramps in your feet, turn your shoes upside down before going to bed. Good thing I never had no trouble with my feet, 'cause she never said what a person done who didn't have no shoes.

"What about them plants hanging upside down in your kitchen? What do you do with 'em?"

"For one thing, I make the best cough syrup they is. Give your Mama some of it last winter when you young'uns was near hacking yourself to death. I take a whole rat's vein plant and a handful each of wild cherry bark and black gum bark. Simmer for near two hours, add a pint of sugar and boil again. Better than the mess they make at Wilcox Drug Store. I sell 'em the cherry and gum bark, but I never told 'em about the rat's vein plant. No siree. I ain't never gonna tell 'em neither. Might put me outta business."

She laughed and threw her head back showing a mouthful of crooked, stained teeth. I figured she was funning me 'cause nobody ever traipsed clear to Foggy Mountain for medicine when we could get doctored by Widow Baker, in exchange maybe for fresh eggs or tomatoes from the garden. What surprised me was them drug store men would buy what they could walk out in the woods and gather for their ownselves, if they had any gumption a'tall.

"They pay you money for bark off a tree?"

"For 'sang too, iffen I can find it. It's getting scarce'n hen's teeth. But there's pennyroyal, boneset, horsemint, and gingerroot. Always asking when I can bring more."

I'd heard tell of digging 'sang, but had no idea of them other plants fetching money. "What iffen I was to gather up some of them plants. You reckon them men would buy from me?"

Widow Baker looked up from fluffing the preacher's pillows with deep frown wrinkles. "Oh, I wouldn't never do nothing to take away from your business," I added. "I'd never think about doing such as that. Reckon my mouth runned ahead of my thinking. But I shore would fancy doing something besides catching snakes. Appears to me the preacher ought to stay away from snakes his own self."

She straightened up, pressing her hands into the small of her back. "Nobody ought to mess with snakes unless he's been touched by the Spirit."

"Papa said I'm touched, but he don't mean it thataway. I'm aiming to leave this here holler one day, but not without some money in my pocket. Might even travel from one place to another, like them gypsies. They're bound to see some wonderous places, even meet up with some folks who love books same as me. Them books we brung to you, why they is falling apart. And I can't abide keepin' my only book underneath my bed much longer."

Widow Baker nodded. She looked down at the preacher and laid her cheek against his. "Good. He's cooled down." She reached over and patted my arm. "Come out to the kitchen. You look like you could use a cup of tea and we'll talk."

When I sank into a chair, tiredness washed over me. Widow Baker filled a teacup and pushed it towards me. I sipped the quar-tasting stuff and gagged. It smelled like an old fishing worm. She sat in a chair across from me and poured herself a healthy portion of Papa's whiskey. After takin' a big swallow she leaned forward.

"Iffen you choose to leave these hills, always remember how to find your way back. These are your folks, good and bad. They're a part of ya."

"You're sounding like my Granny. Miss her something fierce."

"And you always will. You had a powerful love for her." She took another swallow of the home brew. "Aah, that's good," she said with a sigh. "Best phlegm cutter they is."

I wondered how she bought her whiskey since Papa wouldn't abide her comin' around. Mama must've brung it to her in secret.

She stood, poured me some more tea and settled into her chair again. "Hattie, I knowed you're the one's been carrying flowers up to the church graveyard, adding 'em to mine. Lucy Grace. Hard to think she's been gone nigh onto twelve year now. Ain't that about the time you come into this world?"

"I'm fifteen now."

"My, my. That's right. For a minute there, I disremembered your Mama had no arm-baby at the time Lucy passed on. The girl-child was you peeking around your Mama's dress tail. Your Mama. The only one in all of Ashworth who weren't damning me to hell for what I'd done….Lucy was a sweet thing, her skin the color of nutmeg. So smooth..." She stopped talkin', her eyes full and soft. She was looking back, remembering.

"How did she die?"

"Scarlet fever. People said it was because James and me had gone against the law. A white woman loving a Negro man? Not only weren't it allowed, James could've been hung for even lookin' my way. Only he died before that could happen." Her eyes turned hard, her voice cold. "They killed James for standing up to the boss man. Always sending the Negro miner down the shaft if there was any charges not blown. What did it matter iffen the dynamite blew up in his hands? James knowed he ought to keep his mouth shut, stay in his place. He was called many an ugly name. 'No count nigger' was one of the more polite ones."

She raised her head, her eyes flashing. Her words punched me in the stomach, made me want to shout no, Lord a mercy, no.

"Shot him six times because he refused to go. Six times. And him a man who never touched a gun or a knife in his whole life. They killed others, too. Said they was fixing to have a riot on their hands. I reckon that's the truth. When it was all over, eight Negro men lay dead. Talk of a strike swept through the camp, but it never took hold 'cause the next morning two truckloads of armed thugs rolled into camp. Banged on ever miner's front door, aimed their rifles at the women and the children. 'Return to work or else,' was all them men said. And so they did. I understand why them miners had no choice, but I ain't forgot what happened here."

"Mr. Harper done all that?"

"Before his time. They took them Negroes and buried 'em the same day. Nailed the coffins shut and dug the holes before I got word. Never even had a preacher say any words, but the singing…They couldn't stop folks gathering up there in the dark of night. *Swing low, sweet chariot, coming for to carry me home.* Lordy, I'll never forget the singing.

Buried 'em with nary a marker. I'm having a fine marble one made, with ever name on it, ever miner killed. Soon have it paid for, free and clear, and a man's bringing it from Foggy Mountain to set it in place."

"Now I knowed why there ain't no Negroes in our camp."

Widow Baker finished her whiskey, sitting the glass down hard. "I'll be back directly," she said and went out the back door carrying a lantern.

I sipped my tea and gazed at the books lining a shelf over the sink. One in particular caught my interest. *The Home Doctor. The Little Book That Tells You How.* I took it down and returned to my chair. I thumbed through the pages, but the remedies offered used a mixture of ingredients I'd never heard tell of. Disappointed, I closed the book.

I wished Widow Baker would go on talking about Lucy and her Papa, the Negro miner.

After she returned and checked on the preacher, she leaned against her kitchen cabinet. It was stacked with papers and more books that looked tattered and worn. She motioned to the book I'd laid on her table. "I see you been lookin' at one of my doctoring books."

"Don't understand most of it." I reached for one of Mama's fried pies as Widow Baker took a corncob pipe out of her apron pocket.

"Ahhh, but some of it could be useful iffen you've a mind to learn. The school up past Crockett, Red Bird Mission, I brought to your mind earlier . . . They teach new ways of doctorin'." She filled her pipe. "I could learn you the old ways and then if you should go there, you'd have both to pull from." Soon as she got her pipe going, the air smelled as sweet as a cake baking.

I licked my fingers and thought about eating another fried pie. "Ain't got no reason to learn doctoring. Besides, what we done to the preacher made me sicker'n a mule."

"Don't be so quick. Your stomach would behave the more you doctored. You ain't old enough to be sot in your ways. Keep your mind open and don't shut the door just yet." She pulled a chair up to the table and sat across from me.

"Since you're interested in gathering herbs," she continued, "Bloody Cove's one of the few places left unspoiled by coal mining or logging. That's where the best plants is growing. Could be you might go with me next time. Iffen you should go alone always remember, whatever you gather or dig, don't clear a patch clean. Leave some for next time. That's why 'sang ain't gonna be around much longer. Mark my word. People has done got greedy."

She drew on her pipe and studied me. "Drink ever drop of your tea. Help you sleep." Her voice was soft and low like she'd tucked her Lucy and James away for now.

I drained the cup even though the tea was cold and bitter.

She stood, left the room and returned with a pillow and quilt. "I ain't got a bed to offer, but I reckon the porch swing would serve as well."

"Yes, ma'am. That'd be mighty fine."

She fussed over fixing my bed to her liking, smoothing the quilt, fluffing the pillow. I watched with heavy eyes. "Lonesome Creek," I said half-dreaming, "Lonesome Creek's in Bloody Cove. That's where Jim fancied to go fishing."

She untied her apron and folded it in her hands. "Prettiest place I ever did see. They's Indians live back in there, but they ain't gonna bother you none. Some is right friendly. Matter of fact, Goingback showed me a place to dig for 'sang that few knowed about."

I sat on the swing, pulled my legs up, rested my head on the softest pillow I could ever remember. Widow Baker slipped inside and my eyes shut.

Scrapper jumped up next to me and we floated in the air. Scrapper and me together. He set about washing the back of my hand, shivers running clear up my arm. His purring filled me with pure pleasure and I drifted into sleep, deep and dreamless.

• • •

A crow screeched, and I sat up not knowing where I was. Scrapper was gone. Fog moved across the porch like ghost whispers. I hopped out of the swing and hurried inside.

Widow Baker weren't around. Preacher Sam's eyes was closed. He was bare-chested with a quilt pulled up underneath his armpits. His hands was folded on top of his chest with his thumb sticking up. It looked like he held a yellow candle. I thought maybe he was teetering on the edge of dying. I leaned over him.

My nose bumped his, his eyes flew open and I jumped back. "Holy cow," I said. "You ain't dead."

He grinned, his black beard parting to show tobacco-stained teeth. "Reckon the good Lord sent Sister Baker to let me preach revival."

"You ain't fit to do such."

"That's what some of the good Pentecostal folks gonna be saying. Only they gonna be talking about how I ain't got enough faith to refuse doctoring."

"Hadn't they rather have you alive than dead?"

"Not iffen I was healed by a doctor woman instead of relying on the Lord to see me through. I must've stepped away from the Lord, backslid don'tcha know, or I wouldn't have got bit in the first place. I could be forgiven for that. But some won't never forget I give in to doctoring — won't never and that's a fact."

"You still aiming to build a brush arbor for a revival? How you gonna do it by yourself? The people ain't gonna follow you up there to help. And how you gonna preach iffen there ain't nobody to listen?"

"You full of questions, ain't ya? Well, Miss Hattie, it's like this…I have to listen to the good Lord and not worry about what other people think or do."

"And what does he say?"

"To get ready 'cause judgment day's a'coming."

"Birdman gonna help ya get ready?"

"Who?"

"The man who come into Ashworth a few days ago. The man the miners don't want in their bathhouse even though Rae's Pa told him he could stay. The man they was fixing to run off only he left before they done it. He said he talked to you. He's on his way to Tennessee."

"Oh yes, I recollect him. The man with the black bird. Can't say. He's a mite strange, talking to his bird all the time, but I will say the Lord works in mysterious ways. Mysterious ways. I put it in His hands."

"Well, iffen anybody asks me, I'll tell 'em ya got more gumption than most around these parts. Building a brush arbor when there's no way of knowing iffen one soul will be there. To preach when there might be nary one to hear. Some folk might call ya a fool."

"Well he ain't no fool and that's for certain," Widow Baker said, coming in the door. The smell of lye soap and her dusting powder floated around her. She couldn't have slept any during the night, but she'd brushed her long hair and her eyes looked bright and shiny. If I ever needed doctoring, I wanted this woman instead of old Doc Evans. He smelled like the medicine bag he carried and grunted like a sow when he poked someone's belly.

She fluffed Preacher Sam's pillows, her long hair falling over his face but he didn't seem to mind. Then she was up, fluttering about the room, raising a window higher and gathering up the washrags and towels.

"Hattie, go get the preacher some coffee and a bowl of mush from the stove. Iffen he's gonna be in the land of the living, he needs some hot vittels."

While he ate, Widow Baker read from the Bible. "I will take the cup of salvation and call upon the name of the Lord…"

I returned to the kitchen, helped myself to the mush and coffee. Then I washed the dishes and swept the floor. I was fixing to scrub it, when she appeared in the doorway.

"Lord-a-mercy child, ain't you done enough?" She dabbed her upper lip with a hanky. The morning had turned hot already.

"Why I ain't done much a'tall."

She smiled, looking right comely, and took the scrub brush from my hand. "Tell your Mama I couldn't have done it without you. In my younger days there weren't nothing I wouldn't tackle, but now . . . Well now time is movin' on. I ain't gonna be around forever you know. These mountain folks gonna always be needin' a doctor-woman. You might think on that." She smiled and pressed her hand on my shoulder before turning to snip a piece of dried herb hanging above the window.

"You certain you don't need me. . . "

She shook her head. "You scoot on home. The looks of his thumb is bothering me, but I can take care of it iffen the need arises."

Thumping down her porch steps, Widow Baker's words whirled in my head. *Couldn't have done it without you. Ain't gonna be around forever. You could learn doctoring if you've a mind to.*

Have a mind to? How could I? The thought of Preacher Sam puking his guts out turned my stomach upside down even now.

Red Bird Mission? I could never consider goin' to such a place. First of all, I had no money and even iffen I did, Papa would set our hounds loose and track me down. He'd snatch me back home where I belong. Mama wanted me close by, but I had to go a far piece, where he couldn't follow.

CHAPTER SIXTEEN

The Revenuers

The lantern swished with kerosene. My sparing of it would pleasure Mama. Scrapper explored the bushes along the tracks, running to catch up with me time and again. Puffy clouds moved across the sky. Sun and shadows played over the mountains alive with blooming redbud trees. The first sign of spring though a chill was in the air.

Since Jim had left us and Papa was weak and broke up, besides coughing his insides out—we'd have no payment from the Ashworth Coal Company. Mr. Harper fancied Papa's whiskey. Would he be fit enough to cook up another batch? And if he was to do such, would it bring us enough money to get by?

Jim was gone. I picked up a rock and threw it into a ditch. Jim'd left a deep ache in my heart and nothing on this earth could heal it. Like my brother, could I leave these mountains where the coal company ruled our lives? My head buzzed with daydreams of gathering herbs to sell. I could see Mr. Wilcox smiling…taking the bunches I'd gathered . . . handing me a pouch stuffed with silver dollars… Maybe I'd have more than I needed, and I'd fill Mama's tobacco tin. Why she'd cry tears of . . .

Two men stepped out of nowhere. Scrapper took off. Dressed the same, the men wore shiny black suits and sported handle bar mustaches. They carried rifle-guns like I'd never seen before. Revenuers. Government men aiming to bust up all the whiskey stills till there weren't none left in all of Carr County and beyond.

"Where you going, little girl?" one said.

All of a sudden, I felt feather-legged. "I ain't no little girl and it ain't none of your business."

The one who spoke looked stout as a bull. He stepped forward with a quar-looking grin spread over his face. "Why looky here, Vincent, she's not a little girl. And spunky, too. I'd say she was close to becoming a woman. A real woman."

He unbuttoned his jacket with one hand, holding his gun in the other. He then fumbled with the buttons on his fly. His eyes narrowed and he looked at me like Mr. Harper had done standing at our yard gate. My heart jumped about wildly. These men could give me more trouble than I'd seen in my whole entire life.

Sunlight washed over me and my skin looked white as snow. I'd been given a sign. "Thank you, Lord," I said, holding my hands up. "Don't you come no closer, mister."

He laughed. "And why not?" Vincent fingered his mustache and frowned at the big man.

"I just come from the doctor." I held out my arms, lifted my face. "She says I got a rarified creeping fungus. It's eating my skin off. Anybody touches me is bound to get it and there ain't no cure."

The man took his hand out of his privates and stepped back. He weren't grinning no more. "You're lying. Looks to me like we got to teach you a lesson."

Vincent looked at his partner. "What's the matter with you? Let's get out of here."

"Shut up," the man said. Quick as a flash, he cocked his rifle-gun and aimed it square at my head. "Go. Before I blow your brains out."

I turned and ran, all the while screaming inside myself, sweet Jesus save me. I ran back towards Widow Baker's. I couldn't go home. What if they followed me?

Ever breath told me to run…Run…Run…My lungs would surely bust. The curve…the curve…make it past the curve. A pain grabbed my side. I didn't slow down. Just beyond the bend, I looked back. They wasn't nowhere in sight. I spotted the closest hiding place. Underneath the creek's footbridge.

I dropped down to the water, hunkered amongst bushes and weeds. I didn't care if a million chiggers was fixing to have a feast. They had saved me, plus Widow Baker's medicine. I smiled in spite of myself.

Scrapper jumped onto my lap. "Shhh," I whispered, "Don't make a sound."

We waited. Surely Willie had spotted the men earlier. They wasn't sneaking around in secret. Creek water gurgled and splashed, going about its business, giving no answers. I watched a crawdad at the water's edge, doing a sideways dance. A little black snake slipped into the creek.

Them men was as fresh as daisies. They hadn't been climbing no mountain or knocking down no still. They must've looked around camp and the bathhouse, without going any further.

Hard shoes clumped overhead. I didn't dare breathe. They stood above me on the bridge, lighting cigarettes. A match fell through a crack. I could see the bottoms of their shoes, their black socks, their black pants. What if they looked down and seen me scrunched down here, trying to make myself invisible? What if Scrapper meowed?

The men argued. Right off I found out they weren't interested in following me, or in finding a small-time operator like Papa. They was out to make a name for themselves.

"I'm telling you," Vincent said, "we're wasting our time in this godforsaken place."

"How many times do I have to tell you to trust me? If we poke around here awhile, then we can leave like we've given up. Don't you know these people are ignorant? They can't see past the end of their noses. Why we'll even stop by the commissary before we go, to say how this trip was a waste of our time. They'll be convinced we've gone back to Frankfort and word will spread across these mountains like wildfire. We'll ride out of here like we're worn out and defeated."

"But...," Vincent started.

"Hold on. I ain't finished. I've got a place all picked out where we can hide the horses. You and me are going to circle around Panther Mountain on foot, just beyond Ashworth. Know what's there? Why, Big Jim Coal Company, that's what. A reliable source says they're hiding barrels of home brew in the gondolas, under the coal. Bound for Louisville or points beyond. Now what do you think?" He slapped Vincent on his back. "You and me are getting a promotion."

Vincent grumbled low. "You make it sound...a...cake. Speaking of cake, I'm starving. We ain't had breakfast, in case you forgot."

"Quit your bellyaching," the big man said. A cigarette butt was tossed into the creek, another was ground under a shoe. "We'll get us a cold Orange Crush, some thick-sliced bologna and a loaf of bread over at the commissary. No Wonder Bread this far back in the sticks though, we'll have to make-do with what they got. How does that suit you? Then we just might find us a shady spot and rest awhile." He laughed and slapped Vincent's back again. "You sure got a lot to learn about these hollers and the people living in them."

I stayed hidden, counted their steps to the commissary. Now they ought to be crossing the dirt road. Past the horseshoe pits, a burned-up chimney and then the small orchard of gnarled apple trees. Past the trees, the whitewashed company store stood in a clearing. They'd climb its steps, ten in all.

I crept up the creek bank, peeked through thick weeds. The men stood at the bottom of the store's steps, talking to some woman. Elsie Lampert. They'd get their ears full of some crazy gibberish. I couldn't help but snicker.

Scrapper rubbed against my legs. "For pity's sake, if they listen to her, they won't know which way is up."

I run home to tell Mama about the revenuers. She would send for Willie. He'd warn the Big Jim bootleggers. They might return the favor to us one day.

Mountain folks always looked out for each other. Strangers would never do such. Granny had said iffen I was to walk outta these hollers, consider what I might be leavin' behind. Papa and his fractious ways. Yes. But I'd also leave Mama and my sisters, Willie and Widow Baker. The ones most dear to me.

Next to *impossible.*

CHAPTER SEVENTEEN

Death Comes Calling

I run up our footpath. Not only did I need to let Mama know about the revenuers, I'd disremembered what day this was. She'd be needing my help. Today was Monday, wash day.

How had she managed without Jim to tote the creek water up to our yard, and then me not showing up 'til late morning?

I dreaded the work ahead of me. Distant thunder rumbled although the sun shinned bright. Wash day. In good weather, on the hillside out back. If not, the kitchen walls soon wept streams of water.

Coming into the yard, smoke curled from the pipe over the kitchen. I wondered what on earth Mama was doing cooking dinner on wash day. There was no time for such. We was lucky to get left over sweet potatoes and cold biscuits. I runned around to the back of the house. No fire under the big iron pot in the yard.

Inside, Loe and Jewel played a game of peep-pie under the kitchen table. Mama peeled taters and the pie-safe doors was throwed open showing two pies.

'Who died?" I said, not knowing for truth someone had.

"Little Mary Wilson," Mama said.

"Mary Wilson?" I whispered, for shore thinking I'd heard wrong. Any thoughts of revenuers flew out of my head.

"Yellow jackets," Loe said. "A whole mess of 'em come right out of the ground and covered her up when it ain't even summertime yet. Her body swelled like a blowed up hog's bladder. Wait till you see her. You won't believe your eyes."

"Hush," Mama said. "We ain't going up there to gawk. Them that's grieving don't need such."

"Nobody come for Widow Baker," I said in disbelief.

"No need," Mama said. "In maybe ten minutes time, the pore thing had done crossed over to the other side. Flew away with the angels." She stopped peeling and fixed her eyes on me. "What about Preacher Sam? Is he gonna make it?"

"Widow Baker says he would've died without my help. She says I got the gift for doctoring."

"You don't say. Don't you think the Lord had something to do with him getting along so good?" She dropped a tater into the pot.

"Yes ma'am. I expect He did."

I wished the Lord had also taken care of Mary Wilson. The same age as Jewel, almost to the day. Their only baby-child. What would they do upon their ridge without her laughter filling the air? Her yellow hair flying behind her when she run? Mr. Wilson had sold his giant poplar trees to Big Jim Coal Company, timbers to shore up miles of tunnels. Got more money than anyone around these parts. And besides that, he had dug into a vein of coal one-day by accident, when he was plowing to plant corn. Figured he was set for life.

Loetta said, "Some folks is faulting Birdman."

"Birdman? How? You said them yellow jackets…"

I turned to Mama for answers. She was working up a mess of biscuit dough and throwed in more flour. "Mary weren't near the nest. Nobody'd done nothing to stir 'em up, neither. No call for 'em to swarm out of a hole in the ground and sting her all over her like they done. No call."

"You don't believe…"

She shook her head. "Don't matter what I think iffen enough folks get stirred up. Some reckon since he come from out yonder, Birdman drug a curse alongside him. Good thing he's gone. Much as I fancy the little wren he give me, he don't belong in our …"

"Lord-a-mercy, Mama. I clean forgot. I run into some revenuers coming home."

Mama dropped her biscuit cutter and her floured hands grabbed my shoulders. "Where? They give you any trouble? How many? Your Pa… Did you see what direction…"

"Only two men and they never give me much trouble. They headed towards the commissary for bologna and bread. They're messing around here a spell, but they ain't looking for no stills."

Mama went back to cutting biscuits, but she kept looking up at me. "What on earth?"

"They gonna poke around enough to make us think they're doing some actual looking, but then they'll leave. We'll think they've gone back to Frankfort. When for a fact they're circling around to Big Jim to catch 'em hiding barrels of whiskey under the coal."

Mama stopped again as a frown overtook her face. "How did you come by all this?"

"Me and Scrapper was hunkered under the bridge. Them revenuers stood above us, smoking cigarettes and talking."

"Loe," Mama said, "Run tell Willie. He'll know what to do. Quick now. Time's a'wasting."

Loetta clanged the lid onto the bean pot and flew out the door. Mama never asked me to go and I was glad. I'd had my fill of running for a spell.

Besides, it'd be a sight better talking to Mama without Loetta having to know ever thing going on. She could be a pure eejit sometimes. Why soon as she got wind of me making a trip into Bloody Cove, so I could carry some plants to Wilcox Drugs, she'd keep on and on like hounds after a coon 'til she was smack in the middle of my plans. And then likely as not she'd guess and soon know why I was hankering to have my own money. Nothing a secret no more. The longer I kept my nosy sister out of things, the better

Mama slided a pan of biscuits into the oven and set about frying some potato cakes along with onions. She hadn't forgot it was nearing our dinnertime in her doings for the Wilsons, and I hoped some of them biscuits was for us, too. I took one of our ironstone plates and set the table.

"Mama, tell me about Widow Baker. Seems to me I'm old enough."

She flipped the cakes. They sizzled in the hot grease turning brown and crisp around the edges. The smell set my mouth to watering. I cleaned a pile of green onions, fresh from the garden. "Evelyn Baker is and always has been a good woman. Always remember that."

"She told me about James and baby Lucy."

"She must think right smart of you if she done that. Did she tell you they weren't married?"

"I guessed they wasn't."

"Oh, she would've married him, iffen times was different. Against the law for a colored man and a white woman. Even dangerous to be seen together. Good thing they was never caught. Had to sneak around like they was runaway slaves."

"James was murdered in cold blood. Only it weren't because he loved Widow Baker."

"Yes, I knowed that."

"Eight men was shot and buried in the graveyard up yonder with no markers."

"I knowed that, too. It's a terrible thing they done. Reckon you want to know how she lives here without a man to dig coal?"

I nodded. Mama pushed the skillet of potato cakes to the back of the stove and settled into a chair at the table. I scooted my chair up close.

"Evelyn seen James in the commissary one day. And he noticed her too, on the sly of course. Story goes they took to meeting in secret right off. She had walked from Bloody Cove to do some trading with her herbs and....No, she didn't always live in these hollers. No, she ain't an Indian like some folks think. She's dark because she traipses all over these hills, looking for this plant and that'n or looking after sick folks with nary a cover on her head, nor her arms neither."

"Anyway, James walked into Bloody Cove ever Sunday and they'd hide away in the woods for a few hours, a different place each time. After she learned of the killing, and the burying the self-same day, she was determined to live near the graveyard, though she never knowed exactly which grave held his body.

She built herself a brushy lean-to underneath the laurels. People around here wouldn't have nothing to do with her. When I could no longer stand the thoughts of a grieving woman up there with her baby and the nights getting cold, I carried her some food and a quilt. And I made sure they faired well ever day. We've been friends since then."

"You ain't explained how..."

"I'm getting to it. Mr. Sutton, the boss man at the time, swore he heard James talking inside the mines, after him being dead a week or so."

"What did James say?"

"Told him to look after Evelyn or he and all the other Negroes would fix it so the miners would never enter them dark tunnels again. Ain't nothing worse than a spooked miner. Widow Baker got herself a house. For herself and her little girl."

"Only Lucy died."

"Some folks say it was God's punishment. She took up doctoring soon after that. I allow she's gifted with healing."

"You don't think God took Lucy because…"

"She's a good woman who loved a man. A Negro man. Do you think God would take away her child because of that?"

"No, ma'am, I reckon not."

"Lucy died of scarlet fever. Mary died from yellow jackets. Plain and simple. Only it seems some folks got to put the blame somewhere besides where it belongs."

Jewel hollered and Mama jumped up to tend to her. I pondered what she had said. She was right. Seemed people got to put the blame somewhere. Papa faulted Mr. Harper for the timbers falling on his leg, for the death of a young miner and the crippling of another. I reckoned I did, too. He was warned Number Nine needed shoring up, and he did nothing to fix it.

The biscuits smelled overdone. I grabbed a cloth, and reached inside the oven. "Forty damnations," I hollered. I tossed the pan on the stovetop and reached for the lard bucket, a blister popping up.

Mama rushed in with Jewel on her hip. "You hurt?" she asked, her eyes lookin me over.

"Not much. Iffen I'd never seen Papa in my whole life, I could blow on the burn and the fire would go clean out."

"That a fact?"

"It's what I heared."

"Don't think I'd put much stock in it."

Mama fixed a plate for her and Jewel to share. I set across from them at the table. "Ain't you hungry?" Mama asked.

I stared at the tabletop.

"Now what's on your mind?"

I squirmed in my seat. "Well…uh…"

"Go ahead, spit it out."

"What iffen I was to get me some plants to sell? After all my chores was done, of course. And I'd even do extra without you asking, like picking all the bugs off the rose bushes this summer. Would you let me?"

Loe come running in the door grumbling as she came.

"Who's coming into this house all sideways and ornery?" Mama said as she loosened Jewel's grip on a spoon. Go back outside 'til you find our sweet girl-child, Loetta."

She fixed her eyes on Mama, who went about feeding Jewel a spoonful of applesauce. Without a word, my short-tempered sister stomped out the back door. When she returned, she drawed close to the table, eased down on the bench quiet as a mute, without nary a sign of her grumpy self. She filled her plate with potato cakes, biscuits, onions and applesauce like she'd not eat for a month of Sundays. Mama winked at me and leaned to my ear. "We'll talk later."

Her words made me feel near growed up. Like Mama and me had a secret. And it felt good. My stomach growled. I was near about starved my own self.

• • •

We never had our talk 'cause Mama stayed at the Wilson's for Mary's wake and to help dress her for burying. I was left in charge. When it was bedtime, I told my sisters I would read them a story from my book only after they scrubbed ever speck of dirt off their feet.

We piled onto Jim's bed and snuggled under his covers. We'd not heard a word from him since he'd left us. Neither Mama or Papa mentioned his name. Matter of fact they barely spoke to each other at all. It was like Jim'd never lived here in this holler, in this house, playing his banjo, sneaking off to go fishing. Was he walking around on this earth somewhere or had he been robbed of the money Mama give him and was buried in some deep, dark grave like them Negroes? I grieved for Jim's presence, for his teasing me about Willie, for striking up a tune on his banjo, for running up the steps with a string of fish for supper, for his crooked smile and his messy red hair.

Jewel tugged on my night shirt, and I opened my book to the last story. "Once upon a time, when the moon was young and the stars talked together, a wee woman walked by herself on the king's highway and…"

•   •   •

I closed my book and returned it to the tow sack underneath the bed. Then we said our prayers. Jewel fell asleep before we said *Amen*. Loe soon followed her, but my eyes would not close. Too many questions buzzed in my head. Had Willie gotten to Big Jim coal camp before the revenuers? Was Birdman in Tennessee by now or was he waitin' on Preacher Sam who weren't fit to travel nowhere? Would Mama allow me to gather herbs clear up to Bloody Cove? Iffen she did, would Wilcox Drugs pay me money for 'em? Would it be enough? Enough for what? Too many questions with no answers.

CHAPTER EIGHTEEN

The Funeralizing

Mary's fresh-dug grave waited.

Come Wednesday, the miners and their families climbed Wilson's ridge in morning mist. Dozens of crows stirred from the trees and sailed through the woods. It was a wondrous sight. They never made a mislick and struck a limb, but I couldn't abide their cawing, as vexing as cats fighting in the dark of night.

Every person had scrubbed till they shined and they weared the best clothes they had. From clean overalls and shirt, like Papa's, to a dark green dress with real pearl buttons clear down the front and crocheted lace around its collar, like Mama's. I'd seen her wear her dress one other time, to a cousin's wedding. Pulled out of an old trunk, she'd hung it on the back porch to freshen in the air.

I didn't have nothing fine, except for my dress with the dancing ballerina girls. The sight of it would raise Papa's hackles in front of the whole camp. None of the other young'uns had splendid clothes neither. I wore Jim's pants and his shirt, which were nearly threadbare. He had left two pair of pants and two shirts behind since they didn't fit him no more. They didn't fit me neither, but they'd have to do.

The men had refused to enter the mines this day, until Mary was laid to rest. Mr. Harper didn't like it none. Said he'd dock the miners double for the time they lost. They paid him no never mind, and the tipple stayed shut down.

The women and young'uns carried armloads of wild ferns gathered from sheltered places. I carried a bucketful of wild iris. An old woman, Eula Cobb, wove the ferns together and fashioned a covering for the grave. She nestled the purple flowers amongst the green.

The miners toted baskets packed with cakes, pies, biscuits, cornbread, green beans, pinto beans, stuffed squash and fried chicken. Women set the food on two poplar boards, with barrels underneath for a makeshift yard-table. They throwed a sheet over it to keep out the flies and little fingers, such as babies like Jewel. As well as hollow-legged Willie.

Puffed up with his success, my friend thought he could do as he pleased. He had reached Big Jim's coal camp long before the revenuers. The moonshiners scurried around and hid the whiskey in a cave and it was never found. Thanks to Willie, the mountain folks had outsmarted them revenuers once again.

Mrs. Seabolt stood guard over the food. She spotted Willie and my sisters edging closer and shooed 'em with her apron. "Get. Get away from there. Ain't time to eat until the funeralizing's done."

A mess of young'uns run off in the woods to play. After a bit, I heared Loe's high-pitched voice. "Old Granny Wiggins is dead." One of her favorite games.

A half dozen voices asked her, "How'd she die?"

Loe answered, "She died this a way." Laughter tumbled out of the woods. I knew they was trying to mimic the antics of Loe. Most likely she stood on her head by now, her flour-sack bloomers for all to see. The ones who couldn't do whatever the leader chose to do, had to fall down and play dead.

Mrs. Seabolt marched over to the wood's edge and hollered, "Ever one of you young'uns get yourself over here right this minute." All was quiet like they'd froze in place. "Iffen you don't, you gonna die for shore and certain before the sun goes down. You hear me?" They come straggling out. Some of their Mamas was waiting with a switch. Then my sisters, and even Willie, moped around and stopped having fun.

Older folks milled around in little bunches, talking low and visiting, waiting for Preacher Sam. He'd sent word he was well enough to come. And we waited for Mary and her Mama and Papa. The door to their cabin stayed closed.

Somehow, Papa had managed to climb the steep path, though Mama, who'd been at the Wilson's since before daylight, told him folks would understand if he weren't able. I spotted him in the clearing, holding a pint of whiskey to his chest, leaning on his laurel stick. He looked like he couldn't take another step. Mama rushed over to him and helped him over to a bench. His shirt stuck to his skinny chest. I wondered if he'd always been as thin.

After a coughing spell, he caught his breath and took a long drink. Men gathered around him, and he passed his whiskey. Mama glared at him with folded arms. She always said whiskey loosened the tongue until foolishness spilled out. She was right. Talk about Birdman commenced flying from one man to another. I squatted behind a nearby oak and made like I was studying an upside-down beetle.

"I knew he was trouble when I first seen him. He's one of them gypsies."

"No he ain't. He's a nigger come in here to stir up trouble. Ain't you heard tell how they come close to ruining the mines a few years back? Thought they was too good to do the work and a bunch of 'em got killed in there. And the doctor woman figured in it somehow, but it was before my time."

"Them timbers give way and not long after, the gypsy-man showed up. Reckon he had something to do with that?"

"Most likely. Gypsies, and niggers too, can call on evil spirits."

"Whoever he is, quar things is happening around here and, I say Mary's death ain't the last."

The numbers grew. I stayed behind the tree hoping no one spotted me.

A new voice I couldn't fix a name to. "You fellows don't know the half of it. I seen him in these woods late yesterday. Right over yonder matter of fact. I come up here squirrel hunting. He disappeared soon as I fired my rifle, disappeared like a haint."

"What in thunder was he doing?"

"Don't know. Maybe he's lurking around here, ready to dump more trouble on one of us or our little children. I'm gonna have me a look-see. Iffen I find him I'm gonna shoot him dead."

A tall skinny man reached for his gun and slipped into the woods. His felt hat was pulled down and I never seen his face. I asked the good Lord to watch over Birdman if this man tracked him down.

The cabin door swung open. The men left off talking. Women hushed their whispering. Everyone moved to the grave with sounds of shuffling feet, swishing dresses, and the creak of old bones. A baby cried out and was quieted. A man coughed. I wondered if Preacher Sam was coming.

Willie and Mr. Luellen carried the coffin through the cabin door and down the steps. Mary's Mama refused to let anyone close the lid, which made the carrying awkward.

Whispers behind me. Mrs. Cobb said, "Such a waste. Them handles is pewter. Brought clear from Foggy Mountain's hardware. The Wilsons is putting on airs iffen you ask me."

"Shhh," someone said, and she hushed.

Mary's Papa had rubbed the coffin's cherry wood 'til it was smooth as silk and he had lined it with shiny pink yard-goods. It was the most beautiful thing I'd ever seen.

The crowd parted allowing an ample opening for the casket to be eased onto the ground. Mr. Wilson went back for his wife, held her up as she leaned into him. She had always been stout and robust, but now she appeared mighty feeble. During the nighttime hours she had refused to leave her little girl alone, standing beside her, bathing her with camphor, talking to her like she could hear. Mama told me these things for she had witnessed her grief.

A breeze lifted Mary's hair making it seem as if she ought to get up to run and play. She was wrapped in muslin like a new-born baby-child, except for her red, puffed-up face. Pennies rested on her eyelids and death's stink rose above the smell of camphor.

Mama's clear voice lifted above us and filled the air with a soft sadness. The first time I'd heared her sing in many a day.

Slumber my darling, thy mother is near.
I will watch over thee.
Slumber my darling, I'll wrap thee up warm.
Pray the angels will shield thee from harm...

Preacher Sam appeared out of the mist and stepped to the head of the grave. Widow Baker come along behind him. With her hair platted into two braids, she looked more like an Indian than ever. But my eyes never lit on her more than an instant. The preacher drawed my attention.

Mama's voice caught in her throat. She went ahead singing, but her voice slowed as her eyes growed wide. The preacher wore his white shirt and black coat only on his left arm. His garments was throwed over his right shoulder and hanged open. His right arm rested in a strip of petticoat tied about his neck.

Mama ended the lullaby, the spell of her words broken.

All eyes turned to the preacher who closed his. He raised his good arm.

"Dearly beloved, let us pray."

I never heard another word. His right hand lay flat against his stomach. But wonder of wonders, his snake-bit thumb had been tucked underneath his skin. It was hard to take it in. The thumb, laced down back and forth with big stitches, had been smeared with a gob of orange salve. His stomach above the thumb had been shaved in a perfect half circle. Reminded me of a rising harvest moon.

"Lord-a-mercy," a woman whispered. "Preacher's walking around half-naked with his thumb sticking inside hisself."

Mrs. Carver didn't play-like whispering. "Humph. Iffen he was a man of the Lord, he wouldn't've got snake bit in the first place."

Then Mrs. Garland said, "Carrying on with the doctor-woman like it ain't sinful."

Mrs. Wilson never seemed to notice the preacher or the commotion he'd caused. A goodly number of women agreed with Mrs. Seabolt when she said, "Law, that woman's so broke up over Mary's death, she'll never on this earth be right again."

When Preacher Sam finished praying and preaching and praying again, we sung a hymn, *Do Not Pass Me By*. Mr. Wilson held his wife tight against his chest while they nailed Mary's coffin-lid shut. She jerked against his arms with each blow. The men lowered the coffin easy like into the earth. Mr. Luellen throwed in a shovel-full of dirt and then another, the sound turned softer and softer.

Mrs. Cobb laid her flowered covering on the mound. A honeybee, or maybe it was a yellow jacket, lighted on the ferns and disappeared underneath.

While we sung *May the Lord Be With You Til We Meet Again*, two men half-carried Mrs. Wilson inside. Her husband followed behind, slapping his hat against his leg, his head hanging down. Mama went inside, too, carrying the last of Papa's whiskey.

The door closed. The young'uns and the miners swarmed around the preacher, to ogle and ask questions. Out of respect for the family, they never caused a ruckus.

Preacher Sam spoke to the men who gathered around him. "Yes sir, the Lord and this saintly woman here saved my life and that's a fact. This old thumb of mine was fixing to drop off, and let me tell you I was suffering something fierce. Yes sir, mighty fierce." He frowned like he was remembering the pain. "Nothing's going to keep me from preaching revival, though. I need some able-bodied men to help build the brush arbor up near Red Bird. Why, we'll have the finest place for preaching revival in these parts, and we'll have enough room for all the heathens to come hear the Word without stepping inside a church door."

No one said, "Amen." or even "Yes, brother." Or looked the preacher in the eye. One by one the miners fell off, saying they had to eat some of these fine vittles or insult them who brought it, eat fast, too, and head on up to the mines. Would be working late for many a day to make up lost wages. No, sir. They'd help iffen they could, but they had to put bread on the table, and they was sure the Lord and the preacher would understand.

Preacher Sam stood there speechless. He watched the men move to the food table, his hopes for building a brush arbor falling apart in front of his eyes.

The men grumbled, glancing over at the preacher while they ate. I didn't have to hear them. They figured the preacher was in this fix in the first place because he was a backslider and now look what he'd let a doctor woman do. Maybe he weren't a man of God at all. Why they seen themselves as good as he was. I knowed all this and it looked to me like the preacher ought to, even if he was from West Virginia.

The men steered clear of Widow Baker while she fixed him a plate. They looked at her sideways and stepped away quick if she moved their way. They was afraid of being too close to a woman who'd cut on a man and stitched his parts together.

Mr. Collette said, "Unnatural," shaking his head.

Then Papa took a sip of another man's whiskey and said, "What didcha expect? A preacher and a witch sleeping in the same house."

Men fell silent as they set about eating. Papa limped over to the shade of an elm and eased down its trunk to the ground. The miners soon left with a piece of cake or pie as they hurried along.

I took charge of my sisters, fixed their plates and led them to a quilt spread under a big white oak. Then I run back to the table and cut me a piece of Mrs. Luellen's jam cake before it was gone. I walked over to the preacher.

He and Widow Baker was sitting on a bench near the house. The preacher munched on a chicken leg, and talked with his mouth full. Seemed to me he was in a fix about the brush arbor, and here he was acting like everything was hunky-dory. Widow Baker told him to sit still or he'd pull the stitches loose. She didn't fancy doing her needlework over.

"What you gonna do now?" I asked, squeezing in between the two of 'em.

"The Lord will provide," he said, wiping his greasy mouth with the back of his hand.

"Well," Widow Baker said, "the Lord ain't gonna provide no heathen miners to build a brush arbor. Now iffen you was to wait 'til you was rested up, let your thumb heal. Then you could chop limbs and willow poles, work up a sweat while you was eating some crow. Then the men might come around. Might." He winced like he had a sharp pain.

"How far does your thumb go inside your stomach anyhow?" I asked, peering over at him.

Widow Baker smiled. "Just under the skin. Poison had done ate his thumb down to nothing and this was the only way to save it. Wish you could've been there, Hattie, when I pealed his stomach skin back and laid his thumb in there. It was a sight to behold. Maybe you can assist me when I cut him loose."

"Yes, ma'am, I'd be proud to help." My stomach turned over. I didn't know if I could abide the smells and the blood going along with doctoring, but I didn't want to miss seeing the preacher's thumb come out of his stomach. "When you figure that's gonna be?"

"I'd say six weeks' time oughta be enough. Going to be a pure sight."

"Yes ma'am." I swallowed the last bite of jam cake and licked my fingers. "You reckon you could've saved Mary iffen you'd been here?"

She turned toward me and took my hands in hers. "The poison in her body was too quick and too strong. Nothing could've saved her. Maybe one day doctors will . . ."

Mama come out the cabin's door. Her hair straggled about her face and Granny would've said she looked frazzled. She motioned to me and I hurried over to her. "Where's your Papa?"

I looked around. "I don't know."

"Did he eat?"

"I . . . I've been talking to Widow Baker."

"Well, carry some chicken home when you go, just in case he's there. I'm going to be awhile. Go ahead and start supper regular time iffen I'm not back."

"Mama, would you let me help the preacher?"

"Do what exactly?"

"Build a brush arbor."

"Seems to me that's a man's work."

"I'm strong.as . . . well, most any boy."

"Why are you wanting to help?"

"Widow Baker says the best plants grow in Bloody Cove and I'd be close to 'em up at Red Bird. I could maybe even dig for 'sang up there."

"Ain't fit for a young girl to traipse all over these hills with a man."

"What about some other person coming along? Like Widow Baker. Would you let me then?"

"I don't know. I'd have to think on it."

I give Mama a quick hug and run to find the preacher.

The ladies' curiosity had overcome their squeamishness and they circled around the preacher to hear of his brush with death. The same ones who had said he must be a backslid sinner since he picked up the rattler and got bit. And they never mentioned he didn't have enough faith to put hisself in the healing hands of the Lord. Instead of Widow Baker. They must've forgiven him.

One fixed his coat slipping off his shoulder. Another brought him a gourd-dipper of cold water. Yet another, a piece of applesauce stack cake smelling of sugar and cinnamon. They edged Widow Baker aside to get closer.

She talked out loud to herself, like Elsie Lampert, and I hoped she weren't getting addled in her mind. "Well. Appears to me I'm the one that's gonna be around when these buzzards is finished."

Widow Baker glared at the women and fumbled with the purple beads hanging around her neck. They made little clicking sounds.

The preacher was enjoying the attention like a baby takes to a sugar-tit. Then it hit me. The green jealous snake had bit Widow Baker. Her taking a shine to the preacher meant she was bound to want to go wherever he did. Besides, she had more doctoring to do on his thumb.

I hung back on the edge of the crowd, waited 'til ever woman was finally shooed away.

Loetta called to me before heading home.

"I'll catch up directly," I said. "Go on now, Mama said you was in charge."

Mrs. Seabolt walked over and give me Papa's chicken wrapped in a cloth, two legs and a thigh. Preacher Sam, Widow Baker and me headed down the mountain. Hope bubbled up inside me. If I went along to help build a brush arbor, which I didn't care nothing about, I might find some plants to sell. I didn't know how to spot the best ones. Widow Baker did. Could what seemed impossible become possible?

CHAPTER NINETEEN

Brush Arbor

"How you gonna build the brush arbor?" I asked as I come alongside Preacher Sam.

"The Lord has a plan." His voice drug along with no spark of life.

Widow Baker stopped, hooked his good arm over hers and turned to me. "Appears we'll be needing to stop at your house and rest a spell before we head to my place."

The footpath turned narrow. The preacher leaned against Widow Baker and I dropped behind. Scrapper was soon at my heels. I reached inside the cloth, pulled a piece of chicken free from the bone and dropped it.

"I could help you build it," I said in a loud voice.

They stopped and turned.

"You're nothin' but a slip of a girl," the preacher said.

Widow Baker smiled. "Iffen she said she could do it, she'd do it or die trying."

The preacher looked at her and then at me. "I'll swannee, the Lord works in mysterious ways, don't He?"

"You couldn't go up there without no doctor-woman," Widow Baker said as she fixed the preacher's coat where it had slipped off his shoulder again. She stepped toward me. "Your Mama let you go?"

"You went she might."

The three of us looked at one another. I was trying to figure how this could come to pass. One snake-bit man who looked close to death, one doctor-woman, and me building a frame of saplings held together by vines and willow branches. Pine boughs or anything soft piled on top. A magical place. I had been to a brush arbor one time, next to Four Mile Creek, with Granny Guthrie.

We watched as a black bird landed in a nearby holly bush and dropped something shiny from its beak. "Maggie," I said. "Is that you?"

Scrapper crept close and crouched low.

Birdman, wearing an old felt hat pulled low, stepped out from behind a laurel bush. Maggie flew to his shoulder. He peered at the preacher and said, "Hell fire, what happened to you?"

I reckon the preacher forgot to tell Birdman it weren't Christian to cuss.

Scrapper kept his eyes on Maggie as Birdman bent over and picked up a gold belt buckle.

Scrapper sprang for the bird. Maggie flew to Birdman's hat and squawked, "Help me. Help me. Help me."

"Scrapper! Come here! Now!" I'd never raised my voice to him, but he set hisself down by my feet. His eyes stayed on Maggie like he was biding his time.

•   •   •

Birdman hadn't gone on to Tennessee like I had figured. Afraid to show hisself around the church, he had waited for the preacher up at Red Bird. When the preacher never showed hisself, he come back to find out why and happened upon Mary's funeral.

We left the cow path and entered the woods as if we'd agreed to do so. Less chance anyone would spot us. We stopped beside a fallen tree for the preacher to rest, for he was feeling more than a little puny.

Birdman's brown face scrunched up as he squatted to study Widow Baker's handiwork. Maggie danced about on his shoulder and Scrapper crept closer. I reached and caught him but a gosh-awful hissing and spitting come from his stiffened body. I put him down and he shot off into the woods.

Widow Baker stepped forward, looking at Birdman, "You ain't got no business coming back here. Some folks is blaming you for the death of a little child."

He stood and slapped his hat against his leg sending dust into the air. Maggie danced on his shoulder. "Do you know what it's like when folks is afraid of ya? When they think you're less than a no-count? When they lay all manner of happenings at your feet? Call ya the work of the devil and names I won't repeat. Run ya off iffen they catch ya around. Well, sir, the preacher here, when I seen him up on the ridge, he asked me to help him to build a meeting place."

Birdman pulled a bandana out of his pocket and wiped his face. "Do you know how long it's been since a body asked me to lend 'em a hand…like…like I was a regular person? Figured I was obliged to help since I told him I would. I'm a man of my word. Hancock County ain't going nowhere. Once I get back in there with my own kin, most likely I won't never come out again. At least there a man don't have to hide like no escaped convict."

"You come from one of them lost tribes," Preacher Sam whispered. He studied Birdman like he was having trouble believing what he was seeing. "In front of my eyes, up on the ridge…I should've known. Your skin color ain't like nothing I've ever seen. Lord have mercy on my soul. He sent me one of his chosen to lead me and I had so much on my mind, I never noticed. Right in these hills of ours."

We looked at Birdman. I'd never heared of such a person and wondered what it meant.

"I shore don't feel like I'm chosen by nobody, preacher. Some think I'm a gypsy or a devil spirit. The government calls me a 'free man of color.' But what has it got me? Treated as bad as the blackest Negro is what. I got to get moving. You still aiming to build that meetin' place?"

"Workers for the harvest is gathering like mighty warriors around the walls of Jericho. Looks like the Lord is a-willing."

"I'll wait up at Red Bird three more day. Iffen you don't show, I'll be on my way. I thank ye, whether it turns out we work together or I never see ye again. I thank ye."

No sooner had he turned than he disappeared, quiet as an Indian. I wondered how he kept Maggie from jabbering and giving him away when he was on the run. Hanging around these parts, he was borrowing trouble.

•   •   •

Preacher Sam and Widow Baker stayed to supper. Mama walked in the back door just as we gathered around the table. After she changed her pretty green dress into her everyday brown, she told us Papa had slept most of the afternoon in the Wilson's barn. Willie had borrowed their mule and wagon and was taking Papa to Blackjack for a load of corn. A man there owed him for some whiskey Papa had delivered last fall, and he was collecting payment. The trip there and back would take three or four days.

Though Loetta had scorched the potatoes and the cornbread turned out dry, Mama said it shore did pleasure her to have girls pitchin' in. Made us feel right puffed up. Loe warmed up some leftover pinto beans and cooked cabbage while I set the table.

The preacher ate like he was starving, but it never slowed his talking down none. He never mentioned us seeing Birdman. Little pitchers sat at the table with big ears, and anything they heard would get back to Papa.

And Mama? Lord-a-mercy. She had took a liking to Birdman, and the pretty bird he carved her. But what if she knowed he had walked away from Moses and couldn't find his way back? He had to be a spirit, wandering the earth. Didn't the preacher say he was lost?

Preacher Sam talked on and on about the need for revival in these parts and the need for a place to preach the word. Said there was lost sheep all over these hills who had never entered through a church door. He was fixing to brung 'em into the presence of the Lord.

"Haints walkin' these hills is the only ones lost." The words jumped out of my mouth.

He turned and looked at me a long moment. Then he smiled. "Hattie, one day you'll see who's lost and who ain't. Would you pass your Mama the cabbage?"

I held the bowl and he dipped hisself a big helping 'til there weren't hardly none left. He ate without talking for a change. Widow Baker and Mama allowed how they was worried about Mrs. Wilson. They was going to keep check on her.

I cleared my throat and announced. "Widow Baker knows the exact spot where all the good healing plants is growing, just waiting for somebody to carry 'em home." I turned to look at her. "Ain't that right?"

"Well, pretty near. Now 'sang digging ain't good for another week or two yet."

Loetta and Jewel picked at each other. I glared at Loe and whispered, "Go play with Jewel. I'll wash the dishes, clean up the kitchen. You don't have to do nothing." She looked at me like she didn't believe me. "Go on," I added. "I'll read you both a story out of my book later. I promise."

They left in a hurry.

"Mama, remember you said I could help the preacher if another growed-up person went along? Well, Widow Baker's going and I want to, too. Maybe I could dig up some plants on the way back home. We'd pass right through Bloody Cove up past Red Bird. It'd be as easy as . . . as easy as falling off a log."

Mama looked at me and sighed. Widow Baker must've knowed what she was thinking. "I would look after her, Clara, you know that."

Mama sighed again, took her handkerchief out and blowed her nose. "Hattie, I don't reckon I can keep you by my side forever. Don't mean I have to like you going off, even iffen it ain't a far piece."

I never said nothing, held my breath. Mama got up and poured coffee all around. No one mentioned it weren't black, but more like brown water. Nor could we offer any cream or sugar. She studied the preacher. "He don't look fit enough to go nowhere."

Widow Baker leaned over to Mama, nodded her head towards the preacher. "I get him home and fix him a tonic and make him rest a full day, he'll be spry as a rooster."

The preacher smiled and reached for another piece of cornbread as if to show he was mending fast.

"Besides, we got help..." I was about to say too much and fought the urge to slap my hand across my mouth.

"Who?" Mama asked.

The preacher said, "Why, dear woman, the Lord. That's who. How can we stray far when the Lord's on our side?"

Widow Baker stood. "We got to go before dark overtakes us. We're much obliged for the food, Hattie. You girls done a fine job. Made your Mama proud. Clara, iffen you think it best Hattie not make this trip, I understand. I know you're particular about your girls as you should be."

Lord-a-mercy. Widow Baker's done fixed things. Mama can say no real easy. Double Damnation.

· · ·

While Mama made certain Loe and Jewel scrubbed their feet good before getting dressed for bed, I walked to the porch to see Widow Baker and Preacher Sam off. The sky above the mountaintops looked like it was streaked with fire. At the bottom of the steps, Widow Baker turned. "Tell your Mama about Birdman waiting for us. She ought to know. She might keep you home. Not because of him, but because of the trouble folks might stir up. You got to tell her. Promise?"

"Yes, ma'am."

"Iffen you ain't to my place by nine, day after tomorrow, I'll figure you ain't coming." She noticed the Preacher's sling needed adjusting and fussed over it, getting the knot around his neck to her liking. I set down on the steps and Scrapper run up and jumped in my lap. Seems all was forgiven. A tiny puff of a bird's feather floated in the air and I prayed Maggie still had ever one of hers. While I run my finger down the white streak on his head, he licked his paws and washed his face.

"A bit too tight," the Preacher said.

Widow Baker bent down and looked at his thumb. "I'll be the judge." He frowned, but never said no more. She looked up at me. "I been thinking Sarah might favor us taking her boys along. They've 'bout drove her to distraction here lately. Don't you fret none, you hear, iffen you can't go along."

I nodded and watched 'em head down our footpath. Widow Baker throwed her hand in the air and I waved back though she never seen me. The Sharp twins, Cloyd and Loyd. I hoped they was off hunting or maybe on their deathbeds from pneumonia or such. Anything to keep them two from tagging along. I couldn't abide either one. Some would've said they was only rambunctious, but me and Granny called it pure meanness.

Scrapper left off his washing, curled close against me and commenced purring. Widow Baker never said when I had to tell Mama about Birdman. I shore didn't hanker bringing it up when I figured she was on the fence between saying yes or no. She truly liked the old man, but she wouldn't abide the trouble he might bring along with him.

Soon as Loe and Jewel come to the porch, Scrapper jumped down and disappeared under the steps. He knowed to stay away from Jewel's fat little fingers reachin' for his stub tail like it was a play-pretty. I felt her against my back, her arms going around my neck. "Horsey, horsey," she whined.

Half way up to gallop around the house, I seen a red ribbon in her tight little fist. "Where did you get that?"

She didn't have to tell me. With her on my back, I run into our bedroom and throwed her down on the bed. She laughed thinking this was a new game. I tossed a quilt over her and reached underneath the bed. My tow sack was there. I pulled it to me and felt for my book. It was there. I raised *The Treasure Box* to my chest while Jewel jumped off the bed and hugged my neck.

Mama poked her head around the bedroom door. "I'll finish up in the kitchen and you can come dry the dishes later. Go ahead and read to your sisters. I do my best thinking and praying with my hands in dishwater."

Loe skipped into our bedroom and jumped into the bed. After I coaxed the ribbon away from Jewel, we settled ourselves and I opened my book.

I wondered about a better hiding place for it, but could think of none.

•   •   •

The next morning appeared bright and clear and full of promise. I dressed and walked through the kitchen, headed to the privy.

""Hattie ?" I stopped, my hand on the screen-door. "Yes ma'am."

"You can go with Widow Baker and the preacher, but I want you back here inside of two days. Your Pa's gone for now and the rest of the miners gonna be working extra hours for a week or more. They ain't gonna have no time or inclination to worry about Birdman's whereabouts. Maybe it's time you learned a little 'bout people outside of our holler. Mind Evelyn, do as she says. Ye can learn a right smart from her. Especially her doctorin' ways. Something you ought to consider since it comes to you natural."

I never argued with Mama. Widow Baker had bragged on my help when we kept the preacher from flying to heaven. Too much bragging had puffed me up in their eyes when thinkin' of the putrid smells, even now, turned my stomach upside down.

Birdman? I'd not gotten around to telling her. "You knowed about Birdman?"

"After things was quiet around the Wilson's, I walked in the woods awhile. Had to get away from things, clear my head. He was hidden back there out of sight. Name's Silas. We talked a right good spell. Then I went back to the house and brung him some food."

"Why didn't you…"

"I was waiting for you to tell me. Was you fixing to?"

"Yes ma'am. After you decided I could go or not. I promised Widow Baker I'd tell ya, but I never promised when. Mama? Do you reckon Birdman's a haint?"

"No haint has the need to eat or sleep or gets lonesome for someone to talk to or carves pretty little birds out of wood. He's a real man all right. Now where his people come from I don't know, but I don't figure that's my concern. He's determined to help the preacher and I think right smart of him for that. In a few days he'll be gone back to his place in Tennessee, and maybe folks'll stop laying blame where it don't belong."

"Ain't you feared they'll hunt him down while we're up there at Red Bird? Could be you ain't the only one who seen him hiding in the woods."

"The men is full of talk. That's all. Besides, the men are busy making up the wages they lost the day of the funeral."

That night on the front porch steps, I studied the stars and considered Mama's words. I'd never knowed her to be wrong when it come to figuring out people and their intentions. Was it possible she could be wrong this one time? I was the one who had heard the men talking and they sounded like they meant business. Maybe it would be best to stay home after all, where I'd be safe…figure out some other way to make money.

"Hattie?"

"Yes ma'am."

"Bring me some pleurisy root and some snakeroot iffen there's any in Bloody Cove."

•　　•　　•

I lay in bed, my sleeping sisters close around me. My eyes wide open. I put the thoughts of Birdman out of my head and traveled the trails through Bloody Cove with Preacher Sam and Widow Baker. What would we find to put in our sacks? How many coins would I have to drop in my jar when all was said and done? I wondered if for truth I could walk out of Ashworth Coal Camp one day…leave Mama…and Jewel and Loe…and especially Willie. Could I tell anyone I was going or have to sneak away …wander the earth lost…like Birdman? Or some haint?

CHAPTER TWENTY

Moonshiners and Willie

Birdman loomed larger than life in my dreams. He walked across the Red Sea alongside Moses. I was there, too. Walls of water come crashing down. I swam under the sea with fish and big-eyed people. My hair floated peaceful like as water poured into me. I jerked upright in bed, shivered and hugged my knees to my chin. Afraid to sleep, I wondered if I'd been given a sign, a warning.

I slipped under the covers and snuggled against Loe to get warm. Then I smelled coffee, but there was no other signs of morning. Mama wasn't clanging skillets onto the stove and outside it was pitch black dark. A soft rain fell. Water dripped from the dogwood tree outside our bedroom window. A cool breeze blowed across the bed.

Papa's voice found its way through the kitchen wall next to our bed. I sat up and pressed my ear against the old chestnut wood. What was he doing home days before he was due? What was wrong? Mama's voice and then Papa's again. They talked low, and I wanted to know what was going on. I eased out of bed, crept into the front room and scrunched behind the wood-box next to the kitchen door.

Papa said, "I'm telling ya iffen they can find old Tippytoe's operation, they can find anybody's."

"Where do you reckon he's hiding?" Mama asked.

"I don't know, but when them revenuers come crashing through the bushes, word is he run out from under his hat. They bashed his still to bits. One-day they're bound to get him. Just a matter of time before they learn who warned them moonshiners up at Big Jim . . . Willie better watch his back. Revenge lights a powerful fire."

.Mama's chair scraped the floor. "We got to help Willie iffen we can." She poured more coffee. "You want something to eat? I'd give a pretty iffen I could fix you some pork chops and gravy."

"I ain't hungry nohow."

"You and Hattie both need to eat. Want me to go ahead and wake her?"

"Not yet. Give the rain a chance to slack off some."

They left off talking.

The cook-stove fire sizzled and popped.

I stayed in my hiding place, my thoughts running about wildly. Tippytoe Golightly. He lived up near Blackjack. Everyone thought the revenuers'd never catch him 'cause he knowed the woods better than anybody. He could disappear and not be seen for months. But folks said his still would never be found neither and they'd found it. They had his hat. Papa said it was a matter of time before... Willie. Was he for truth in danger? What was they gonna wake me for? This was the day Preacher Sam and Widow Baker was planning to head up to Red Bird. Maybe they'd not leave out in the rain. And for shore I'd not go even if they did. Papa was home.

Mama stirred about in the kitchen. She added kindling and coal to the cook-stove. Then she sifted flour into her dough bowl, opened the lid on the lard bucket and set about making biscuits.

Papa's chair scraped the floor. He thumped down the back steps, headed to the privy.

I walked into the warm kitchen as Mama filled her baking pan with big, thick biscuits. One would fill up your whole hand. Cat-head biscuits we called 'em.

"What's happening?" I asked.

Mama jumped, dropping her biscuit-cutter. "Oh," she said like she'd been deep in thought. "Uh…it's them revenuers. They found Mr. Golightly's still. Smashed it to useless scraps. Poured out a new run of liquor, too. Now they're searching for him."

"Why's Papa home?"

"No need for a load of corn now. He's aiming to move his still."

"But why? He's got it hid already. He said not even a bear could get back in that laurel thicket."

"Them two revenuers you seen? Well, since they never found one barrel of whiskey up at Big Jim, they was smart enough to know somebody warned 'em. They took it personal and I reckon it turned them two as mean as all get out. Somehow, they found a still everbody figured would never be found. Talk is they aim to wipe out ever small operator they can find and folks told your Papa there was a slew of revenuers coming from Frankfort to help 'em."

"Where's he gonna move it to?"

"A cave. Got it picked out. This rain's a blessing. Might keep them revenuers close to their fires, trying to stay dry and warm. But you and your Papa won't have the comfort of no fire." She looked me over. "After you eat, get some of Jim's old overalls and one of his worn-out shirts."

"You reckon Widow Baker'll…"

"I don't know. Don't matter none. You ain't going off nowheres now."

"But…"

"Hattie. Sometimes your own desires got to be put aside for the family's. One day maybe you and Evelyn can walk up to Bloody Cove…one nice sunny day when things ain't in such a turmoil."

"Yes, ma'am," I mumbled, holding my hands over the cook stove. My heart fell clear to my feet. Mama cut a sausage casing with her sharp knife, and I moved aside while she slipped two pans of biscuits into the oven. Why was she cooking up our last bit of sausage this day? She'd said just yesterday she was keeping it back 'cause Papa might not find no piney-woods rooter like he done last year right before Thanksgiving. I never asked her. My mind took off in a whirl.

Here I was, stuck. Widow Baker and the Preacher going on without me, while I toted copper coils, barrels, gallon jars filled with sugar…out of a laurel maze up to some cave…I allowed it'd take us all day, with Papa crippled up like he was and this rain besides. Why couldn't he have asked someone else? Maybe Willie or old man Johnson. I'd never sell plants to Wilcox Drug Store. I'd never have any money to put in my jar…never hold any wondrous books in my hands…never have a new ribbon for my hair…I'd be right here in Ashworth Coal Camp forever and a day…

All of a sudden, everything broke loose. Papa thumped up the back steps and into the kitchen, water dripping off his hat, asking Mama why in thunder was she frying sausage when there might not be no more. Loe, her hair like a stirred-up bird's nest, run through the kitchen and out the back door, the screen slamming behind her. Jewel stumbled toward me, whined and threw her arms out. I lifted her up to rest on my hip, glad Loe had changed her diaper. She scrambled higher, nuzzled her warm face against my neck.

Loe soon appeared back in the kitchen, dripping wet from her trip. "Why's Mama cooking sausage?" I throwed my sister a flour sack towel to dry herself.

Then Willie busted into the middle of us, shouting, "They're coming! They're coming! Trompin' up the holler, a dozen lanterns swinging."

Everything stopped. We looked at Willie. "Ma sent me," he said as if we allowed he was telling a black story.

Papa said, "They walking with a purpose or ambling along?"

Willie smiled. He enjoyed being the center of news. "Well," he said, rubbing his chin like an old man thinking.

Papa growled, "How fast and exactly how many?"

Willie snapped up tall. "Like this." He took three long strides, his shoulders square. "And there was…" He stopped to count on his fingers. "Five. Exactly five."

Papa moved near the back door. From a shelf, he took a box of shells, poured them into a front overall pocket, and lifted his rifle gun from its hook. Mama swept past me, smelling of cooked sausage. She pushed a paper bundle, tied with string, into one of Papa's side pockets. Then she took a plug of tobacco out of her apron, slipped it into another of his front pockets. She rested her hand on his face.

He reached up, took it away. "I'm gonna keep an eye on their whereabouts is all, Clara, scare 'em if need be. I'll bring ye some fat squirrels 'fore I head home." He squared his hat, turned and ducked outside into the rain, into the dark morning.

Mama hurried back to the stove, to the skillet hot and smoking.

"Might as well make yourself to home, Willie, and eat 'fore you head back." But she must've took no notice. He was at the table already, pouring more than his share of molasses onto a plate and reaching for a hot biscuit. Soon as he swallowed the last mouthful, he stood and brung me his plate.

"Looks like you licked it clean," I said dropping his dish into the water and turning my back to him. My feelings was in a tangle towards Willie. Did he think highly of me or did he not think of me 'atall? I couldn't tell which one.

As if he knowed my thinking, he moved close to my side and slipped his arm around my waist. "I've got to go," he whispered in my ear. "Chopping wood and toting water plus other chores gonna take all day." He added as he pulled his arm away from me. "I'll be back tomorrow morning. You can count on it!" He leaned close and planted a wet kiss on my cheek before he ran out the back door.

I could hear him hollering as he went.

•   •   •

Soon after Willie left, I spied Papa's walking stick by the back door. I handed Jewel over to Loe. "Fix her a bowl of mush." I grabbed the stick and run out the door, a newspaper over my head. Scrapper come meowing from under the steps expecting to be fed, but he followed me anyhow.

The rain had slacked off to a fine mist and fog rolled up the hill. If them revenuers ever learnt Willie was the one who warned the moonshiners up at Big Jim, his life wouldn't be worth a wooden nickel. I hoped them revenuers'd get tangled in a laurel slick and never find their way out—till one day somebody'd come across their bones. Jim said it could happen, even to a regular person like one of us who had lived in these hollers our whole life.

Papa was up ahead leaning against a sycamore tree and coughing. He'd not made it far. He looked old and broken, not as a strong miner swinging a two-headed pick, loading twelve ton or more a day.

Colonel and Neverblue danced beside him, their tails wagging, anxious to get moving. Scrapper disappeared into the woods. Papa turned and fished a small bottle out of a pocket, took a long drink before returning its stopper. I walked up to him, held out the stick, wondered if he was for truth aiming to shoot them revenuers if they got too close to his whiskey operation.

I never asked him, though. He put the bottle back in his pocket, took the stick from me and pushed hisself away from the tree. "Hoping you'd come. Got somethin' to say to you and you ain't gonna like it. Neither is your Ma, but she's got enough worries without worrying . . ."

I hugged my arms and stepped back.

He coughed, spit a gob into the darkness, and then swiped his sleeve across his bearded mouth. The rain had stopped and fog swirled around us.

"You ain't goin' up to Red Bird. You ain't goin' nowhere with that gypsy Birdman or that witch of a doctor-woman and her preacher. Get any such notions outta your head. You hear what I'm saying?"

His words slammed against me. I stumbled back. "How did you . . .?"

"Don't matter. No call to run to your Ma. She ain't gonna help ya."

Papa picked up his rifle, leaned on his stick and limped away. He disappeared into the fog. He whistled one time, sharp and loud, but his dogs had already took off after him.

CHAPTER TWENTY-ONE

The Commissary's New Shoes

Willie appeared on Saturday morning as Mama started a fire in the cookstove. "Appears you need more kindling," he said as he turned and went back outside. I followed him to the pile of pine knot.

"It was you. After Mary's funeral. You heard me talkin' to Preacher Sam and maybe to Birdman. And you told Papa. How could you . . ."

Willie throwed another piece of wood into the bucket. He picked it up and stepped close bringin' along the smell of fresh-cut pine. His eyebrows raised up and his eyes growed big. "What in tarnation are you talkin' about?"

I folded my arms and glared at him. "Papa's done found out I was goin' up to Red Bird with Preacher Sam and Birdman and . . ."

"Holy moley, Hattie. He's put a stop to it and it's good thing he did, but he didn't learn nothin' from me. You ought to know better."

He turned and huffed inside. I felt like goin' after him to explain myself. Had he said Papa was right? I had no business going up there?

I stomped up the back steps as Willie come back down with an empty water bucket. "Your Ma's 'bout out of water and she could use some more coal," he said as he kept going.

I carried a bucket of coal into the kitchen while Willie toted water from the spring until Mama declared we had enough.

Willie never said much during breakfast, but he kept lookin' over at me. Ever now and then he'd frown and shake his head. I had accused my friend of something he didn't do. I had to figure out how to make things right between us.

When Mama picked up Jewel and carried her to the privy, I poured Willie another cup of coffee and sat down on the bench beside him. I swallowed hard and jumped into explaining. "You need to know. Widow Baker was comin' along. And the reason I wanted to go was to gather some herbs and maybe sang to sell in Foggy Mountain. That's all. And I'm mighty sorry I accused you of tellin' Papa."

"I'd never, never do anythin' behind your back, Hattie, but I'm much relieved you ain't goin' and that's the truth."

He pulled me close as Loe run through the kitchen. "Lawdy, lawdy look who's sweet on Freckle Face." She kept going out the back door, likely headed to the privy.

•　　•　　•

By mid-morning clouds moved across the sky and the sun broke through. Mama sent Willie to Widow Baker's so they wouldn't wait for me. I moped around the house, pulled the ribbon out of my pocket, tied it in my hair, figured Mama would never notice.

I slumped against the doorframe, watched her working up a peck of apples about to go bad. The big pot on the stove steamed with the makings of applesauce, filling the kitchen with a smell of sweet and sour all mixed together. Jars of sugar set in the woods waitin' for Papa's brew, even though makin' whiskey again might not ever come to pass. Now we had nothing to use for sweetening them apples. Mama rummaged in the pantry, come out with a jar, the insides dark and crusty. The last of our honey. The last of our sausage. We'd give out of both and that's how I felt inside myself—give out.

After Papa left yesterday, I asked Mama if she could talk to him, explain how I wanted to gather some herbs and maybe sang.

Mama stopped brushing Jewel's tangled curls and looked at me. "Your Pa has spoken. You ain't goin' against him this time. You'll have to find another way to earn some money."

Papa was right. She weren't gonna be any help.

All of a sudden sunlight flooded the kitchen, then disappeared into shadowed darkness again. Light flickered through the window and then settled down to stay. Wind had swept the rain clouds away like a giant's broom. Mama dropped her spoon on the floor. She was probably thinking of government men on the move, searching the hills, and Papa out there somewheres with his rifle. I figured they'd never find Papa's still in a hundred years of looking. I fretted and stewed over my own worries. The walls of the house closed in around me.

Scrapper meowed from the back porch, his nose pressed against the screen. Jewel squealed and crawled towards him, but he disappeared before she'd got halfway. I'd not fed him yet, had plumb forgot. I reached for a biscuit on back of the stove.

"Ain't fitten to keep something that ain't yours." Mama said.

My face burned as hot as the applesauce bubbling, and I fumbled with the ribbon caught on a tangle. "I...I found it."

"You must return it, and tell her you're sorry you ain't returned it 'fore n..."

Willie hit the back door with a thud. He slumped over double into the kitchen. gasping and wheezing, his hands on his knees. We hurried over. He'd not had time to run to Widow Baker's and back. Mama fanned him with her apron. He looked up and tried to grin, but his face looked pained with the trying. I fetched him some water and he drained a dipper full.

He took a deep breath. "Them revenuers has taken off up another holler. Spotted Golightly and took off after him. Old slippy man'll lead 'em on a wild goose chase. Ever last one of them Revenuers. Tippeytoes done it again." His words lifted a great burden.

"You certain 'bout this?" Mama asked.

Willie stood up straight and puffed out his chest. "Shore as rain falls from the sky. You got any more of them biscuits?"

"I never knowed you to be wrong, but you for shore and certain?"

"Yes ma'am. I never made it as far as the tipple 'fore I seen 'em running through the woods after ol' Tippeytoes...headed towards Bear Holler." He laughed showing his buckteeth. "I stood on a rock outcropping and watched a spell. They took off like hounds after a coon."

I stuffed the red ribbon into my pocket. "You never made it to Widow Baker's house."

He shook his head. "Nope. Followed them government men awhile to make certain they didn't circle around and come back. Figured it was more important." He plopped on a chair at the table, and commenced eating a biscuit and our last piece of sausage. With his cheeks stuffed with food, he managed to finish off a full glass of milk. He wiped his mouth on his sleeve and stood. "I'd be obliged iffen I could head home instead of Widow Baker's. Told Ma I wouldn't be gone long. She'll be worried."

Mama nodded her agreement and rushed over to stir the applesauce and scoot it off the fire.

"His Ma don't care where he is," I grumbled. "And he's done eat the last bite of our sausage and I never got more'n a smell."

"Appears you eat some wiggle-tongue soup this morning. You know perfectly well Willie's a right smart help to all of us, and it's the least we can do to share whatever food there is. Now you tell him you never meant them hateful words."

"Yes ma'am." I stood beside Willie, looked at the floor instead of his silly grin. "I...I had no call to talk to...to you like..."

He plopped his hat on his head. His grin was gone. "Ahhh don't make no never mind, Hattie. Your Ma makes the best biscuits they is. My Ma's sickly a good bit and she can't ..." He cleared his throat and shuffled his feet.

Mama walked over with a small poke. "A jar of applesauce and some biscuits. Now don't you eat 'em 'fore you get home."

His face reddened as he took the food. "Much obliged," he whispered. Then he turned and headed toward the back porch. "See ya, Hattie." He threw his hand in the air and he was gone. Just like that. When I weren't done talking to him.

Now I wouldn't know if Widow Baker and the preacher had left or if they waited on me. What difference did it make anyhow? My ornery self had jumped on me with both feet makin' me out of sorts, not only with Willie but with the whole dang world.

Mama went back to the stove and poured hot applesauce into jars. "I never knowed Willie to be wrong. Iffen he says them revenuers is gone into Bear Holler, that's where they're gone. Now maybe your Pa can head towards home tonight for some vittles and dry clothes. He'll not go to his still just yet for fear they might have staked some lookouts." She screwed the lids onto four jars, applesauce ready for pies or cakes or sharing with a neighbor.

She stopped wiping off the jars and looked at me. "Seems like those long legs of yourn need something to do. Make sure they ain't waiting on you. Let 'em know you won't be going. Then return what ain't yours to Rachel Elizabeth." She reached in an apron pocket and handed me a piece of scrip. "On your way back home, get me a bag of cornmeal. We're 'bout out and it would shore pleasure me to make up a big skillet for your Pa tonight."

"But them revenuers…"

"They ain't nowhere around camp. Willie said so. They might come dragging in tomorrow, though. You go on now. No tarrying, neither. You hear?"

I nodded, took the thin coin, glad to go even though I'd only be gone for a short while, instead of a wondrous trip with Widow Baker and the preacher. And to make matters worse, I'd have to say I was sorry to uppity Rae and no longer have a ribbon.

Loe's head of bouncy pigtails poked out from underneath the table. She held her cornhusk doll and played like it could talk. "Did she steal it?"

Loe answered her doll. "Don't you know nothing? That's why she's got to take it back."

I run out the door and down the footpath. Scrapper followed along behind me. Patches of fog swirled through the air. Granny Guthrie called such fog the breath of ghosts. Halfway down the mountain, I stepped out of the fog. The sight took my breath away.

Wet from last night's rain, the houses behind the commissary looked like a sparkling, golden place, a place fit for its name of *Silk-Stocking Row*.

I stood under a tall pine and watched the sun suck ever bit of fog up and up and up the mountains, up into itself. Then a drop of water splattered on my nose and I looked into the tangle of boughs overhead. Hundreds of webs swayed and each one was sprinkled with thousands and thousands of sparkling stars. It was a wondrous sight. Almost caused me to forget what had brought me down the mountain this day. Then I touched the ribbon curled in my pocket and sighed.

The mountains around me, the same ones a moment ago seemed like a magical place, now seemed to rise up to hold me here forever and a day. How did I think I could go beyond them? Read stories in all them books out there somewhere? What good was my book anyhow, torn and hid away like it was? Might as well not have it. Maybe I should go ahead and burn it, save Papa the trouble.

I hurried towards Widow Baker's though I dreaded tellin' 'em I couldn't go.

•   •   •

I leaned against her wire yard-gate. She was gone. Her windows was partway open to let cool air in at night and some of the hot air out during the day.

Scrapper slipped through her fence and helped hisself to a pan of scraps at the back door. She put food out ever day for any animal happening by. The pan was near full. She'd not been gone long.

Something in her yard told me she planned to be away a right smart while. A tinkling sound rose and fell. The morning breeze lifted tiny bits of music to the blue sky. From scrawny branches of an old apple tree hung dozens of bottles. All shapes, sizes, and colors, they sparkled in the sunlight while they swung and twisted and tapped each other, their sound as satisfying as cow bells ringing on a far-off mountain.

A sudden puff of wind set the tree all a jingle, like shivers in the air, coming out of nowhere and then gone. I wondered if Preacher Sam knowed Widow Baker tied her bottles in this tree to keep the evil spirits away while she was gone. Some folks, like Papa, called her a witch because of such things as this, but I just thought it pleasured the ears and eyes and surely could do no harm.

Inside her yard, I pumped some water, drank two dippers full, and enjoyed her tree as much as a play-pretty. A crow cawed overhead, a mess of crows behind him, but they flew on. Leastways them bottles kept the crows out of her garden.

•   •   •

I stood outside another gate, this one wood and freshly white-washed. I pulled the ribbon from my pocket. The sun burned on my head, but this house was shut up tight. Nobody did such in Ashworth Coal Camp unless it was in dead of winter. I bet their closed-up house was hot as a firecracker. Papa said outsiders didn't know how to use the sense they was borned with. In this instance, he was right.

I decided it'd be best to leave the ribbon. I weren't hankering to come back another time, to say I was sorry for stealing it, when I weren't. Wasn't like I took it from her. Bet she ain't even missed it. I opened the screen, knocked lightly on the door. I'd tell Mama I'd tried. Nobody answered. Probably gone to Foggy Mountain again, to buy a new hat or dress they fancied. I looped the ribbon around the doorknob.

"Just what do you think you're doing?"

I jumped around and faced Rae and her Mama, the ribbon in my hands, my face on fire. Scrapper shot past Rae, his stub tail in the air.

She jumped back, her eyes on Scrapper, her mouth hanging open. At least she knowed Scrapper was real, and not a made-up story.

"See, I told you. You can't trust these people," her mama said. She wrinkled her nose, took her big hat off, shooed me like I was a mangy stray about to mess on her porch. "Get away from there. Go on home. Go on, now."

I dropped the ribbon, run down the steps and out the gate, never looking back.

•   •   •

I stopped smack in the middle of the creek's footbridge, its loose boards and rope sides all a-quiver. I'd disremembered Mama's cornmeal, couldn't return home without it. Had no choice but to turn around, go back to the commissary I'd just skittered past.

The commissary was dark and cool, empty except for Mr. Emmett. He threw pink sprinkles over the floors like he was feeding a mess of chickens. I waited while he worked his broom back and forth and then swept a pile of gomed-up dirt out the door. Seemed to me Mama could show him a thing or two 'bout scrubbing, but I reckoned in a store it was enough to settle the dust. Besides, I liked the smell and the feel of oiled wood.

Mr. Emmett rested his broom and walked to the other side of the counter. He sucked on his teeth while he eyed me, his arms folded over his chest. I ordered a measure of cornmeal, handed him the piece of scrip and yearned for a piece of peppermint stick kept in a big glass jar. He returned with a small brown poke and smacked it down on the counter.

"Be off with ye," he said, "You come one day when you got a powerful hankering for a new pair of shoes. You're growing up, getting old enough to try 'em on. Upstairs in a room custom-made for such." A quar looking grin stretched across his face as he looked me up and down. Then he righted hisself and bent over a hoop of cheese with a butcher knife. He raised his head and shooed me with his knife. "Be off, I say. I got me a real customer."

I picked up the cornmeal and turned as a man stood against the sunlight flooding the doorway.

He walked close, bent his face and looked into mine. The poke slipped out of my hands and plopped at my feet. With a crooked smile on his face, he said, "Looks like you've been cured. What was it now? Some contagious skin disease?"

My feet felt rooted to the floor. Willie was wrong. One Revenuer, Vincent, had stayed behind, had not chased after Tippeytoes.

Mr. Emmett frowned, one eyebrow raised. He weren't gonna be no help. He looked at me like I was the one causing trouble.

Vincent picked up the sack and handed it to me. "I wouldn't have let him hurt you, if it had come to that. He's my boss, I had to play along, but I would've stepped in, only you did a fine job taking care of yourself." He laughed, a full good-hearted laugh as I edged towards the door. "I've got a girl myself back in Middlesboro, about your age. Named Sally," he added.

I nodded, but could not speak for the knot growing in my throat.

"I know your father makes whiskey. Hell, how's a man to make a living around here? Not from mining coal. I know he's got a still somewhere. I know that. But it's hid so good we may never find it. Yes sir, may never and that's a fact."

He turned back to Mr. Emmett and I flew out the commissary's door and down the steps. I heard Vincent say, "Yeah, you got that right. It's a hell of a job."

When I reached the footbridge, I looked back to see Vincent riding away on his horse, his saddlebags bulging with supplies. He must've left with the others, then his boss sent him back for victuals. Them revenuers was fixing to stay in Bear Hollow a good long spell. I hoped they got lost back there in the wilderness Tippeytoes knowed ever inch of, knowed it all his life. Then I thought of Vincent's daughter and I weren't sure what I wished for.

•   •   •

Papa never come home that night, nor the next. But at first light of the third day, we heard Neverblue and Colonel barking, their yelps coming closer and closer. Papa climbed the porch steps, slow and heavy. He carried a jar of sugar and two fat squirrels.

Mama fixed us a fine breakfast and announced she was aiming to bake applesauce pies this day, one for us and one to take up to the Wilsons.

Loe, always flapping her jaws when she ought to keep 'em still, said, "Papa, didya see any of them revenuers? Did ya? Hattie seen one. In the commissary. Talked to him, too. Told me his name. Didn't ya, Hattie?"

Papa set his coffee cup down slouching dark liquid onto the table. He looked hard at me. Mama pulled Loe aside, gave her the gardening basket, told her to not come back till it was running over with anything she could find in the garden. Then she took Jewel in her lap. All this happened, though it seemed far away and slow as in a dream while Papa studied me and I studied my toes.

Silence hung heavy in the air.

Finally, Papa said, "What Loe says is true?"

"Part true."

"Which part?"

"I seen a revenuer, but I never said one word to him."

"When? And how come you knowed his name? And how come you passed it to your sister? Tell me that."

"I...I don't rightly know why I told Loe. Mr. Emmett. He must've spoke his name, I reckon." I hadn't intended to lie, but I couldn't tell Papa I knowed his name because his boss called it when I met them two revenuers near the bath house.

He slammed his fist on the table, tipping his cup. I watched the coffee rush across the table, splash onto the floor. Mama sat up straight, but she never jumped up to get a rag. Jewel tuned up for a good cry. Papa's hands commenced quivering, then shook like he was afflicted. He grabbed the table's edge and stood, tipping his chair.

Jewel squalled, but Mama took no notice. Papa turned toward me, his eyes burning into mine. "Don't ever repeat the name of a revenuer in this house. They ain't fit to be called by a name. They ain't like a regular person."

Mama placed Jewel in my lap. She stuck her thumb in her mouth and whimpered as she pushed herself against me. Mama righted Papa's chair and helped him sit. He seemed like a spent, old man, unable to breathe. Mama fanned him with her apron.

"Damn them revenuers," he whispered. "Damn them all to hell." A coughing spell overtook him.

•   •   •

Two days later, word spread up ever hollow like a wind-swept wildfire. The revenuers had captured Tippeytoes Golightly and bound him up tight with strong ropes. Some said they threatened to hang him, as an example to all the other moonshiners. They slung him across a pack mule and carried him off to Frankfort. The judge would have no mercy and Tippeytoes would most likely die in prison.

The unbelievable had happened. Something folks thought never would. The only good news was Willie seen ever last Revenuer strut—that's what Willie said they done—strutted— out of Bear Hollow, shouting and hollering, celebrating their good fortune, not noticing him hiding behind a clump of spruce, counting.

Gone. They was all gone for now.

CHAPTER TWENTY-TWO

Voices in the Mines

Days and weeks passed. Quiet, ordinary, routine chores filled our hands and our time. Inside ourselves we mourned for Mr. Golightly, though we'd not received any word of his fate.

Papa paced back and forth across the front porch, the thump of his stick and the drag of his leg getting harder and faster with each passing.

He stopped at the screen door, peered inside. "Clara? Clara," he hollered. "I'm going after that load of corn."

"Lord help us," Mama said. She stood sending bean scraps to the floor. We'd been snapping a mess of green beans, the last of the garden, while Jewel played with a pile of strings under our feet. Mama had sent Loe to search the vines for any pods we had missed.

Mama busied herself wrapping up cornbread and sweet potatoes and filling a jar with pinto beans. "Hattie, run down to the spring and fetch your Papa a jar of buttermilk." We was thankful the Wilson's had a milk cow and had more milk then they knew what to do with. Mama shared our tomatoes with 'em or anything else we could spare from the garden.

She stopped, wiped her hands on her apron, looked off into the distance. "Why can't he stay close to home this day?"

I left to do her bidding, knowing she weren't actually asking me why. We knowed without saying it aloud. He had to shake his fist at them revenuers for taking Tippeytoes. The only way he knowed was to go about the business of making whiskey, whether or not it made any sense.

"Now, Clara," he said, taking his leave, "one good thing 'bout them catching such as Golightly. He's the biggest prize there is to them and they're gonna be satisfied for a while. Now's not the time to lay low. Now's the time to make a run of whiskey. After it's done, I'll hide it in the cave I was telling you about. Take my still apart and hide it, too. Then they can look till their eyeballs fall out and they'll never come across a trace. We got to stay a step ahead, outsmart 'em."

"What iffen Mr. Golightly has already broke? What iffen they know the whereabouts of ever still?"

"Shhh. Don't think such. He'll carry all he knows to his grave, don't matter what they do to him."

•   •   •

Soon after Papa left, Mama counted her canning jars. She decided most might be needed for whiskey instead of beans since Papa would be set on doing as big a run as he could manage.

She threaded me, Loe and herself a needle with her strongest darning thread. We spent the afternoon stringin' beans and hangin' 'em from nails driven into the wall behind the cook stove. They would dry into leather britches, ready for cooking on a cold winter's day. Mama allowed canned green beans tasted the best, and maybe so, but I was glad to have no water boiling on the stove, filling the air with steam. Makin' the whole kitchen weep.

We moved to the floor and sat like Indians, a great pile of beans in the middle of us. Mama made Jewel a bean necklace. A stiff breeze blowed through the house bringing the smell of honeysuckle growin' along the garden fence. Most times like this Mama would tell us a story, but somehow even Loe knowed not to ask for one. A wren flew to the back porch eve, filled the air with its song.

A voice called from the front yard. "Hello. Anybody to home?"

Widow Baker. We jumped up and run to the porch. She lifted two tow sacks off her shoulders as light as air or leaves or…

"I brung these for Hattie. You gonna need lots of hanging space."

In the front room we spread out bunches of pennyroyal, peppermint and all manner of things I couldn't call the name of. But Widow Baker named each one and said they was gathered fresh this morning and to not delay getting 'em hung to dry.

I looked at Mama.

"Well, go on. Them beans'll wait for us."

Widow Baker rested a spell in the kitchen before heading back down the mountain. Mama fixed a fresh pot of coffee. Then she reached inside a basket and handed me a ball of rag strips she was saving to make a rug.

"I'll be careful, Mama, fix ever piece back before going off to Foggy Mountain's drugstore."

"I'll not have enough for a rug no way till maybe come winter. You go on and use what you need."

I pulled a straight chair to the front room, stood on it and throwed the rag ball over a log rafter. Loe handed me one bunch after another. The plants looked right pretty hanging upside down, tied by all different colors of cloth and the smell was like stretching out in a summer meadow.

Loe found a milkweed pod on the floor. She opened it and commenced blowing the insides. It looked like little feathers floated in the air. In her dancing around, she stepped smack onto a pile of pennyroyal.

"Stop it," I hollered. "Look what you done."

Jewel squealed and tried to catch the feathery pieces. Mama come to the doorway. "Gather up the rest of them milkweed pods, Loetta, and carry 'em outside. Hattie's gonna have enough to sweep up. And let Jewel have a turn blowing."

"Yes ma'am," Loe said.

Mama returned to the kitchen. She talked to Widow Baker about the revenuers, Tippeytoes, and Papa.

"Lord'a mercy. I knowed something was a'miss when I heard a whippoorwill calling the other evening 'fore dark."

"How's the preacher fairing?" Mama said like she just this minute recognized he weren't sitting in her kitchen.

"Resting at my place. Fixed him a strong tonic to build up his blood, seen to it he drank ever drop and told him not to move out of the bed till I got back. He's over done things and has got to build up his strength iffen he's gonna preach revival up at the brushy arbor. And his thumb is worrying me right smart. Don't look like it ought to."

"Maybe his thumb's healing slower than you thought it would. Did Silas help ye with the building of the brushy arbor?"

"Law, yes. We couldn't have done it without him. It's as fine an arbor as there ever was on this earth. Silas is skilled with his hands, more than anybody I've ever knowed in all my borned days. In the evenings, he'd whittle the most handsome birds I've ever laid eyes on."

"Like this'n?" Mama took the wren out of her apron pocket and held it out.

I hung a plant with daisy-like flowers as Loe returned searching for any more milkweed. She stopped, looked into the kitchen and then up to me. "Papa don't know she's got it. Does he? Like your book." She hurried back to Jewel. There was no more milkweed.

Widow Baker continued, "Silas couldn't do none of the heavy toting, after he stepped in a whistle pig's hole and twisted his foot."

"I'll swannee that man has more bad luck. He hurt bad?"

"I wrapped it good. He'll mend iffen he stays off his foot a spell. I doctored him while we was there and left him some vittles. The preacher won't be leading revival up there for a while yet and there ain't nobody gonna be up there to disturb him."

"Folks is blaming Silas. Saying Mr. Golightly getting caught is due to a hex he put on us all. They say iffen times was regular, iffen Silas had never passed through our camp, it would've never happened," Mama said. Her coffee cup clinked in her saucer.

"Tippeytoes is getting old, maybe he got a little careless, too."

Mama agreed it could've happened. "Or maybe he got hisself snatched up on purpose, sacrificed hisself for all them other moonshiners."

"Hmmmm," Widow Baker answered as she slurped her coffee.

My thoughts turned to Birdman up at Red Bird, resting under the brush arbor while his foot mended. And Maggie. Did he still have her or did she fly away?

I jumped off the chair and went into the kitchen for a drink of water.

"Hattie, it's a shame you couldn't have been a part of it all. You would've been right smart help. More than them two boys I took along. All they wanted to do was stir up mischief, tease Silas's bird or go off fishing somewheres. Though I will admit we enjoyed them sun fish more'n once."

"What about Maggie? She all right?"

She laughed. "Got the best of Cloyd. Button fell off his overalls and the bird swooped it up 'fore he could bend over. She wouldn't give it back, neither. Left her alone after that."

"You wouldn't have had any such trouble from Hattie. She's a worker and that's a fact. Like her Pa, she don't let go soon as a task grabs hold of her. Sets her mind to do it. In this world it serves a body well to be mor'n a mite stubborn."

I felt my cheeks burn as I went back to the front room, to the task unfinished.

"You're looking peaked. You sleeping at night?" Widow Baker asked Mama.

"Yes. No. A little. Too much on my mind, I reckon."

They went on talking, Widow Baker giving advice and handing Mama a brown bottle. "Put two drops in a cup of catnip tea before bedtime."

I hollered into the kitchen. "When's all this gonna be ready for carrying to Foggy Mountain?"

"Patience, girl-child, patience. Iffen it don't rain much and the air stays pretty dry, I'd say maybe two weeks."

"Two weeks? That's forever."

"Why you in such a hurry?"

"I ain't in no hurry," I mumbled, wondering what I was going to do for two weeks' worth of waiting.

Widow Baker wrapped me in her arms before she took her leave. "Birdman's gonna be gone to Tennessee soon as he's able. He's not your way to leave these hollers. Not him nor them gypsies."

I squirmed loose and looked into her eyes. "I know they ain't. I do. I don't belong in Tennessee with Birdman and them Melungeons. But what is my way? Seems to me there ain't one."

"Listen to your heart, Hattie. Sometimes the Lord shows us how when we give up trying to make things go our way. He can even use a bad thing in our life for our good."

"You sound just like Mama."

She smiled and squeezed my shoulder. We had no more time to talk. Widow Baker had to tend to the preacher.

•   •   •

Near about suppertime, Willie run up the back steps and into the kitchen, his usual way to come calling. He brung some unsettlin information.

"Elsie's gone. Poof. Disappeared off the face of the earth." He stopped to catch his breath.

"What on this earth are you talking about?" Mama said as she fixed him a bowl of soup beans and a piece of cornbread.

He plopped down on the bench beside me, ducked his head over his food and ate like he was starving.

"Well?" I said holding my hands up in the air. His lollygagging was makin me purely edgy, which it seemed he could do without even trying.

He swallowed and gulped some water. "Mr. Wilson found her coat, all folded neat like, on a tree stump near his house. Her hat and latch pin laying on top. No sign of Elsie nowhere. She never knocked on their back door to ask for food, neither."

"Forever more. What do you reckon happened to her?" Mama asked.

"It's like she's disappeared into thin air with nary a trace. You know she never went nowhere without her coat and hat. Some say she must have been lifted up to heaven and is up there alongside Moses and Elijah. I don't put no stock in such tales. Ain't that where the old gypsy man was seen last? Up on Wilson's ridge? Odds are he's the one. Got mad 'cause the miners wouldn't let him set up housekeeping in the bathhouse and look what he's done. Put a hex on ever one of us is what."

"He ain't a gypsy. He's got a home in Tennessee." I give Willie my best glare.

All of a sudden, I weren't hungry. I didn't like being around Elsie Lampert. She acted touched in the head and smelled like rotten cabbage, but I felt awful thinking about her wandering around without the coat and hat she had put such stock in.

Willie reached for the big bowl of beans, dipped more into his bowl with lots of juice. "Pass me the cornbread, Loe."

He settled into eating again like he'd not had a bite. "Well, all I can say is, things is happening around here and they ain't natural. Look how Mary died. And Tippeytoes. He should've never been caught. Now Elsie's disappeared. Things is happening all over. Even inside the mines."

"What? What's happening? Willie had taken on a parttime job at the mines since a number of moonshiners was layin' low and had no money for a runner.

He reached over and patted my hand. "Don't you fret none 'bout me. I ain't in any danger. Pickin' slate outta the coal ain't nothin'. I ain't never going past the drift mouth. No, sir. Even iffen Mr. Harper says I got to. I heard them miners talkin, headed to their shift before the tipple started rumbling."

"What was them miners saying?""

"They been hearing voices. Some say it's them Negroes killed back years ago when they refused to work. Mr. Case won't go back inside no more. Matter of fact, he's quittin. Moving his family 'fore the company throws all their belongings out in the road, breakin' ever dish and stick of furniture they got. The Case family'll leave in the dead of night. He and most of them miners figures them haints was stirred up by Birdman."

He laughed, but it was a quar-sounding laugh. "We ought to be feared of . . . of them big coal companies. They own us, Hattie. Our lives ain't worth a mountain of slate. The truth is I ain't got no say in what job I will or won't do at the mines. No say a'tall." He pushed his half-eaten bowl of beans and cornbread aside, run his hands through his thick hair, and stood up like he didn't know what to do with hisself. "I got more trouble than worrying over haints or gypsies or ghosts and that's the gospel truth." He glanced around. Seems we was alone. Mama and my sisters had headed to the privy.

Willie leaned to my ear. "I could use a swallow of whiskey."

Papa always kept a jar under the back porch steps, but I never offered to get him any. Liquor would do him no good. I give my friend a hard look and shook my head.

He plopped back down, his elbows on the table, and held his head in his hands. He had scrubbed his hands before supper, but the tiny cuts had dried blood and coal dust in 'em. Slate had edges sharp as a knife.

I should've noticed sooner. I jumped up, returned with a pan of warm water and a piece of lye soap. I went to work. He winced a few times and gritted his teeth. When I patted his hands dry and then rubbed Widow Baker's ointment over 'em, he sighed. He smiled over at me. "You done a good job. Like a real doctor woman."

"Ain't nothin'." I laid his hands easy like onto the table. "Should've seen 'fore now you needed tending to." I carried the dirty water to the back porch and throwed it out. When I returned, Willie had settled in a kitchen chair and closed his eyes.

For all his bluster earlier, Willie had fears deep inside hisself. More than them voices in the mines. I was fearful too. Would he be swallowed up by the drift mouth one day? Would he have no choice but to leave these plundered hollers before such a thing happened? Like Jim? I laid my hand on his arm. His eyes flew open. He grinned and pulled me down to his lap as Mama and my sisters come inside. I jumped up. Heat flew clear to the top of my head. Mama looked at me with raised eyebrows. Loetta snickered.

"Hattie, get some water boilin. Willie could use a strong cup of tea." Mama pulled a chair close to him and sat down while I built up the fire underneath our teakettle.

"You know all us coal camp people, as well as those makin' whiskey, are beholden to you. Mr. Harper'll not send you into the mines iffen we got anything to do with it. You ever decide you got no choice but to leave us, we'll look after your Ma. You don't got to worry over her."

Willie nodded, sucked in a deep breath and blowed it out.

I fixed three cups of Widow Baker's tea, Mama adding a splash of whiskey to Willie's. He took a long drink, his cup doing a dance on its saucer when he set it down. "I ain't scared, Miss Sizemore. Ain't nothing in them dog holes 'cept putrid water and rats. And I an't feared of haints neither. He took another swallow.

"I'll tell you one thing for shore," Willie said as he stood. "A good number of the miners is scared 'cause of them voices, even threatening to walk out. Mr. Harper says iffen the men quit, he's bringing in armed men from Frankfort…by the boxcar loads. Force them miners to work whether or no."

"And if they refuse?" I asked as I looked from Willie to Mama. Would the armed men kill them all?

Her face turned white. "Convicts," Mama said. "From the State Prison. When the railroad was built through these mountains years ago and the locals said the work was too dangerous and walked off the job. Cutting and blasting up these hollows, pushing hard with no value put on a man's life, they brought in criminals thinking nobody would care. Men chained together like animals and treated worse by men on horseback carrying rifle-guns."

Mama took a long drink of tea. "Good family men out of work, standing and watching from afar. Many a convict found his grave under them tracks. It was a dark time in these hills, I tell you that. A dark time. I reckon somebody like Mr. Harper could bring it all to pass again. Lord help us iffen he does."

CHAPTER TWENTY-THREE

Laying Blame and
a Flaming Skillet

A few days later, Willie stopped by our house after his workday of picking slate from tons of moving coal since the break of day. He walked as bent over as a hunchback and he was covered with coal dust. He set his lunch bucket down and straighten hisself as a groan escaped his scrunched-up face. The whites of his eyes was streaked with red and his teeth looked pearly white in his black face. I couldn't take my eyes off 'em while he talked on and on to me and Mama.

I brung a pan of water, lye soap and ointment and went to work on his hands.

Willie said the voices inside the mines, iffen there was any to start with, must've quieted down because none of the other miners had threatened to quit since Mr. Case left. But the men seemed too quiet—the quiet hangin' heavy in the air—standing outside the mines each morning, waiting for a young miner to give them the signal. Their stations could be worked—no gas leaks. The job had once been Jim's.

Instead of laughing, joking, slapping each other on the back, bragging about who was going to load the most ton, the men shuffled in without a word of good will passing between them.

I patted his hands dry and Mama spread the medicine over 'em. She asked him to stay for supper.

"Won't your Ma be worried 'bout you?" I asked.

"Nah. Told her this morning I'd be late. Figured I might get an invite."

"Humph," I said as I walked outside to pitch dirty water onto the hillside. I returned to the kitchen and got the taters frying

Willie talked on and on while he ate his supper, Mama sitting across from him. She sat real quiet, her eyebrows bunched up, not offering to tell him the miners had Birdman figured wrong. Why didn't she set Willie straight about this man who give her the pretty little wren she hid in her apron pocket?

I was glad nobody knowed he weren't far from us this minute, camped under the brush arbor, his foot mending. The Preacher, Widow Baker, Mama, and me was the only ones who knowed. Well, maybe Loe, but she was more caught up in my doings, wondering what I might be up to, than Birdman's.

I figured the voices was there in the mines all right, amongst the sounds of water dripping, rats scurrying, and picks cutting into a vein of coal. The miners was quiet because they was afraid to go inside the earth, afraid they'd hear them voices again. Listening. Listening, but scared to talk about it. Talk would make the voices real and not imagined.

How did I know all this? Granny Guthrie. She said as long as men was killed in the mines, their voices would be trapped in them dark tunnels. She said it like it was the gospel truth. Forever and ever, amen.

•   •   •

Willie carried every bit of our leftover food away in his lunch bucket. I stood on the front porch to see him off. He stopped halfway down on the steps, turned and looked up at me. "Five old men, some even older than your Pa, has banded together to get ever still amongst 'em up and running since nobody knows how long they got before them revenuers return."

I moved closer to the steps. "I thought most of 'em, except Papa, was laying low. You ain't said this to Mama. Why not?" I crossed my arms and glared at him.

"Sorry, Hattie. Just now recollected it." He sprang up the steps and grabbed me tight. "Iffen it comes to pass, your Ma'll know soon enough. No need to heap more worries on her than she's already got. But if you think it's best . . . well, I got confidence you'll know what's best." He turned and hurried away, his bucket thumping against his leg.

"How did you come by this information?" I hollered into the shadowy half-light.

Willie stopped at the wood's edge and looked back. The white of his eyes shined. Then he lifted his hand, blew me a kiss and was gone.

"Looks like I weren't worth your time to give me a real kiss," I said. Most likely he never heard me, but I felt better for having said it. He's got confidence I know what's best? Humph. He'd better have enough for the two of us.

That self-same night I told Mama all Willie had somehow forgot. She listened, but never spoke until I'd finished. "We got to pray for all them men, revenuers and moonshiners alike."

•   •   •

One afternoon she made two of her vinegar pies.

"Jim's favorite." I whispered to Scrapper's ear as he lay in my lap licking his paws. Soon as Jewel squealed when she spied him there, he jumped down and disappeared.

Men come into the house in the dark of night and sat around our kitchen table. Mama told us girls to scoot to bed when they pulled out their liquor and got down to serious business. We crawled under our covers with blackened feet, but I did not sleep for a long time.

Their voices rose and fell and rose again. Mr. Seabolt said the fields was ripe unto harvesting and it was time for gathering in the sheaves. I thought this was quar talk, for I knowed these men never darkened a church door, never sang hymns or listened to the preacher's fire and brimstone hollering. Unless they give in to their wives' nagging and went to revival once a year. The other men seemed to agree with whatever Mr. Seabolt said.

•   •   •

Five old men, including Papa, had banded together. They vowed to get every still up and runnin' one at a time. And as soon as the whiskey was hid out of sight, they'd move on to another and do the same 'til they was done. They planned to use Willie for a lookout 'cause he had the sharp eyes of an eagle and the swift legs of a bobcat. Leastways, that's what he said. Whatever the reason, he was beside himself and whenever he could, he'd run to our house with his report.

"What about your job up at the mines? Won't you get fired?"

"Nah. Got the Gash boy to take my place."

"Billy? Why he ain't but nine-year-old."

"Mr. Harper says he's the best slate picker he's ever seen. Maybe they won't need me no more." Willie laughed like he'd told the best joke ever, but I knowed different. He and his ailing Ma needed his pay, pitiful as it was.

•   •   •

Most of the whiskey operators had made liquor all their lives and before now, they'd always worked alone, proud to be independent and not beholden to nobody. Papa said times such as this called for extreme measures.

Talk was the revenuers would return with a vengeance, armed with information as to the location of many a still, information they'd beat out of Mr. Golightly. Nobody called him ol' Tippeytoes any more nor laughed at his funny way of running through the woods. No, he'd earned something kin to sainthood. In school I'd read about them who died for a cause only I didn't think the revenuers would burn him at the stake. I asked Willie what he thought would happen to him. He said they'd probably build a scaffold beside the capitol building. The governor and folks from all around would watch him hang. And they wouldn't put no black cloth over his head neither and they'd watch his eyes pop out.

I didn't believe any of these tales.

I worried just the same.

•   •   •

The miners under the earth digging for coal — as well as the men up on top cooking sour mash into white lightning — was scared. They seen Birdman as the cause of all their troubles. Not to mention him being the cause of little Mary Wilson dying or Elsie Lampert disappearing. I knowed Birdman had no reason to inflict such heartache on Mr. and Mrs. Wilson or to harm a touched old woman. And him spreading a hex over all of us? Why, all of Granny Guthrie's talk about the haints made more sense than that.

•   •   •

I didn't talk to Mama about all I had figured out in my own mind. Here lately she had closed up into herself and shut the door. Not only did she not hum or sing or tell stories — she was unusual quiet. I wondered iffen she was scared, too, like the miners and the moonshiners. I studied her moving about, but she never noticed me doing it. Her mouth was clamped together, her lips pressed tight and she set about scrubbing everything in sight.

She even got after Scrapper with her broom, said he was messing up her porch and threatened him with a bath. A bath. Scrapper washed hisself all day long when he weren't chasing something in the woods or eating a mole or a bird he'd caught.

*   *   *

One night, after another moonshiners' meeting, I woke up and heard her in the kitchen washing canning jars. They swished and clinked together. I smelled fatback frying. What on earth was she doing? I hoped she weren't getting addled in her head like Elsie Lampert, getting her nights mixed up with her days.

Someone knocked softly at our back door.

I scooted out of bed and watched out the window as moonlight spilled over Willie. His dark hair shined. Scrapper appeared out of the shadows and rubbed against his legs. He bent down to pet him until Mama opened the door. She handed Willie two tow sacks full of jars and a flour sack full of food. I could smell the fatback, and it made me hungry for a piece between a hot biscuit. I figured Willie must be carrying them jars and food to one of the men's stills, or maybe to Papa's in the laurel thicket.

*   *   *

The next morning, Scrapper never meowed at the back door. I called and called, but he didn't come. Had he followed Willie last night, hoping for something else to eat? Even Loe asked where Scrapper was and Mama admitted she missed that rascal. I set to worrying maybe something had happened to him.

Soon as I finished my chores inside, I set on the front porch steps and called Scrapper. Loe and Jewel lined up on the porch, sounding like echoes of each other. "Scrapper, where are you? Where are you, Scrapper?"

Their hollering got louder and louder and they took to giggling when there was no answer. I could stand it no longer. "Hush," I said. "Hush or ever one of you will burn in hellfire and damnation."

They looked at me with eyes growing wide. Loe grabbed Jewel's hand. "Come on. Hattie's mouth is getting her in trouble and we certainly don't want to be around her, do we?"

I hated Loe when she acted all growed up. I heard Mama talking to my sisters, but the only words I caught was "…go play…later."

She never come out to the porch, but I figured "later" meant she'd deal with my cursing soon enough.

The morning felt hot and close. No breeze stirred the leaves on the sycamore tree close to the house or the tops of the tall pines along Wilson's ridge. Hot as all get-out. And it weren't even dinnertime yet. The heat would build, bring great thunderclouds over our mountains by mid-afternoon, even though there weren't many clouds in the sky yet and the rain weren't close enough to smell. I could feel it coming. Maybe the brewing storm, as well as Scrapper being gone, had made me hateful to my sisters.

Even the birds flying about seemed skittish—and as it turned out—Mama acted skittish her own self. I noticed right away when I finally went inside. She didn't seem herself a'tall.

First, she dropped two eggs on the floor lifting 'em out of the egg basket, fixing to stir 'em into cornbread. "Oh, Lord, what a mess."

After breakfast, she'd decided to go ahead and bake while the cook stove still had fire in it. When it came time to eat again, she'd not have to build another fire and add more heat to the already hot kitchen.

She bent down, wiped and cleaned. I toted water from the rain barrel. I offered to lend a hand, but she shooed me away. She set about scrubbing the spot with lye soap and a brush. It appeared she was hopping mad at the whole kitchen floor and wasn't gonna quit till she scrubbed ever last inch.

Loe, coming in the back door, was the one who noticed smoke rising from the skillet sitting on the stove's eye.

"Mama," Loe hollered.

All of a sudden, grease whooshed into flames. Jewel laughed and reached up like it was a play-pretty. Mama screamed, "No, baby, no," pushing her to the floor as she ordered us, "Open the door!"

Jewel squalled while we squeezed ourselves between the screen door and the house. Mama stopped on the edge of the porch and pitched the flaming skillet into the yard. Chickens squawked and flew in all directions. We laughed at the sight, but then Mama turned, holding her hands out in front of her. She looked like she'd been branded, the shape of the handle burned into her flesh. She hadn't thought to grab a cloth first.

In front of our eyes, blisters rised up, filled her right hand and puffed up like they was fixing to pop. The flaming skillet had burned her fingertips on her other hand. Mama looked at her hands like she couldn't take it all in.

I pushed Loe towards the steps. "Run for Widow Baker," I said. "Run!."

•   •   •

I eased Mama down on her bed. A groan slipped from her lips, but she never cried out. Her face looked like she'd worked outside in the wind all day, while other places was as white as her pillow casing. Her eyebrows and eyelashes had been singed clear off. Thank the Lord she'd had her hair pulled back in a tight bun...if she hadn't...just the thoughts of her thick black hair flaming like a torch ... I felt my stomach heave and run to the back porch. I leaned over the rain barrel, splashed water on my face and returned to her bedside.

The first thing Widow Baker done was to give her a spoonful of medicine out of a little blue bottle. She placed pillows under both arms and went to work. She broke the blisters and bathed her hands in a clear salve.

Mama shut her eyes and relaxed a little. Widow Baker commenced wrapping her right hand and the fingers of her left one using the strips of cloth Mama had boiled just the day before. Today, Mama had aimed to tie them pieces together to add to the rag ball, the same rag ball I'd used a few days ago, hanging plants from the rafters. The colors and patterns of cloth had turned the whole room pretty. Today, seeing the same colors and flowered prints around Mama's hands made me hurt clear to my bones.

Jewel wouldn't go near the bed and hid behind my legs. I reached around and picked her up. She buried her face in my neck and whimpered. I felt like crying my own self.

"Your Mama's a strong woman," Widow Baker said. "She will heal. She's mighty fortunate. Remember that. Mighty fortunate."

I nodded, knowing what she said was so, but looking at Mama hurting and helpless made her words pass on by me and fly out the window. What if we lost Mama and had to bury her alongside Granny Guthrie?

All of a sudden, I didn't have no worries as big as Mama's. What was it she said one time? Sometimes concerns over the family had to come first, before any of my own. Mama was the one who kept things together no matter what. Now it was up to me, me being the oldest, to look after our family. Maybe when she was well. Maybe then I'd think again about them foolish plants hanging all over this house and why I thought I had to have such. How could I ever think of leaving now? It wouldn't matter if Papa burned a hundred books of mine. I couldn't leave.

"Hattie, are you listening?" Widow Baker said. "Whenever she gets too restless, give her three drops from this bottle, right on her tongue. It'll settle her down. She ought to sleep maybe two, three hours at a time. Make yourself a pallet on the floor beside her. You can tend to her during the night. Loe can be in charge of Jewel. Don't you try to do it all. Promise me?"

"I promise. I'll do everything just like you said."

"You got it in you to be a good doctor woman. Maybe you can learn your calling before you get as old as Methuselah, like me." She laughed. "I seen it clear as day when you helped me with the preacher."

I looked at her like she was speaking in tongues. What did she say?

"I'll be back in two days. Iffen she's done sufficient healing, like I hope, we'll unwrap her hands to finish healing in the open air. But just in case we need to wrap her up again, have plenty of clean cloths. Unless of course she starts a fever. Iffen she does, you send for me."

I nodded.

"When's your Papa due home?"

"I…I don't rightly know."

"I expect Willie will stop by soon. He's taken a fancy to you Sizemores. Especially you, Hattie. When was he here last?"

"Last night, I think. Yes, last night. The only hankering Willie's got is for Mama's cooking. He'll come when he's hungry enough."

"Maybe you ain't paying attention to the young man. Good vittles ain't the only reason he's always hangin' around." Widow Baker patted my arm. "Your Mama's restin'. Walk me to the door."

I opened the screen door for her as she fit her doctor's bag underneath her arm. "Iffen Willie don't show up by tomorrow after dinner, send Loetta to my house and I'll go fetch your Pa myself. We've had our differences, but all that don't matter now. It's certain he dearly loves Clara and he needs to know what's happened." I stood on the porch and watched her leave until she disappeared down the footpath.

I prayed for Willie to somehow know I needed him. My heart ached for him. I felt more alone than I'd ever felt in all my borned days.

CHAPTER TWENTY-FOUR

The Storm

It come late afternoon, like I figured. Angry, purple clouds hung low over the mountains, swallowed the sun, turning day into an unnatural looking twilight. I thought of the wicked giant snuffing out the sun like a candle.

Something terrible was fixing to happen.

I pulled a straight chair close to Mama's bed. Loetta appeared and stood beside me. She begged me to light a lamp. Said Jewel was afraid. I told her we couldn't spare the oil and she was old enough to comfort a little one with stories and such, like Mama would do. Loe looked at me, but instead of putting up a fuss, she turned and gathered Jewel, and they hurried as fast as doodle bugs to bed.

The wind whistled around the windows. The porch swing banged against the house. I bent over Mama and listened to her breathing. She was restin' good. My sisters' singing growed louder. A song we'd learned in Sunday School back when we used to never miss.

"This little light of mine, I'm gonna let it shine…let it shine…let it shine. Put it under a bushel, no, I'm gonna let it shine…let it shine…let it shine."

I eased away from Mama and peeked into our room. The two of 'em was a shadowy hump in the middle of the bed, covers over their heads, even though the air in the house was near to smothering. We'd shut everything up tight.

I returned to Mama. Lightning flashed, filled up the house with light. It flickered about, danced about the room and throwed shadows over Mama's bed. And the thunder. Lord-a-mercy. The thunder boomed, rattled the windows, set the house a trembling before the whole thing started over. I couldn't see how Mama could sleep, even with Widow Baker's medicine.

Wind blowed the rain sideways against the bedroom window. The top of a pine tree snapped, hit the ground with a thud. Then another done the same. Please, God, I begged, don't let no tree fall on our house. I soon had other worries. Rain found its way underneath our tin roof. A 'plink, plink' hit on top of the warm-morning stove between the two bedrooms. Then a big drop splattered on top of my head.

"Loe," I hollered, jumping up. "Come help."

By flashes of lightning, we searched the kitchen. We gathered ever pot and pan we could find. Soon we had at least two more leaks and nothing to put under them. I opened the back door to grab the washtub and a bucket. Something dark streaked past me. I snatched what was needed, and slammed the door against the rain.

Loetta screamed.

"Yeeoow," Scrapper hollered.

I squatted as my heart thumped wildly. "Come here, Scrapper. It's all right. Come on."

His eyes glowed under the kitchen table.

"You must've stepped on him," I said glancing over at Loe. "Scared him half to death."

"I scared him?" she huffed as she grabbed the washtub and the bucket and placed 'em underneath the drips.

"Come on, Scrapper. You can stay inside with us. Come on." I done my best to speak easy and gentle.

He jumped into my arms, cold and wet and stinking, but I didn't care. He'd come home.

"Mama's not gonna let him stay in the house," Loe said as she left to take care of Jewel who'd started whimpering.

"Hattie?" Mama called from her bed. "What's happening?"

"Just a minute, Mama. Don't you try to get up. I'm a'coming."

I ran to her bedside, Scrapper still in my arms. Mama was bound to have a pure hissy-fit when she seen him.

She never took no notice. "Hattie?" she said, trying to rise up. "Is that you, Hattie?"

"It's me, Mama. You got to stay still and quiet. Lay back down. How you feel?"

She sank back onto her pillows. "Terrible thirsty. It's powerful hot in here."

Just then a bolt of lightning hit closer than ever. I runned to the bedroom window. A big poplar tree had split down the middle. It was black and smoking. Thunder shook the house. Scrapper jumped down and run under the bed. Jewel squalled and Loe shouted at her to hush.

Soon as I come to my senses, I run to get Mama a dipper of water. When I returned, she was asleep again. I prayed she weren't getting a fever. I dipped a rag in the water and wiped her face and neck. Then I throwed the quilt and sheet clear off her. I laid my cheek on hers, and I thought she felt warmer than she ought.

Finally, I was able to rouse her. I slid my arm under her head and held the dipper to her lips. "Drink, Mama. You got to drink."

She took two sips, though much of the water ended up on the bedcovers. I eased her back on her pillow and she slept.

I sank down in the chair, not knowing what else to do. I felt tuckered out all of a sudden. How I could get hold of Widow

Baker in this storm? How late in the day was it, anyway? Would Wille stop by like I hoped? I'd not done anything towards supper. I couldn't remember, did we eat any dinner? This day seemed as long as a hundred. Scrapper appeared from underneath the bed and lay on my feet.

Just when I thought maybe the storm was letting up, without warning, something—like thousands of creek pebbles—poured onto the roof. The pounding growed louder and louder till it was like a thundering herd of horses. I covered my ears. Then the sound of pebbles, blown by the wind, beat against the window. I looked outside. The air had turned a pale green, like a willow tree leafing out in spring. Balls of ice covered the ground. Some of the pieces was as big as the coal we burned in the cook-stove.

All of a sudden, we heard glass breaking. Screams rose from our bedroom. Mama didn't stir. I hurried to our bedroom door and couldn't believe what I saw.

Our window was filled with large, jagged holes. Balls of ice bounced across the floor.

I grabbed a folded quilt laying across the end of the bed, glad Mama had lots of 'em. I throwed it on the floor over the glass. "Bring me another one," I hollered at Loe.

We held a quilt over the window, as best we could. Hail beat against the quilt and against our arms. Then the storm quit. Just like that. All was deathly quiet. We lowered the quilt. It was one Granny made the year before she died.

The sun shined and glimmered against the ice-covered earth. I squinted against the brightness. The outside air was cool and as fresh as a spring morning. It smelled like pinesap. I remembered to thank the Lord. Nary a tree had landed on our house.

"Loe, fetch the water bucket! Run outside and gather up the ice balls for Mama." I swept up the glass and then wadded up newspapers and stuffed 'em in the jagged holes. Tomorrow I'd have to nail some wood to cover most of the window. Maybe I'd have to use some from our chicken coop or from our yard gate. If the commissary carried glass, most likely it would cost far more than we could manage.

I opened the back and front doors and all the windows. The fresh air felt like it'd swept us clear to heaven.

"Hattie?" Mama called.

I run to her, carrying ice wrapped in a tea towel, glad to hear she was awake again. "I'm powerful thirsty. What is this? Ice? Lord-a-mercy. I must be dreaming."

After Mama drank two dippers of water, I laid the icy towel over her forehead all the while telling her about the thunderstorm, the fierce wind and then the hail and the air turning cool and fresh.

"Ah, Hattie, the Lord is good, ain't He? Have you children eaten anything? What time is it anyway? I 'spect I could manage to eat a bite iffen you'd stir up some cornbread."

I leaned over and kissed her on her cheek. "I could fry us some hoe cakes in no time."

"Sounds mighty fine."

Just as I turned to leave her room, she called, "Hattie?"

"Yes ma'am?"

"What's that cat doing under my bed?"

But she smiled and I felt like shouting or singing a joyful song. Widow Baker had said Mama was a strong woman.

•   •   •

I built a fire in the cook stove and then one in the front room fireplace. The whole house felt damp clear through. Some of my plants hanging from the rafters dripped water, but I was too busy to consider they might be ruint.

I set about fixing a decent supper of corn bread with some left-over sweet potatoes and cooked cabbage. I even opened up a jar of Mama's applesauce. We had reason to celebrate our good fortune.

Willie thundered up the front steps, through the house and into the kitchen. "Where's your Ma? I just come from Widow Baker. Did ya ever see such a storm?" He looked at me and Loe setting supper on the table while Jewel crawled after Scrapper. "Where in tarnation's your Ma? Where is she? She gonna be all right?"

"In her bedroom," I said. "She…" He dropped his dinner bucket and run to see her.

Scrapper commenced meowing and walking around in circles. I opened the back screen door. He zoomed past like he couldn't get out soon enough.

Jewel whined and fussed.

"Hush, now. He'll be back come morning. You'll see." And I knowed he would. Maybe even this night iffen I went out by the garden and called his name. He'd be back for sure. Didn't he return after going off with Willie, following the smell of fatback?

Mama insisted on coming to the supper table. She soon found out she was as helpless as a newborn baby-child, her hands wrapped in rag strips.

●   ●   ●

Before Willie left us to carry the news to Papa, I followed him to the porch. I touched his shoulder. When he turned, I throwed my arms around him and squeezed him tight. "Everything's gonna be all right, Hattie," he whispered in my ear. "Your Ma's gonne be all right. You got the gift of doctoring. Don't you worry none. You hear?"

He eased away. "I got to go."

I'd made certain some of our supper left in his miner's bucket. He always carried his pail wherever he went even though he'd left his breaker boy job.

"Got more important work to do now," he told me one day. Maybe, but a lookout for the moonshiners put him in a different kind of danger. His lungs wouldn't rot away from years of breathing coal dust, but a revenuer's bullet could snuff his life out in an instant.

"I'll be back soon as I get word to ya Pa," he hollered from the wood's edge. "I'll help ya fix the winder. Don't you go to worryin' 'bout me while I'm gone." He disappeared without making a sound as if I'd conjured him up standing in our kitchen with his sideways grin.

"Now why would I do such as that?" I said into the quiet. But I knowed I would until he returned. A far-off whippoorwill was my only answer. Since it weren't pitch black dark just yet, Granny would say the bird's call was a sure sign somebody was fixin' to die. A shiver run clear through me. I hurried inside to tend to Mama.

CHAPTER TWENTY-FIVE

Jim's Home

I blew the lamp's flame out and lay down on the pallet beside Mama's bed. I'd drifted off to sleep when Papa hollered from the kitchen. Was I dreaming? He cussed at the chair he'd knocked over and thumped his walking stick against it. "Damnation! Clara! Where are you?"

I jumped up. Where did he think she was in the middle of the night? I fumbled for a match and lit the bedside lamp as Papa stood in the doorway. He gasped for breath and then was overtook by a coughing spell. We waited for it to pass. Mama raised her arms and Papa stumbled to the bed. He fell onto his knees. His head rested across her chest.

"Did Willie fetch you?" I asked as I placed a straight-back chair near the bed and helped him sit.

"Ain't seen Willie."

"Then who?"

"Widow Baker. When the storm hit, all four of us men had hunkered down in my cave. Lucky for us she knowed where it was."

He turned to Mama. "Came as soon as I could. You hurtin' much?"

"No," Mama whispered as her eyes fluttered and shut. She sighed and was soon asleep.

Papa looked over at me. "Seems your Ma's had some good doctoring."

"We're beholden to Widow Baker. She came to us right off."

"She declares you're gifted your own self. What have you got to say about it?"

"I . . . I reckon I don't know."

"Humph. Anything left from supper?"

The beans, taters and cornbread had turned cold, but Papa never complained. After he finished eating, he checked on Mama, returned to the kitchen and picked up his walking stick. "Send Willie if you should need me. Iffen you see him. Can't figure where he's gone off to."

He limped to the back door and turned. "You done a fine job takin' care of your Ma."

He was gone before I'd taken in what he'd said. My whole life I'd never done nothing to please him. Matter of fact, all I seemed to do was make his anger rise up and spill over. I tucked his words inside myself. I'd save 'em for another day when I might need 'em more.

•   •   •

One day bled into another, all of my doctorin' and housekeeping chores much the same. One marvelous thing kept me going. Mama was healing and getting stronger. I continued sleeping on the floor beside her bed and rised up before daylight to cook some porridge. We had give out of coffee, even chickery, and of course that's what I yearned for the most.

Our chickens had quit layin' eggs since the storm and the old rooster had quit his crowing. I kept listening for Willie's boots thumping up the steps and commenced worryin' about him in spite of declarin' I wouldn't do such. Neither did Papa darken our door. Was he and Willie laying somewhere out in the woods? Hurt or dead after them revenuers smashed Papa's still to bits? I imagined the worst.

My worries cast me into a daze, and I moved about my duties like some other Hattie had took over my body. I was eat up with fretting.

After supper, twilight slipped into dark sudden like. As if the devil hisself had dropped his black cloak over our house. Far off heat lightning flickered across the mountain ridge, but no thunder grumbled in reply. Even the katydids had turned mute. No breeze stirred the bedroom curtains. Even though I'd throwed the back and front doors wide open, the air inside our house growed smother-some thick and pressed upon us. Whatever was going on was unnatural, and the sum of it all made me plumb jittery. I feared another storm was coming.

Loe commenced whining. "I got to go to the privy. Now." She danced around holding herself as I struck a match and lit a lamp in Mama's bedroom.

"You ain't going. Use the chamber pot." I spit my words at my sister sounding like a short-tempered hag. Seems I weren't able to bridle my tongue. I huffed around Mama's bed and straightened her bedcovers.

Loe fussed and sassed me until Mama said, "Do as she says. This instant. Then you come back here and tell your sister you're sorry for not minding. Hattie's doing the best she can with what she's been dealt, and you ain't helping none."

Loe scurried away to our bedroom. We heard her jerk the old chamber pot from underneath our bed, its lid clanging onto the floor, no doubt adding more chips or dents to the beat-up enamel.

"Humph," Mama grunted shaking her head.

After giving Mama a birdbath, I helped her into her nightclothes and rubbed her neck and back. She closed her eyes and sighed. Our routine helped her relax a little, and Widow

Baker's medicine would help her fall asleep. Jewel stood at the foot of her bed watching us. Mama was mending, but her youngest child kept her distance from this helpless person she no longer knowed.

A clamor on the back porch caused Jewel to squeal. She runned over and grabbed my legs. I pressed my hand onto Mama's shoulder. I figured a bear must've knocked over a pan of apple peelings I'd left on the porch, forgotten until now. Their scent must've drawed this lumbering creature to our door.

Loe hightailed herself to us, her bloomers around her ankles. She stumbled into Jewel as the back screen door opened and slammed shut. My sisters screamed. I pulled Loe close as Jewel scrambled into Mama's bed.

Then he stood in the middle of us, out of breath and wet, most likely from tromping through rain on his long journey home. We stared at him like he weren't flesh and blood, but only a spirit. Mama first spoke his name. "Jim," she said.

He dropped his banjo before he fell to his knees beside the bed and eased his head onto Mama. She wrapped her arms around him, her hands stuck up in the air. Jewel squeezed in the middle of 'em and tears streamed down Mama's face.

•   •   •

I pulled our rocker close to the kitchen table and as soon as Mama sank into it, Jewel climbed onto her lap, squirmed a little and promptly fell asleep. Mama's face beamed with happiness as her eyes fell on her youngest and then on each of us in turn.

Jim and Loe settled around the table while I filled our brother's plate with cold leftovers. He didn't seem to mind the beans and cornbread was no longer hot from supper for we'd not have another fire in the cook-stove 'til morning. Then I remembered the apple peelings on the porch and brung 'em inside. I'd cook 'em tomorrow morning and add a jar of applesauce, kept for a special occasion. Yes, we had a powerful reason to celebrate. Our Jim was home.

While he ate, questions spilled out of me and Loe while Mama rocked and listened. "How did you know we needed you?" "How long can you stay?" "How long did it take to get here?" "What's it like where you live?" "Where do you work?"

Jim smiled, shook his head, and kept eating until he'd swallowed the last bite and gulped down two glasses of water. He pushed his empty plate aside. "I'm here 'cause Willie come for me. Said my family was pining for me something fierce. That true?" He looked around at us with a big grin and then reached over and ruffled the top of Loe's hair. She smiled all over herself. Jim was thinner now, his red curls had growed clear to his shoulders and he had the beginnings of a mustache, but he was the same, inside where it counted.

I carried his plate to the dishpan, added a dipper of water and returned to the table. Now I knew where Willie had gone. I leaned toward my brother. "Who told Willie to fetch you?"

"Widow Baker. She fetched Papa since it was closest and told Willie to come get me. He says he'll return to the mines if Mr. Harper'll have him. Else they'll throw him and his Ma out of their house. Don't know why he thought he'd get away with working for the whiskey operators."

"Oh my," I whispered. I could hardly take it all in. Mama sucked in her breath and squirmed. "Are you hurting?" I asked. I stood and went to her. "You needing some medicine?"

She shook her head. I brung Mama a dipper of water and held it while she drank it dry. Fear for Willie and for Jim, and for Papa too, had twisted my stomach into a hard knot and I suspected the same fear had brought on Mama's distress. I returned the dipper to the water bucket and eased onto the bench next to Jim. He clasped his hands in front of him until they turned white. The quiet hung over us. I was afraid of his answer, but I had to ask.

"What about you? Will you return to the mines?"

He raised his head and looked at me for a moment. Then he nodded. Mama gasped. "Got no choice," he said. "Willie's got word the revenuers will return. And soon. Papa and them other moonshiners never got their stills up and running. They did help move each one into caves or into the middle of laurel thickets. Won't be long 'fore Mr. Harper insists we have a workin' miner or we can't live here no more."

"But the coal company don't own our house," I said.

"What good is that? They own the mountain underneath us. Counts more than what's sitting on top. The mineral rights was give up years before we was borned. Our people, and many like 'em, never knowed what they was putting their X to."

I thumped my fist on the table. "It ain't right."

"No, but there's nothing we can do to make it right."

•   •   •

We kept talking late into the night before Jim took up his banjo and played ever tune we fancied and twice he played Jewel's favorite, *She'll Be Comin' 'Round the Mountain*. When he finally laid his banjo down, I carried Jewel, heavy with sleep, to our bedroom. Loe stumbled along behind us and I tucked them both into bed. A breeze found its way into our room even though the window was half way boarded up. Part of the chicken coop had done the job and me and Loe had nailed the boards in place without Willie's help. I'd been feeling ornery against him, not knowing why he'd not showed his face around here but I could no longer be such. Now I felt most grateful he'd left us to bring Jim home—even if it meant my brother'd surely return to the mines. At least our family was together. The curtains swayed, the air cooler.

When I returned to the kitchen, I give Mama some extra drops of her medicine to help her sleep through the night. Even though she was wore out from all the excitement, I was afraid she might lay awake worrying about our family.

Scrapper meowed at the back screen door and I let him inside as Jim stood and stretched. The old cat shot through the kitchen and disappeared underneath Mama's bed.

Jim laughed. "That creature still around?"

"He is and always will be. Even Mama has taken a liking to that rascal."

"You don't say." But Jim had no sharp edge to his words and his grin was as big as a sunny sky. I laughed too, and Jim give me a quick hug.

"I'd give a pretty iffen I could fix you some coffee."

Jim picked up a knapsack, reached inside, and pulled out a leather pouch. He untied a knot in the drawstring, lifted out two coins and dropped 'em in my hand. I could hardly believe my eyes.

"Been saving all I could since I left home. What else you needing from the commissary? We can't be foolish about spending it, but it just might get us through any rough spell knockin' on our door."

I grabbed Jim around his waist nearly knocking him off stride. "I'll be careful. I promise. We can't let old Mr. Emmett get suspicious about how we come by all this money. Coffee, cornmeal, and dried beans. That's all for now. We can wait on window glass."

Jim was agreeable and said my growing up was remarkable. Remarkable. Made me all puffed up. "Mama's the only one who can know 'bout this," he added. "We'll need us a good hiding place."

"There's a loose board underneath my bed."

"Perfect." He handed me the pouch. "Make certain it's tucked in there good.

Tomorrow you can make a trip to the commissary. I'll sleep on the floor beside Mama tonight. Rest in your own bed for a change

. . .

I stood on the front porch in a thread-worn dress as my nightclothes and shivered in the foggy damp. Jim had managed to dig up a gob of fat fishing worms before he vanished down our footpath carrying a pail of bait and his cane pole. His footsteps sounded soft as a whisper and a nearby bush trembled. The early morning sky held one bright star. Brought to mind the times we climbed to the top of Wilson's ridge and spied for shooting stars until the sky give way to a pale, silvery light.

No need for Jim to wait around until Mr. Harper knowed he was home and demand he return to the mines. To check each and ever tunnel for gas before he raced to the tipple as a breaker boy. No need for my brother, who had no heart for mining, to enter a dark drift mouth or to work over a chute of fast-movin' coal any sooner than necessary.

Jim's plan was to stay out of sight until the moonshiners' fate was certain. Maybe them revenuers would finally give up and go home, and Pa could go about his whiskey-making business. Jim could leave us again, go back to his job as a clerk in a general store, in a foreign place far from here. I doubted any of these had any more chance of happening than me leaving these hollers one day. Why did I ever consider such a thing? Seemed I'd be right here forever and a day, my dreams of reading dozens of books nothing but pure foolish.

Granny declared one time, 'These mountains has got a powerful pull on us that live in 'em.'

Yes indeed. When I'd been a mere child, they'd been a comfort, like her quilt throwed over my back. Or like slipping on my flour sack dress covered with dancing ballerinas. Or touching anything that'd been stitched by Granny's strong blue-veined hands. Each and ever one had pleasured me to no end.

Yet at times like this, since I was no longer a child, I felt as helpless as them sorry mules forced to pull coal out of the mines, until they give out one day, no use to anyone. Their end would certainly come as a shot to the head and never mind wishing it weren't so.

These mountains bound me here. They felt like a curse.

•   •   •

Sunlight bathed the commissary's fresh-oiled floor, made soft from years of scrubbing and miners' boots tromping across 'em. The sharp smell of coal lingered in the air, but the floor smells rose up strong. It reminded me of the earth's breath after our storm left dozens of broken pine trees.

Mr. Emmett turned from feeding hunks of fatty meat into a grinder. He folded his big arms across his bloody apron. A dark scowl was writ across his face.

"The Sizemores ain't got no more credit in this store. You'd best skedaddle."

"Don't need no credit." I thumped Jim's fifty-cent piece onto the counter makin' a jar of picked pigs' feet dance.

His eyebrows rose until they disappeared underneath his shaggy hair. He smelled worse than a pack of wet, mangy dogs. "Who'd you steal that from?" He spat his words like a snarl and my stomach lurched from his stink.

"Don't matter none. Spends the same," I swallowed the foul taste in my mouth.

"Watch your tongue. Half of your money has to go toward your family's debt, though it won't make a dent. Soon you freeloading Sizemores'll be broke again.

You'll never walk outta here with new shoes. Unless you're willing to bargain for 'em. Mark my words. They's a shiny pair sitting right over yonder. Appears to me they's 'bout your size, too. Yes sir, won't be long and you'll be begging for them shoes. Ask ya ma. She knows. Yes sir, she is well acquainted." He laughed and I thought of a wicked king in a story book, only Mr. Emmett weren't make-believe.

Prickles run all over me. Even so, I couldn't help myself but turn and gaze upon shoes like those worn by Rachel Elizabeth. Mr. Emmett talked gibberish and pure foolishness. And how would Ma know about such? For certain he had told me a puzzling story.

I turned back to the matter at hand. "I come for cornmeal, dried beans, coffee and a sizeable piece of fatback. I expect a full measure for my money . . .or . . . "

He throwed back his head and laughed. "You'll take what you get, missy. And be glad fer it. A mighty wonder I ain't requiring all of your money against what's owed."

He scooped the cornmeal, coffee and beans into three small cloth bags and tied each with string. Then he piled them on a piece of brown paper and commenced wrapping 'em. I straightened myself and stood as tall as I could. "What about the fatback?"

"Humph," he said. He huffed to the meat case. He returned with a scrawny, oily parcel and threw it on top of the bags. After wrapping and tying my purchases, such as they were, he shoved the package across the counter. I had no way of knowing, but felt certain he would keep whatever money was left instead of using it toward our debt.

Heat rose inside me until my face burned hot as fire. "I need to see our family's record inside your ledger book." It was propped against the cash register, but he'd not touched it.

"Not 'til the end of the month. And it's not for your eyes. Only your Pa's. Or if he's not able, your Ma can take a look."

I clamped my jaws shut and ignored the flies swarming onto a pile of ground up meat. I fixed my eyes on the shelf behind Mr. Emmett. Bags of snuff and a stack of twisted chewing tobacco waited for a miner to pay double what they ought to cost. Pa would most likely never have enough money to buy his favorite chew. Not now. Our debt would never 'be settled.' As long as we lived in this place it would keep on growing until it buried us.

We was no better'n slaves, just like Jim declared. No miner could ever earn enough wages to satisfy what he owed. And now iffen Pa could no longer make his whiskey for Mr. Harper, our family was standing on a cliff's edge with a herd of wild hogs chargin' toward . . .

"Are ye deef, missy? Didn'tcha hear what I said? Get your sorry hide out of here or I'll call on a company man that'll help you along."

One of them men always hung around the commissary to keep a miner or a family member from getting out of line. Except on payday when there was a half dozen or more with rifle guns at the ready. Papa said they wasn't nothin' but thugs who wouldn't think twice about beatin' a man to a pulp or pitching him and his family out on the street—iffen that's what Mr. Harper wanted.

I clutched the measly purchases to my chest and turned, ready to be shed of this place. My resolve to leave straightaway flew out the door as them shiny black shoes drew me over to eye 'em closer. I reached over and touched a buckle.

"Ahhh, seems you do fancy them shoes," Mr. Emmett hollered. I jumped like I'd touched a hot stove. I scooted towards the sunlit porch, sorry I'd lollygagged.

"Ask your Ma!" His voice thundered after me. "She knows all about new shoes." I glanced back. His face twisted into a grin. I hightailed myself away. I thundered down the front steps and nearly tripped over a man sprawled out there. A man with a gun strapped to his leg. Mr. Emmett come to the porch. His peculiar laughter nipped at my heels.

CHAPTER TWENTY-SIX

Shoes of Shame

I crossed the creek, the railroad tracks, hurried past the bathhouse and trudged homeward. Clouds darkened the footpath. Undone by what had took place at the commissary, my muddled thoughts pressed heavy upon me. Them shoes in the commissary had a hidden meaning and had me stumped. The prettiest things I'd ever laid my eyes on, but they was bound to something shameful.

Mama somehow knew, but I wouldn't ask her until she healed and felt more herself. Until she wasn't weak and teary-eyed over the least thing. I had no doubt she'd once again be like a strong tree to lean against.

When I reached our yard and looked up to the porch, Mama was wrapped in a quilt and sitting in a rocker with her head thrown back and her eyes closed. Her face looked drawn tight. Maybe she was hurtin' along with frettin' over our family and what might become of us — not to mention what might become of Jim if he returned to work in the mines.

I climbed the steps and she jerked up straight. "I didn't know where you had gone. Seems Jim's been fishin' and has lit out again. There's a pail of Sun Grammies in the kitchen waiting for your knife. Best see to 'em before they're ruint."

"Yes ma'am."

She squinted her eyes at me and the bundle I held. "How did you manage to buy anything at the commissary? We ain't got no more credit."

"Jim give me some of the money he's been saving." I wasn't about to tell her Mr. Emmett was a no-count cheat who refused to show me how much we owed. Most likely she knowed about his lowdown ways already.

She leaned back and shut her eyes. A smile teased her lips. "I declare. The Lord has provided."

I hurried inside to lay our provisions down. Now wasn't the time to argue with Mama. No matter iffen it was the Lord lookin' after us, which she always declared, or my brother, which I figured made more sense, I had some food to put on the table.

Toting the fish and Mama's sharp knife to the chestnut stump beside the garden, I went to work. Loe and Jewel weren't around, most likely playing in the woods somewheres. I was glad to have some time to myself, time to sort through my tangled, miserable thoughts.

I gutted the fish and slung their insides into the garden. "Take that!" In my mind, the mess slid down Mr. Emmett's wicked face. Scrapper bounced out of the woods and had hisself a feast. Since the fish would start stinkin' by suppertime, I lit a fire in the stove, stirred up some cornbread and got busy fixin' a generous dinner. Didn't matter we'd eat a mite early. Soon as some of the fish sizzled in a fry pan, the oven was hot. I slipped a skillet of cornbread inside.

"When you finish up in there you'd best go see about your sisters. Time they was home," Mama hollered from the front porch.

I flipped the last fish onto a plate and peeked at the cornbread. "About ten more minutes," I said toward the front screen door as little feet clambered up the steps. "Fish 'bout done?" Loe yelled. "We smelled it clear down to the creek and we're starving. She and Jewel tromped into the kitchen with Mama moving along slow behind 'em. "Not with them dirty hands. Go wash up before you eat one bite. And Loe, you're fixin' to clean up the kitchen when we're done since you've made yourself scarce all morning. Now scat."

Mama was sounding more like her old self and it weren't the hot kitchen warmin' me all over.

When we all settled around the table, Mama looked my sisters over, mud-splattered except for their fresh scrubbed hands. "Makin' mud pies again, I see. I hope they was good'uns." They squirmed, but Mama smiled and thanked God for our fine dinner of fish and cornbread. Before we'd finished, Jim slipped in the back door and I handed him a plate. He ate like he hadn't eaten in a month of Sundays.

Next thing we knowed Willie appeared in the kitchen, grabbing a plate and helping hisself to our food. He squeezed between Jim and Loe on the bench. I was beholden to him. He'd traveled a far piece in order to bring our Jim home.

I let him swallow his last bite before I asked. "What news you got for us? What've you heard?"

He held up both hands and started talking.

"First off, your Pa ain't able to leave his sour mash right now. Has to tend to it pretty near ever minute of the day and night. He says this might be his last run and he's got to stick with it." He glanced my way and grinned. "He also said he's mighty grateful you took charge, especially of you takin' care of your Ma."

Once again Papa's words surprised me.

Willie stood and paced the floor with his hands clasped behind his back. That meant there was more and most likely not good news.

"Tell us," I said. "Get on with it."

He looked at Jim. "No need for you to stay around here expecting work up at the mines. Mr. Harper ain't gonna hire you on. Somehow, he found out you'd come home. He says you're not only a slacker, but your talk about the miners needing a union has stirred up a hornets' nest. I heard him talkin' to your Pa my own self. I know this for truth."

"What else did you hear?" Jim asked. He stood and peered out the kitchen window.

"Why ain't you come here sooner?" I shook my finger.

Willie's grin vanished. "Weren't more'n an hour ago I come by this information, and I figured Jim ought to finish his dinner before he lit out."

"Mr. Harper showed up at your Pa's still to see how the whiskey was comin' along. Seems he's runnin' low on 'the good stuff.' Mr. Sizemore assured him he was fixin' to light the fires and start cooking. As you know, revenuers can't spot smoke as easy in the dark and they're purely skittish about gettin' lost in these hills. Don't know how Mr. Harper, him being a city man, found your Pa's whiskey operation when no clear path leads to it, but he did. Mr. Sizemore come right out and asked him iffen he would consider puttin' Jim back on the payroll."

Willie took to playing like he was the bossman hisself. He puffed out his chest, smoked a pretend cigar, and looked over pretend glasses. "That Sizemore boy best keep his hide out of this camp or any coal camp up in these hollers. He ever shows his sorry self around here again, I'll set the law after him and tell 'em to do whatever is necessary to teach him a lesson he won't forget. We'll not abide any union talk around Ashworth."

The armed company men was the law in camp. They done whatever Mr. Harper told 'em, like the one I'd seen at the commissary. Jim had no choice but to leave us once again. It was plain to see he had spoke up for a union more than we'd realized. All those times we thought he was off fishing or traipsing here and yonder, he was talkin' to the miners or their wives and he hadn't been quiet about it. When he turned and put his arms around Mama, I asked him if this was true. He straightened up, looked me in the eye and nodded.

"That's what I figured you'd done." My brother certainly weren't no slacker. I wondered iffen Papa would credit him any for his gumption, even though now his life was in danger and our family's future uncertain.

Mama stood. "Hattie, wrap up some fish and cornbread for your brother. Be quick about it."

Along with the leftovers from dinner, I added a small jar of buttermilk, two boiled eggs, and three green tomatoes to a flour sack. Then I pressed a buckeye into Jim's hand. "For good luck."

"Best be praying, Sis." He dropped the buckeye into his shirt pocket and pulled me close for an instant. He smelled of sweat and the whole outdoors he dearly loved. He turned to Mama and rested his head on her shoulder. He lingered there a spell. No tears was shed, except for Jewel who squalled more than enough for all of us. She didn't understand what was happening, but she knowed something was terribly amiss.

Our redheaded, skinny Jim grabbed his food sack and his banjo before he hurried out the door and disappeared into the woods. We grieved his leaving, but his union talk had put his life in mortal danger. As much as it pleasured us to have him home, even for such a short spell, I wished Papa had never sent Willie to fetch him.

•   •   •

Willie was skittish to be on his way. According to him, the moonshiners counted on him as a look-out day and night until the white lightning was ready, and poured into jars or jugs and hid in the back of caves, along with all evidence of their doings. I packed his lunch bucket with leftovers from dinner, and walked to the front porch with him. He clambered down the steps.

"Next time you show up at this house you come with good news. No more bad. And that's a fact." I knowed it weren't his fault Jim had to vanish from our sight and from our lives, but a purely mean spirit had took over.

He turned and looked up at me and studied me for a moment. "I'll keep my eyes and ears open 'til I find you some good news. And that's a promise, Hattie Mae."

He placed his ragged felt hat, that had once been his daddy's, on his head and with a quick wave was gone. First Jim and then Willie going off had took all the starch out of me. I sank onto the porch steps. Scrapper jumped onto my lap until Mama opened the screen door. She asked would I help her and we headed to the privy.

•   •   •

The next morning Widow Baker come callin'. "You hoo," she hollered from the yard gate. "Anybody to home?"

Me and my sisters raced to the porch. We jumped around and squealed and clapped our hands. Visitors was a rarity to our house seeing as we lived off to ourselves, but the doctor woman hadn't come by to pass idle talk or to while away the time. She had healing powers and we were beholden to her for looking after our Mama who joined us on the porch. Her face shined like the sun.

"Hattie, light the stove and put a pot of chickery on. And get the jar of honey the Wilsons give us. . . and . . . don't we got some biscuits left from breakfast?" Mama was beside herself with pure happiness and I rushed to do her biding. Mr. Wilson had brung the honey soon as they learned of Mama's accident. Kept the burns from getting' infected and Widow Baker was mighty pleased when she learned we had a quart jar full. Now we had about a cup left, but no longer was it need for Mama's hands. We'd use the rest for pure pleasure.

While the coffee bubbled on the stove, I gathered the cups and saucers, biscuits and honey and arranged everything on the table.

Mama sat in a straight-back chair. Widow Baker unwrapped her right hand, the one burnt the worst. "Ahh," she said lifting her arm and turning her hand this way and that. "Before long you're gonna be as good as new. The good Lord, along with Hattie's help, has done worked a miracle."

Mama's eyes filled up and spilled over, but she was smiling at me through them tears. "Hattie's done some mighty fine doctoring."

To me her hand looked ugly, pink and wrinkled, though I weren't about to say so. Loe also had enough sense not to speak her mind, but she chewed her bottom lip as she watched. Then she turned and ran out the back door. She rushed up the hill towards the privy, which was not unusual for her. But I knowed she could not abide looking at Mama. Jewel was the one who surprised me. Instead of running away, she leaned against Mama and patted her arm.

Widow Baker reached in her frayed leather satchel and handed me a small jar. "Open it."

I done as she said. Inside was a gob. It looked like the snot Loe blowed out of her nose when she had a powerful cold. "What is this?"

"Come from a plant growin' out west. Traded some of my 'sang for it at the Foggy Mountain pharmacy and don't know if I'll get my hands on any more. But don't be stingy using it. Softens the skin and helps the scaring."

I held the jar in one hand and used my fingertips of the other and worked the slimy mess gently over Mama's scars. "You're not gonna hurt me, Hattie. I ain't a china doll."

"Trying to be careful is all."

"I ain't faulting you. You've took good care of me and I knowed the load on you weren't easy neither."

Loe joined us before we'd taken one bite of our biscuits. I showed her the gunk and she made a face. "Looks like snot!" We laughed and Loe gave Mama a peck on her cheek. My sister seemed more like herself.

Widow Baker set her coffee cup down. "Best be on my way. Got two more stops before I can rest these old bones. These hills could shore use another doctor woman." She looked at me, but I commenced stacking the dishes and played like I never noticed. How could I take care of people when the sight of blood made me feather-kneed and when Preacher Sam puked his insides out?

"I ain't had no training to be no doctor and don't plan on getting' any," I grumbled not knowing anyone had heard.

"Someone's doing a mighty job protesting." Widow Baker closed her satchel and handed me a pouch. "Something to help ease your Ma's worries a little. Nothing to do her any harm. You might fix it for your own self, too. We'll talk some more later. And you need to listen. Red Bird Mission's a mighty fine school. You could learn far more than I could teach ya 'bout nursing folks, even midwifery. You could live there while you studied. Earn your keep by cooking or cleaning. Wouldn't have to have a nickel in your pocket. You think on it."

My mouth opened, but no words come out. Loe walked her to our yard gate asking about the snot in the little jar.

CHAPTER TWENTY-SEVEN

Willie, Good News, and More

The days drug by as slow as a garden slug inching up a cornstalk. School would be startin' up again 'fore long and I especially grieved for the poetry and stories I'd never hear. It seemed like my feet kept trying to pull my body through a bog like we'd once come upon in Dead Man's Holler—the time Jim took me there fishin'. He'd spotted the deep, nasty mud and kept me out of it. Now his cane pole leaned in a corner where he'd left it, where he'd most likely never touch it again.

"You might try your own hand at fishing," Mama said making me jump at her voice. "Even iffen you didn't catch nary a fish, it'd be a good place to talk to the Lord. Peaceful by a stream don'tcha know. You moping around the house ain't doing any of us any good. I know you're grieving for your brother. All of us is, but we can't give up on livin'. Jim would somehow know we was wallowing in our misery. Besides, he's where he ought to be. Clerkin' in a store instead of becomin' a miner and old before his time. We need to be thankful for that. Mighty thankful."

I looked at Mama who had more faith and more gumption in the little finger of her scarred hand than I could ever imagine having. I hugged her quick and hollered for Loe. "Come help me dig for worms!"

Two shovelfuls of damp earth uncovered some fat ones in the deep shade cast by our privy, but my sister wouldn't touch 'em. I scooped 'em up and soon had a can full. I took Jim's pole and the bait and set out for a spot upstream from our coal camp. Widow Baker's words had planted a kernel of hope inside me, but that old word *Impossible* kept whispering in my ear. Mama was healing, but slowly. I couldn't leave her when she couldn't carry a bucket of water from the creek or chop kindling or manage wash day without me.

I found a spot along a scooped-out part of the bank where the creek lay still and deep. Jim had showed me how to bait my hook and to drop it in easy like before wiggling the worm to catch a fish's attention. In no time a'tall, I had a strike and a powerful pull on the line. I jerked the pole and fell backwards into a prickly bush. An empty hook swung in the air.

"Dad gum," I swore at my luck.

The next try weren't no better. It seemed I'd use up all them fat worms and have nothin' to show for my efforts. The fish was in that deep hole, and I was determined not to let 'em get the best of me. Maybe now was the time to talk to the Lord, like Mama said.

I backed away from the creek, sat down like an Indian, and went to whispering since Jim declared fish couldn't abide any loud noises. Maybe they didn't like my earlier fussing.

"Lord, we're in a powerful mess down here. It appears to me you might be the only one who can straighten it out. No need to tell you what all's been happenin' since you knowed it already. Mama says you know everything about us, even the number of the hairs on our heads. Is that true? I'd be beholden to you for any help you could give us starting with a big 'ol fish for our supper.

Or iffen you're so inclined and ain't too busy, one of your miracles for our family would be mighty fine. I know you allowed your Son to turn water into wine. Seems you ain't dead set against drinkin'. Papa's got to cook his sour mash into whiskey for Mr. Harper or the Sizemore's'll be throwed clear out of Ashworth. That's our family's troubles in a nutshell. My own worries has got to be put aside for now. Like Mama said, takin' care of our kin has got to come first. Ain't no way I can walk out of these hollers, not now, maybe never."

The sun bore down on my head since in my haste I'd forgot my straw hat. Weren't no time to be fishin' in the heat of the day. Another saying of Jim's. I baited the hook whether or no with my last two worms. They looked dead, but I plopped them into the same good for nothin' hole. The water had turned still.

"Might as well give up and throw them worms out." No sooner had the words left my mouth then something struck hard and held on.

Instead of jerking the line, I pulled it in easy like until a big 'ol trout lay flopping in the weeds. My catch would feed our family tonight. Jim would be proud. I was proud my own self, but I remembered to give thanks. This here fish was nothing short of a miracle.

·   ·   ·

Willie must've smelled the fish frying to a mouth-watering crispy goodness 'cause soon as we gathered to the table, he come tromping into the kitchen.

I put my fork down and stood up from the bench ready to fix his plate.

He motioned me to sit. "Ain't gonna to eat one bite 'til I deliver some good news." He flashed me a grin and his blue eyes danced. "Didn't I promise you I'd do such the next time I come?"

I plopped back down. "Well, out with it!"

He grinned, enjoying hisself more than he ought. Then he drank a whole glass full of water, and wiped his chin on his shirtsleeve. We waited. Except for Loe and Jewel who gobbled their food.

He raised hisself up tall resting his chin in his hand like an old man. I couldn't help but smile in spite of myself. "Do you recollect when the miners was spooked by them voices they swore they heard in the mines? Been going on for weeks now iffen I figured right."

Me and Mama nodded. How could any good come out of this?

He continued. "Not only had they heard them fearful voices, some miners had their lunches stolen from their buckets when they wasn't lookin.' Made 'em mad as hell." He glanced at Mama. "Sorry Mrs. Sizemore. It weren't me sayin' them words, but one of them miners."

She smiled and raised one hand. "Do go on."

"Elsie Lambert come walking out of the mines this morning. Pretty as you please like she was lollygagging through a field of wild flowers. Them strange voices was hers all along. Not no haints or a hex from Birdman. Not the spirits from them dead Negro miners from years ago. Don't it beat all you ever did hear? How long's she been missing anyway?"

I jumped up and give him a hug for delivering such good news. Then I piled him a plate full of trout, cornbread, wilted lettuce, and fried green tomatoes. He pulled a straight-back chair up to the table and dug in.

"Been a month of Sundays or more I expect," I said around a mouthful of cornbread. "Didn't she leave her coat and latch pin on the Wilson's doorstep after little Mary's funeral?" I helped myself to more tomatoes before Willie ate them all. "Where is she now? We can't let her pass right through these hollers and disappear from us forever. She wouldn't have nobody to look after her."

Willie held up his hand. "No need to fret. I run and fetched Mrs. Pritcher. She took Elsie to her house like a mother hen. Said she would feed her and clean her up. She was one awful dirty woman and smelled worse than ten dead skunks. Worst I ever did smell."

I finished off the fried green tomatoes and leaned toward Willie. "I'm obliged you come here bringing good news, just like you promised, but what business you got up at the mines? I thought you quit your job."

"Shorely did. Long as I got breath in me, I'll be the whiskey runner. They sent me with a message to give Mr. Harper, and I come upon Elsie waltzing out of the drift mouth followed by a string of miners. It was a sight to behold." Willie grabbed the last piece of cornbread and stuffed his mouth.

"Do we have to beg you for ever speck of information? What was the message?"

Before he could answer Mama said, "It was about this particular run. Right?"

Willie nodded while he chewed and slurped his water. He finally swallowed his last bite. "Mr. Sizemore sent me to assure Mr. Harper when he could expect his whiskey delivery. No need for him to get all crotchety 'bout the time it takes to make the best there is. He's made threats to call in them revenuers, if something happens he don't get his whiskey."

Mama's hand flew to her throat and her mouth fell open. "Would he do such as that?" Her voice rose into a squeak.

"For certain he would," I said stacking the dirty dishes and carrying them to the wash pan. "He's 'bout as mean as old Mr. Emmett in the commissary. Hard to say which one would be declared the worst evil man in this entire world." Mama commenced coughing, her face scrunched up and red. I rushed to her, thumped her back and lifted her water glass to her lips.

She shook her head. "Swallowed wrong," she squeaked out. Tears run down her face and I brung her a wet rag. She soon settled down, but I figured it was the mention of Mr. Emmett's name had caused her choking spell.

"Well? When will the whiskey be ready?" I asked Willie as I set about scrubbing the dishes. In all the commotion with Mama, Loe had gotten out of her chore to dry. She and Jewell had disappeared, off to play out of ear's reach.

Willie picked his teeth with a broom straw. "Mr. Sizemore says three weeks or maybe a little less. Mr. Harper agreed to wait, but no longer. Seems he's about to run dry, and he don't like it none when he does. Thanks for supper, Hattie. It was mighty fine. I'd best get back to my job. Since it's the only one I got, can't afford to get laid off." He grabbed his old felt hat and turned to go.

"I'll see you to the gate," I said and throwed the dish rag into the pan.

"No cause for Loe to shirk her duties. Mark my word, she'll not be getting away with it." Mama said. "Soon as she shows herself, she'll wish she'd done her part 'round here. She took our broom, hugged it to herself and started sweeping the floor. Love for her flooded my heart. She was on the mend for certain.

Willie and me stood in the yard unable to speak over a woodpecker's racket, drilling in a dead tree.

Soon as it flapped away, Willie creaked the gate open and shut it behind him. He'd kept his promise about bringing some mighty good news, but I was at a loss of any words to thank him proper.

"Wait," I yelled as I caught up to him at the wood's edge.

Before thinking, I grabbed him and planted a big ol' kiss on his lips. His hat went flying and he nearly lost his footing.

I scooped up his hat, dusted it off, and held it in both hands.

"Golly durn, Hattie. What you do that fer?" His face turned a firey red as he took his hat and plopped it on his head. Then he was gone into the woods, disappeared from sight. But his whooping and hollering could've reached the heavens. Why had I kissed him like that? Willie was like a brother to me. Wasn't he? Or had something shifted? Had something changed and now we could never go back to the old way?

CHAPTER TWENTY-EIGHT

No Clear Way

"Yahoo! Anybody to home?" Widow Baker called out early one cool morning, even though she knowed we was inside.

Mama and us girls gathered on the front porch to welcome our friend, as well as our doctor, standing in our yard. Her presence always brought us pure pleasure.

We never had much use for old Doc Evans hired by the coal company. Iffen he weren't passed out drunk, which happened more often than not, he treated his patients rough and spoke to 'em with a sharp tongue. And he always smelled like horehound candy he sucked on, which I couldn't abide.

Widow Baker huffed up the steps toting a basket and her worn leather satchel. She pulled her shawl back onto her shoulders. She looked older than I ever remembered. Her hair, normally in a long plait hanging down her back, was flying about her head like it had been stirred by a fierce wind. I lifted the load from her arms and she sank into a straight-back chair by the screen door.

Loe brought her a dipper of water. We stood nearby and waited 'til she caught her breath.

"These hills has got too steep for the likes of me. Used to think nothin' of running up and down 'em like a young Billy goat. Now it takes me twice as long to travel half as far. And I don't like it one smidgen."

She rested her hands on her knees and studied her dusty, lace-up shoes where her big toes had pressed clear through. Scrapper meowed underneath the house.

"Even my own tonic medicine don't help none," she continued as she shook her head and pushed herself upright. I reached out to steady her, but she swatted my hand away. "No need for me to keep on grousing. Don't do nobody no good." She picked up her doctoring bag and walked over to Mama, her exhaustion seeming to fall away. She acted more like her old self and I was much relieved. "How you fairing, Clara? Sleeping like you ought to?"

Mama nodded, smiled and held out her hands to be examined. "Hattie's a right good doctor woman her own self."

I glanced over at Widow Baker. "I...I only done what you told me."

She cut her eyes at me while holding Mama's hands. I couldn't tell iffen she agreed with Mama or maybe she was fault-finding. Either way, I weren't no doctor woman.

After rubbing a sharp smelling ointment into Mama's scarred hands, Widow Baker handed me the jar. "Three times a day without fail for nigh on two weeks. After that, once before bedtime ought to do it until the cream is gone." She turned back to Mama. "Should make a powerful difference, but no working in the garden, hoeing and such, or wringing out clothes on wash day. Use some good judgment about what you allow your hands to do."

"I will. Hattie has took up the slack around here, and Loe's gonna help her sister more than she's been doing. And that's a fact of the matter."

"Glad to hear it," Widow Baker said as she reached in her basket and handed me a loaf of bread and a small jar of honey. "Baked this morning. Save the honey to mix with a little whiskey in case any of you should come down with the croup as it seems you Sizemores is prone to do."

"Yes ma'am," I said already tasting the salt rising bread spread with a smidge of molasses left in a jar Miss Wilson give us for Christmas.

Our friend fixed her basket of more bread and honey to her liking and set it down. She pushed it toward the porch steps with her foot. She stood gazing toward the ridgeline pressing her hands into the small of her back. Then she glanced over at Mama. "I'll return in two weeks. See how you're getting' along. Could be you won't need no more doctorin' and you can return to your regular way of doing things, within reason. If I determine that be the case, would you allow Hattie to accompany me on a trip into the hollers along Red Bird Mountain? We'd be gone maybe two days iffen you could manage without her."

"Why I expect I could. It's past time Loe stepped up anyhow, and Isom ought to be home by then. His whiskey makin'll be done and Mr. Harper will be comin' to lay claim to his share. Maybe then we can all settle down to our ever day lives. We ain't done much settling here lately."

"Truer words was never spoken," Widow Baker said. "Birdman's walked pretty near halfway to Tennessee by now with Preacher Sam beside him on his swayback mule. Between the two of 'em they shore stirred things up around here."

"You certain they're gone?" My voice rose into a dry raspy sound.

"Walk a ways with me, Hattie. I'm headed to the Wilson's place. Since little Mary died there ain't been no peace up on their mountain. No medicine can fix sorrowful hearts, but I can sit with 'em a spell before I head over their mountain to Four Mile Creek. Like to check on a few families over there when I can. I'm the only doctor they got."

I looked at Mama. "Well, I uh . . . I don't . . ."

Mama waved her hand. "You go on. I'll be just fine. Iffen you come across your sisters, tell Loe she'd best skedaddle on home or she'll be pickin' a switch from the cherry tree. I expect a switch will fit just fine in my good hand. Just fine. You tell her that."

"Yes ma'am." My sister would learn the hard way to do her part instead of running off ever chance she got, tending to Jewell as her excuse.

• • •

We entered the woods behind our house where an old wagon trail edged upward around the mountain. It was weedy and briar filled, but still better than climbing straight up with no path a'tall. I offered to tote the basket and was surprised when Widow Baker never protested.

After we walked a bit further, we stopped. "Spect I'd best be headed back home. Mama might be needing me."

Widow Baker nodded. Her face looked flushed and shined with beads of sweat. She eased down on a pine log as a big 'ol black snake took its time getting' out of our way. Birds fluttered from a clump of Sumac, the first in the mountains to show a change from green to red.

"Hand me that brown bottle," she said in a nearabout whisper. After two big swallows, she wiped her mouth on the back of her hand. She looked up at me. "You still heartset on leavin' these hollers?"

"Can't leave Mama now. I considered following Birdman and the preacher into Tennessee where the gypsies and them Melungeons live. But I decided it was too far a piece, even though the air there is as sweet as honeysuckle."

"Do tell." Widow Baker stood, looked at me square on and placed her hands on my shoulders. They's some rough folks living in them settlements in Tennessee. Maybe the preacher can do 'em some good and long as Birdman's with him they'll not do him no harm. You're not old enough or tough enough to take on them folks. I predict one day soon you'll have no choice but to leave us. Now's the time to consider where you might go."

"Papa's not gonna let me go nowhere."

"Iffen you wait for his permission, you'll never leave. Your Mama's a strong woman. She loves you more than her own life, but she knows you're growing into a woman unafraid of people different from us. There is good and bad people in them gypsies, in the Melungeons, in these hollers of our own kind. All outsiders ain't bad, like your Pa believes. Reading and learning new ideas ain't bad neither. Consider where you might go before you have to decide in haste. Just remember, iffen you should need my help, I'll do whatever I can."

She picked up her basket and her satchel and continued on her way. I watched her until the woods turned thick and I could no longer spot her wispy hair lifted in the breeze.

I trudged toward home. Where could I go to be shut of Papa and his hateful ways, but close enough to keep watch over Mama, Loe and Jewel? How did Widow Baker know I'd have to leave soon? What iffen she's right? Will I be ready?

CHAPTER TWENTY-NINE

War in the Woods

Worrisome thoughts lay heavy upon me—like a gunnysack of coal across my back. I paid scant attention to the little used footpath thick with fallen leaves. Birdsong in the undergrowth seemed like far off prattle instead of the usual pleasure.

My breath hitched when a man stepped out of the woods holding a rifle-gun across his chest. Vincent. The revenuer who had stopped his partner from doing me harm months ago. And the same man I'd seen in the commissary not long ago. He looked scruffy and dirty instead of clean and shiny. Leaves and twigs had caught in his hair, his shoes and pants muddy.

His face twisted into a scowl. His dark eyes bore into mine. "What do you think you're doing up here? Get on home where you belong!"

"You can't tell me . . ." I swallowed my words and backed away. I had no idea what had made him purely hateful, but no need to rile him any further.

"I'm headed home this minute. Mama sent me to fetch my two sisters. You ain't seen 'em have ya? One is pretty near up to my shoulder and the other ain't but a baby child." I knowed they never wandered up this way, but it was all I could think of on short notice. I was much relieved Widow Baker was most likely up to the Wilson's place by now and out of harms' way.

I edged around him. He turned as I did until we faced each other again.

"I doubt your sisters would play way up here in these thick woods. Maybe they'll be home when you get there." He leaned his rifle against a giant elm and pulled a scrunched-up handkerchief out of a shirt pocket, shook it and wiped his face. He no longer looked fierce and angry, but wore out and sad.

I hurried away scattering dried leaves into the air. I stopped short and looked back. Vincent was slouched against the elm rolling hisself a cigarette.

"You up here in these parts all by yourself?" My words rose up sharp and hung in the air. Fear gripped me. Other revenuers must be around, close to where Papa as well as some others, was makin' their runs of whiskey.

He struck a match on the tree bark and lit his cigarette before his thunderous eyes glared at me. "You don't need to know . . ."

Just then shots rang out, sounding nearby. Cursing and shouting were followed by more sharp gunfire.

"Go!" Vincent yelled jabbing his finger toward me. "Get home!" He grabbed his rifle, turned and ran toward the confusion. For a long moment I never moved. Gunfire slacked off, but the yelling rose amongst breaking glass and crashing metal. Spilled whiskey would run like a flooded creek down the mountain until it soaked into the earth and disappeared. Nothin' left but the smell of it.

Papa. Willie. I couldn't do nothing to help 'em. It pained me not to follow after Vincent. But iffen I ended up takin' a bullet my own self, I'd not be around to help Mama. I took off at a run. Headed home.

Why hadn't Willie warned the moonshiners before them revenuers swarmed over the hillsides? Maybe he was shot trying to do just that and now lay dying or was already dead. Willie.

Sometimes a pest, sometimes too cocksure of hisself, but always a friend and for certain something more. I never got to tell him so. Then I fretted over Widow Baker. Had she made it to the Wilson's and stayed clear of danger?

I kept running. At last, I seen the tin roof of our house.

• • •

Loe and Jewel huddled together on the front porch steps while Mama paced back and forth behind them. Another rifle shot rang out as Mama looked up and seen me. "Hattie!"

I run up the steps. "I'm here. I'm all right." I throwed my arms 'round her waist careful of her tender hands.

The woods around our house turned as quiet as an empty church. I led Mama over to the swing. "Sit down. Now." She was all trembly and I feared she was about to give out. "Nothin' we can do but wait."

"Pray," Mama whispered. I flopped down on the swing beside her, scooted close and wrapped my hands around her arm.

Loe and Jewel ran over to us. The four of us held onto each other. It seemed like forever and a day though it could've been only minutes. A jumble of prayers was lifted to the heavens amongst Jewel's whimpering. Then someone or something lumbered through the woods and we hushed.

I jumped up as Vincent appeared. He carried a limp Willie throwed over his shoulder. "He's alive," he said easing him down onto the porch. "A blow to the head, but he ain't shot. I checked him over."

Willie groaned. Mama knelt beside him while I rushed inside to fetch some water and rags. By the time I returned Vincent had disappeared. I gave thanks for him and prayed he'd live to return to his little girl. And I asked the Lord to spare Papa. As much as he caused anger to rise up inside of me, I had to admit he also claimed a piece of my heart and even more of Mama's.

I bathed Willie's face and wrapped a wet rag around his head. It had growed a good size lump. At last he opened his eyes. He looked up at me. "Hattie . . . I'm . . . I'm sorry. I should've . . ."

His eyes closed and his whole body slumped down. I grabbed his shoulders. "Don't you go and die on me. I won't allow such. You done the best you knowed how. I'm certain you did. You hear me?"

His eyes fluttered open again. They took on a great sadness. "Them revenuers surprised me. I let your Pa down and . . ."

"Hush such talk. Nobody could know what them sneaky revenuers was up to. You got to live. You got to. For me."

A sigh escaped his lips. He reached for my hand. His eyes closed.

•   •   •

Before the dark of night laid its cloak over our mountain, the crickets, tree frogs, and katydids took up their singing. Everything seemed a usual end to a day turned catawampus, as if we had only imagined the sounds of fighting nearly upon us. But as evidence, Willie was here holdin' his wrapped-up head, sitting at our kitchen table.

I come inside from the back porch after going from front to back peering into the woods, holding my breath and listening. Our fear was that ever moonshiner had been shot dead during the raid. Nobody had put our fear into words, but it filled the air like a thick fog and swirled around us. Willie pushed his supper plate aside. He'd not eaten a bite.

Heavy clomping up the back porch steps. Papa and Widow Baker stood amongst us as the screen door slammed behind them. I shut the solid door and latched it in case a Revenuer had followed 'em. Papa slumped onto the table bench. Mama rushed to his side. His clothes was torn and covered with dried blood. "Tell me where you're hurt," she said. Her hands hovered over him.

He shook his head. "Neverblue. Held him in my arms til he breathed his last. Then we buried him."

Widow Baker poured him a drink of his whiskey. He gulped it down as she told us more.

"Soon as I heard the ruckus, I turned back from the Wilson's. Figured I'd be needed here worse. After I tended to the wounded men, we buried Neverblue proper. Colonel wouldn't leave his grave, but I expect he'll find his way home in a day or two. If not, somebody'll have to fetch him."

"None of our men was killed?" Mama asked as I filled two plates of pinto beans and set them on the table. She nodded to Widow Baker. "Sit. Both of you need to eat. Get some strength back before you tell us more."

They done what she said, but mostly they moved the beans and taters around on their plates. I pulled a chair over to listen. "Silas and Homer was wounded, but not mortal. Only one man was killed," Widow Baker finally said. "A revenuer. That's when the fightin' stopped and they carried him off the mountain."

Fear squeezed my chest. "Which one?"

"Vincent," Papa said. "The only decent one in the bunch. He tried to stop them others and one of 'em put a bullet in his back. I seen it myself. One of our moonshiners'll get the blame for sure and certain."

"No! No! Why, Lord? The only good one." I stood tipping my chair. A sob caught in my throat. Widow Baker stood, moved over to me and pulled me close.

"He won't be forgotten for the good he done," she said. "When the air clears and the funeralizing's past, you got to let his widow know what he done for you, for Willie, and for us. He was an outsider, yet he took it upon hisself to look after us. He seen us as folks who was doing the best we knowed how in this old world."

Willie reached up and took my hand. "For certain I'm beholden to him. I'll go with ya."

Papa turned toward Willie like he was just now seeing he was there. Willie dropped my hand and cowered like he expected a thrashing. He scooted to the end of the bench. My stomach lurched and I held my breath.

Papa pushed hisself up from the table. He was weak-kneed and about give out. Mama rushed over. She turned her shoulder toward him and his hand pressed upon her to steady hisself.

"You ain't to carry the blame for what happened," he said at last. My breath rushed out of me. Was this my Papa talking? "I expect they broke old Tippeytoes, and he told 'em where to find us," he continued. "All of us was took by surprise. Even . . . even Neverblue. The only good thing out of all this is they never found the whiskey we'd already hid in them caves. We've got a right smart back in there, and we'll find us other places to set up our operations again. Mark my word."

Papa took on a coughing spell after his long talk and he sank back onto the bench. He dropped his head as his body shook with a terrible hacking. Widow Baker pulled a bottle out of her doctor's bag. She poured him a big spoonful. He swallowed it without any fussing, surely another miracle. Perhaps she was no longer a witch to him, but a friend who had helped bury our Neverblue. With all our troubles fallen upon us, we had much to be thankful for.

Later that night, Papa returned to his spiteful ways. Back from his trip to the privy and headed to bed, he knocked a bundle of pennyroyal to the floor. All my plants I'd gathered and hung from the rafters was dried and ready for toting to Foggy Mountain, only I'd not got there yet. A mess of dried leaves had scattered in every direction. "Hattie Mae! Get rid of them weeds or I'm a fixin' to do it myself. You hear me?"

"Yes, Papa. First thing come morning."

He thumped his way to bed grumbling as he went.

CHAPTER THIRTY

Gypsies Again

Willie slept in Jim's bed, and Widow Baker took Granny's. Our doctor friend planned to stay on a spell and I was much relieved. Early the next morning Willie left us, and returned home to his Ma even though he was not his spry self. He refused my urging to rest another day with us.

As promised, I gathered the dried plants with Widow Baker's help and we filled two gunny sacks while Papa retired to the front porch. Loe and Jewel followed him and hollered into the woods for our grieving hound, but Colonel never showed hisself.

• • •

After two days passed without a hint of more trouble, Papa limped his way into the woods. He carried the last few pieces of fatback to convince Colonel to leave Neverblue's grave. Then he and his hound dog would head up to the mines. Papa aimed to let Mr. Harper know his whiskey was in a safe place and he'd get it to him as soon as he was able.

Widow Baker left us and climbed back up to the Wilsons since she'd never made it to their place.

I kissed Mama on her cheek, picked up my sacks and headed to the Pharmacy in town. Maybe I'd even have enough money to spare Vincent's widow some of my coins.

•   •   •

Turned out coming to town was a pure waste of my time. The hours Widow Baker had spent tromping up near Red Bird Mission gathering thornapple, belladonna, and bloodroot, not to mention me tyin' each bundle and stringin' 'em up plus weeks of drying . . .

•   •   •

A few lonesome coins clinked inside my pocket. I stomped out of the Smith Brothers Apothecary and slammed their green door. The milky white glass with raised green letters, shuttered in protest. A ball of fire rose inside me until I feared it would bust open. I stomped down the wooden steps and planted my bare feet on the dusty street. Sun had not yet warmed the dirt on this cool, fall day.

Come winter would I have to wrap my feet in rags? I grieved for them fancy shoes at the commissary, the shiny black ones with buckles. Even though they wasn't made for trapsin' all over these hills, my heart was set on 'em just the same. I fussed at myself. How could I think I'd ever wear such shoes? They was no count to a mountain girl like me. I'd live in these hollers 'til the day I died without shoes, without readin' books of my chosin', without learning the ways of folks who weren't my kin, without any money in my . . .

I whirled around and faced the store. Them Smith brothers in white coats had cheated me as shore as my name was Hattie Mae. "Take our offer or peddle your weeds elsewhere," the hefty one said while he glared over his wire rim glasses. The skinny one with a monstrous mustache folded his arms and nodded toward his brother. "You heard him."

What was I to do? No other place wanted my dried bundles. They could be poison in the wrong hands, or a relief from pain in skilled ones. Maybe Widow Baker was right. A doctor woman could mix her own medicine. Better'n any apothecary.

A good size rock found its way into my fist. I griped my fingers around its rough edges, tossed it up in the air and caught it again and again. I eyed the fancy glass and considered its colors shattered into a million tiny pieces. I sighed. The rock slipped from my hand and thudded onto the road. "You sorry men ain't nothin' but cheats!" Scrapper meowed in agreement.

I scooped him up in my arms and nuzzled my face close to his. "We got to head home before Papa gets there. He's bound to get all fractious iffen I'm seeing to these weeds instead of doing my chores."

No sooner had these words left me then the earth rumbled makin' my feet and legs quiver. I looked up to the sky. . . It was a clear fall day without one cloud.

The noise growed louder. The merchants and customers poured out of the stores along Main Street and looked toward the racket. Scrapper wiggled out of my arms and vanished.

While everyone waited and watched, the jumble turned into braying mules, neighing horses, slapping of reins, yelling men, and creaking wheels. The first gypsy house rolled into sight. Then another. Some was much like the one I'd seen last year with Granny. Mixed in between the houses was a few wagons, cows, and men on horseback. The line kept coming. The merchants, as well as their customers, ran inside the stores, slammed the doors. Some folks peeked out the winders.

A handful of young'uns eyed the gypsies along with me. It was a wondrous sight. Ever woman wore bright red skirts and red scarves tied around their necks and red head coverings. The sun shined off of their gold bracelets, necklaces and earrings. My eyes could hardly take it all in. The men wore mostly black pants, boots and big hats. They also wore gold around their necks and hanging from their ears.

The caravan slowed to a crawl, but made no sign of stopping. I moved closer to one of the wagons and walked alongside it. A weathered old man with a red bandana around his neck and a ring of gold in one ear looked down at me.

"Watch your toes there, Missy!"

I danced away. "Where didcha come from and where ya going?"

"From West Virginia. Headed down to Mississippi. Got to make it in time."

"Time for what?"

"Our Queen has died. Gypsies from all over the country is gathering to pay their respects. Thousands upon thousands is bound to be there."

"You got a Queen?"

"We did. Now she's gone and not old neither."

I stumbled, but righted myself and caught back up with the wagon. "How'd she die?"

"Slipped out of this world and into the next during childbirth. Took her baby girl along too, 'fore it took a breath."

"What was the woman's name?"

"Queen Mitchell. Never gonna be another'n like her."

The driver of the wagon had fallen behind while we talked. I stepped back while he clicked his teeth and urged his mules to pick up their pace.

A pretty house rolled along next, painted yellow with red trim. A hefty man with a beard rode up high on the seat. He lifted his black hat and smiled. "Climb up here beside me, pretty lady, and we'll see some sights from these hills clear to Mississippi and beyond. No telling where we might go."

The house kept rolling while I stood rooted to the ground. The man turned around on his seat and waved. "Catch a ride with one of us if you've a mind to. Name's Henry. Look me up. I'm a man of my word."

I raised my hand and waved. He kept looking back while he moved forward. Was this my chance I'd been waiting and hoping for? The money I'd managed to earn this morning was a pitiful amount, not nearly enough to strike out on my own. Maybe these gypsies coming through while I was here to see it all happening was a sign. Granny said to pay attention to . . . Granny. She'd also declared iffen them gypsies offered to take me away from these hollers, I must find a better way. "Drat," I said to Henry and the folks trailing out of town. I kicked at the dusty road before I continued on my way.

I grumbled as I went. "Now what? Them gypsies is gone. My dried weeds ain't no count. I ain't ever in my lifetime on this earth gonna have enough money to leave these hollers. Even Preacher Sam took off for Tennessee with Bird Man. Left me without so much as a fare thee well when they had declared they'd take me along." I turned around to watch the last gypsy leave Foggy Mountain.

•   •   •

Then a house on wheels turned around. It passed a line of travelers who hollered and waved their arms at the driver, but it kept coming towards me. The yellow house, Henry holdin' the reins, rolled closer. He pulled up by my side and lifted his hat in greeting. His long black hair steaked with white hung in a tangled mess. He grinned down at me.

"You never answered where you're headed. Can you speak your name? I'd sure enjoy your company if you'd ride beside me to the edge of town. Then you can jump off and be on your way if you've a mind to. I'll not try to stop you. Promise." He raised his right hand.

"Name's Hattie Mae." I squinted up at him. "My feet could use a rest from traipsing about for certain." Besides, what would it hurt to learn more about these gypsies? The urge to know about faraway places bubbled up and there was no stopping it. I buried Granny's warning deep inside myself and shut the door. Then I give him my hand and he pulled me up to sit beside him.

CHAPTER THIRTY-ONE

Choosing

Henry turned his house around once again as the long string of gypsies passed us by. Most of 'em waved and smiled as they went. One man hollered, "Woo hoo! Look who's got himself a woman! A pretty thing, too!"

"Pay no attention to him," Henry said. He laughed as his large rough hands snapped the reins. Elmer's jealous is all. We both lost our wives a while back. Flu epidemic. Yes sir. A man's no good all alone." The stink of Henry's dirty hair took my breath. A sour taste rose in my throat and stayed there like a knot. The mules seemed in no hurry, and the string of gypsies was soon way ahead of us.

We swayed along in silence. The end of town was in sight. I took a gander at this man. His clothes was slick with dirt. Not to mention he stunk worse than Elsie Lampert. Henry's face was pockmarked and as wrinkled as dried up leather. I must've been blind not to see his intentions. He was an old man lookin' for a young wife. "I'll be on my way. You ain't nothin' to me but a stranger."

"Whoa!" He jerked up on the reins and stopped his mules. He turned and looked at me. "Don't you hanker to see faraway places? Meet all kinds of different folks?"

"Cer . . . Certainly."

"Thought so. Now's your chance. Besides we'd have plenty of time to get acquainted." Henry grinned, clicked his teeth and urged his beasts onward. "I predict you'll be thanking your lucky stars I came along when I did." I never answered him. Granny appeared in my mind as clear as if she'd never died. *"This ain't the way, child. This ain't the way."*

I pushed her words away. Maybe it wouldn't hurt nothin' to ride along a little further. Maybe past the edge of town. That's all. Besides, I hankered to learn more about these gypsies.

As we bounced along, Henry's tongue loosened. Soon I knowed all about the Gypsy Queen birthing a baby girl who never drawed a breath. And the gypsy women traveling to Mississippi wearing red 'cause they was in mourning. But I didn't learn scarcely anythin' about Henry 'cept his first name. No, that weren't all. He was set on getting' hisself a wife, and a young one to give him children.

"I aim to see places clear across this country, even the ocean one day," he said as his little house swayed behind us. "Stick with me and you can too."

Was this my chance like he said? Could it be as easy as riding away with Henry and this band of gypsies? More of Granny's words come to me unbidden. *Consider what you'll be leavin' behind.* Mama. And most of all, Willie. My heart thumped faster until I could not breathe. I tried to reason with myself. Me and Willie hadn't made any promises to each other. He was my best friend, but here lately he had become more. If I left, would grief overtake him? Would I wander the earth searching for someone to fill the big hole in my heart?

Jolted by the rough road, I gripped the wagon seat. Reckon I was lost in my thoughts when Henry reached over and clamped his rough hand onto mine. I jerked away coming close to toppling over and onto the creaking wheel.

"Stop and let me off right this very minute. I ain't going nowhere with the likes of you. I ain't fixing to get hitched to no old Gypsy man."

"Hold on. You've got no call to . . . I've not done nothing wrong. What do you expect when a pretty girl like you asks for a ride? And a friendly girl at that I might add."

"You got a way of twistin' words to your way of thinking. Stop this minute. I'm gettin' off."

His face turned red and he clinched his jaw, but he never slowed his mules. I was fixing to jump when a front wheel dropped into a hole. The two of us slid across the seat and onto the dirt road. He landed smack on top of me. I kicked and pushed and rolled away until I popped upright. He groaned as he managed to stand. We dusted ourselves off. The mules was pitchin' a fit. Their hollering and screeching filled the air as they pulled against the reins to no use. The wheel was stuck.

Henry rushed over to his animals. "Shh you're not hurt. Scared is all. Shh now. You gals is gonna be fine. You're both strong and I need your help." He rubbed their snouts and kept whispering to them. All of Henry's anger seemed to have disappeared, but I kept my distance. The mules snorted and stomped their feet.

He turned and squinted at me. "Reckon you're strong enough to help me push? You can't leave me like this." Even though the air had cooled, sweat trickled down his forehead. He pulled a dirty rag out of a back pocket and wiped his face and neck as he bent over and eyed the cause of his troubles.

"I could leave you, I ought to leave you, but I won't. Not in the fix you're in." I raised my chin and squared my shoulders.

"Let's get to it then," he said.

The two of us lifted a flat rock beside the road juttin' out of the dirt. We huffed and groaned our way over to his house sitting catawampus. We wedged the rock into the hole and against the front of the wheel. All them times I'd helped Jim clear a garden patch, throwing rocks into the woods, I'd growed muscles I didn't know I had.

·   ·   ·

Mr. Collett, a hefty man from up Four Mile Creek, come along the road leading a brown and white cow with a bell around its neck. He eyed our trouble and kept on walking without any offer of help. "Aint you ever heared of the good Samaritan?" I said in a loud voice, but he only stepped up his pace.

"Come on," Henry motioned. "Time's a wasting."

Crows cawed as they headed for their roostin' place. The trees around the bathhouse would be filled with them black shiny birds, chattering and fussing as they settled their feathers.

A cool wind picked up from the North. Clouds gathered. I wished for Mama's corncakes and a bowl of soup beans.

"Hattie!" Henry hollered. He waved his arms in the air. "Ain't you heard me? What's wrong with you? I've got to get on my way 'fore bad weather sets in."

"Humph. Serves you right for not paying attention . . . for trying to get familiar. Serves you right." I stomped over to the hole.

All of a sudden, my name rode the wind sounding far off like I was imagining such. Henry, his face bent to his mules, never raised his head.

"Hattie Mae." Closer this time. I turned toward the sound.

"Here! I'm right here!" I said.

I held my breath. Willie appeared from a curve in the road. When he seen me his eyes growed wide. His face looked like a dozen haints chased after him. He took off runnin' towards me and near about knocked me over before he could stop hisself. He grabbed my shoulders.

"Hattie," he puffed out with a whispery breath. I thumped him on his back.

"What's happened? Is it Mama? Them revenuers?"

He shook his head. I managed to steer him over to a stump beside the road, but he wouldn't sit. He cast his eyes toward the gypsy and scowled. "What are you doing with the likes of him? Dang, Hattie. Ain't you got any sense a'tall?"

"Tell me why you come for me. Now."

Willie took a deep breath and blowed it out. "Two of them company lawmen, along with Mr. Harper, is threatening your Ma. She sent me to stop you from comin' home."

"Stop me? Why? What was them men saying? Where's Papa?"

"He and three other men left this mornin' to tote your Pa's whiskey to Mr. Harper's, but I reckon whiskey ain't gonna make no never mind. Ashworth Coal Company is set on claiming the land underneath your house. Your Ma's afraid iffen you was there, you'd get square in the middle of it all and do something foolish. I promised I'd keep you away."

For a moment I had no words. One thing I knowed. I had to go home. I waved my arm toward Henry's tilted house. "Quick! Help us push!"

Willie looked at me like I spoke in tongues, but he nodded and we joined Henry. The three of us used ever muscle and ever grunt we had. The wheel caught hold. The house shook itself as it settled back onto the road.

"Much obliged," Henry said as he stuck out his hand. Willie refused it. They glared at each other.

"Take your house out of this holler and don't never come through here again. Never. You got it?" Willie said. He turned to me. "You comin' Hattie?"

"You knowed I am," I said taking his hand.

"If you go, I'll not be waiting for you," Henry said as he climbed up to his seat. He thumped his hat onto his head and gathered the reins.

"No need. I'll not be traveling nowhere with the likes of you. I got to choose a better way if I ever leave these hills. These mountains, these hollers, they got a pull on us. They is a part of us. Forever and ever. Besides, I considered what I'd be leavin' behind."

Henry shrugged and shook his head. Then he snapped the reins and hurried his mules to catch up with the gypsy travelers.

•　　•　　•

Willie had promised he'd keep me from getting' in the middle of trouble, but he knowed me and never tried. Mama needed me. Needed us. Henry takin' me away from here? Away from Willie? How could I consider such? At least I hadn't for long. Granny was right. Gypsies weren't the way.

The dusty streets of Foggy Mountain soon fell behind us. We ran down the railroad tracks all the way into Ashworth. We stopped on the swinging bridge to catch our breath. Our feet bled from running on railroad cinders, but we hadn't noticed 'til we seen blood smeared on the wood.

We could take care of our feet later, but I could no longer ignore the hitch in my side and leaned against Willie. He rubbed my back. "Something I got to tell you . . ."

I pushed away from him. "Tell me. Now."

"Them coal company guards pulled your Ma and your sisters outta your house. I witnessed it myself, but I couldn't stop 'em. They both toted rifles."

"Mr. Harper?"

"Stomping back and forth on the porch. Chewing on his cigar."

"What are they hanging around for? Papa?"

"Don't you tell your Ma I told . . ."

"What? Tell me what?"

"You Ma's gonna be madder'n a hornet at me when she sees you. She told me to keep you away. I . . . I never broke a promise 'fore now."

"Spit it out."

"It's you Mr. Harper wants to see."

CHAPTER THIRTY-TWO

In the Lion's Den

A cold rain started up and we hastened our steps. The fear of what we might find when we got there burned in my chest. What did Mr. Harper want with me?

Seemed my brother Jim was right all along. The ground underneath our house, the rights to whatever was there, had been sold to the coal company long ago and that meant they could do as they pleased with our house sittin' on top. Papa's whiskey, we thought would allow us to keep on livin' there, weren't enough. Mr. Harper had led us astray while he drank his fill, always wantin' more.

• • •

Mama and my sisters huddled together on the porch swing. Mama gripped her rolling pin in her good hand and her eyes shone like fire. Jewel had wrapped herself tight against Mama's chest. Loe was near invisible, lost in Mama's skirt. Neither sister sobbed or even whimpered.

I throwed my arms around them. "Where's Papa? Why ain't he here?"

Mama shook her head. "Ain't laid eyes on him. But it's a good thing or we'd have some dead company men and your Pa on a hangin' tree."

"First sensible thing I've heard out of your mouth." The screen door slammed behind Mr. Harper. He dusted crumbs off of his jacket. He was followed by three rough looking men toting rifles. They thumped down the porch steps and stood in the yard.

Mr. Harper walked over to us.

I stood and faced him. "Helped yourself to Mama's biscuits I see."

"Your mouth's gonna get you in a heap of trouble," He announced. "I'm here to keep you folks from being thrown out of camp. You might ought to listen."

Mama stood up and raised her rolling pin. "You and your thugs get outta here and leave us alone. None of my kin wants anything you got to offer. We'll get along just fine without any help from you."

Mr. Harper smirked at me. "Hattie's old enough to talk for herself. That right?"

"Let me go!" Willie hollered from the yard. He squirmed against a man who held him tight. "Leave 'em alone or . . . or . . ."

Mr. Harper laughed and turned his eyes on Willie. "Good thing you're here, my boy. Save me a world of time searching for you. Seems you're never in one place for long. Since you're out of a job, thanks to the revenuers, Ashworth could use someone your size. We're in need of another breaker boy. Three days a week could become five if things go as planned. You think on it."

Willie wretched hisself free and run up the porch steps. He stopped short of striking Mr. Harper with his balled-up fists. His face had turned red as a forest fire. "You . . . you leave us. Now. And . . . and I ain't never gonna be no breaker boy for nobody."

"You'll come to your senses when you and your Ma don't have anything to eat. I heard she's been sick lately. A pure shame if she . . . "

"Get out of here," Willie said between clinched teeth.

Mr. Harper raised his eyebrows and smiled. Then he turned back to Mama as he pulled a fresh cigar out of his shirt pocket. "I'm leaving. For now. I'll be back in two days. You talk to your daughter. Convince her it's the only way. You understand me?"

Mama glared at him as she pulled me close.

The company men tromped away. We hurried inside. I didn't know the particulars, but fear growed inside me. What was the only way? Was my time to leave these hills drawing neigh? Was Willie's? Mr. Harper was right about one thing. The moonshiners and their runner had been put out of business.

"Stay with your Ma," Willie said. "I'll find Mr. Sizemore. He needs to get home." He touched my cheek and looked into my eyes. His face looked tender and sad all mixed together. He left in a cold, driving rain, slipping into the woods and out of sight. I begged the Lord to go alongside him.

I followed Mama into the kitchen. The men would need some food whenever they returned. She started a fire in the stove and sent Loe to gather more coal. Jewel latched onto my legs while I peeled taters. I glanced over at Mama. "What was Mr. Harper talkin' about? The only way? What's he talkin' about . . . about me? You got to tell me."

She turned away, shook her head. "Not now. Loe don't need to hear 'bout such evil in this world when she ain't growed up yet. It'll break my heart to tell you, but I ain't got no choice. I'll tell you everything. Later. After everyone's turned in."

There was nothing I could do but wait.

•   •   •

Boots thumped up the front porch steps. Before anyone could get to the door, it was pushed open. Papa and Willie wobbled into the midst of us. They looked like they'd been drug out of a ragin' river and through bramble bushes and then mud by a wild horse. Mama rushed over. She led Papa to the fireplace, set him in a chair and wrapped a blanket around his shivering bones. No words come from his chattering teeth and Mama never pressed him to speak.

"Mr. Harper," Willie hissed as he shook his fists in the air. "He . . . he ain't fit to go on livin'."

He mumbled a string of words makin' it near impossible to catch enough of 'em to make sense. I planted myself in front of him.

"Spit it out! We got to know. What happened?"

"Mr. Harper and some of his men showed up at the cave where the moonshine was hid. He demanded a taste." Willie cast his eyes over at Papa who had his hands on his knees and his head bent. He looked like a sick old man who'd had no more fight left in him.

"Go on," I whispered into the chilled room. The fire had died to a simmer. I poked the embers and added a log.

Willie stared at the dancin' flames. "As ever one knows," he said at last. "The Sizemore whiskey's the best they is. Mr. Harper claims this last run ain't no count. He's a lying dirty dog, and his men are in the cave right now toting ever drop of whiskey to his house. We couldn't do nothin' to stop 'em." His shoulders slumped, but he clenched his jaw. My Willie had fight left in him, he'd not give up.

"What on this earth are we to do?" I asked. The only sound was the fire crackling as the flames danced higher.

"No sense in trying to think on empty stomachs," Mama said as she busied herself at the stove. "Loe, fetch me some bowls and spoons. Be quick, now."

I set a plate of steaming cornbread on the table while Mama dipped up bowls of cabbage and potato soup. I disremembered seeing or smelling anything so grand. My stomach rumbled. Loe's eyes growed wide and she licked her lips. Jewel jumped up and down and clapped her hands.

We bowed our heads. Willie took my hand in his. Then I took Mama's. She and Loe reached for Jewel's. Even Papa joined us. Mama prayed.

"Lord, as You knowed we're in a mighty fix down here. We've been throwed into a lion's den, but you're stronger than any wild animal, even Mr. Harper and his company men. Show us the way, Lord Jesus, and we will follow. Amen."

"Amens" followed all around, the cornbread was passed and we slurped our soup and stuffed our mouths full of the crusty, warm bread.

Then, out of nowhere it seemed, Widow Baker appeared with a quart jar of buttermilk. She poured Papa some first. Crumbled cornbread added to buttermilk gave him great pleasure.

"Much obliged," he said turning his face up to her. His eyes took on a softness I hadn't seen since . . . since I disremembered when.

As soon as our spoons scraped the bottom of our bowls, Mama scooped 'em up and filled 'em again. It seemed the soup was never ending, like one of them miracles in the Bible.

After supper, Papa drug hisself to bed. I watched Mama tuck him in like a little child. Seeing him near helpless instead of grousing about my sinful dress or the words of foreigners comin' into my life, caused me to hope against hope he'd changed. Was it possible?

Jewel cried out for Mama. When she left their room to tend to her, Papa throwed the covers back and managed to sit on the edge of the bed. He looked over to the doorway where I stood. His bloodshot eyes bore into mine.

"I'm needing a drink," he said. "You know where it is." Before I could do as he said, he had more to say. "You ain't goin' nowhere, Hattie Mae. Might as well get that notion outta your head. I seen what you been doing. You ain't fooling nobody. You belong here. In these hollers."

A chill ran through my body. How did Papa know I was fixin' to leave here soon? Didn't he know he was drivin' me away, makin' me more determined than ever to leave this place, to leave him?

I returned with a pint jar of liquor. His hand shook as he took it from me. I turned to go.

"Wait. There's more you got to hear."

"Some of the men got plans for Mr. Harper. He'll not be bothering nobody again, includin' you."

Me? What did Mr. Harper have to do with how I lived my life? Papa and Mama both knowed some things I didn't. Maybe I didn't want to know any particulars of such. Mr. Harper was hated by most everybody, including the miners and the moonshiners. But murder?

After a mighty swig, Papa screwed the jar lid on tight and wiped his mouth on his nightshirt. I set the liquor on the floor within his reach. Why weren't he sparing of it when there would be no more?

Seems he knowed my thoughts.

"Mr. Harper don't know where the best is hid. He'll not find it. Besides that, I got my eye on the perfect place to make another run. He ain't put me out of business yet. No siree."

"Who you figure's gonna buy it? Mr. Harper was your best customer."

"Some city slicker Big Jim knows. Since Willie warned him about the revenuers closin' in, he can't do enough to help us. Don't you fret none. Us Sizemores ain't going nowhere. That includes you. You ain't following after no gypsy or Birdman or preacher. Never. You understand me?"

"Yes sir," I whispered.

"What did you say?"

"Yes. I understand."

Did Papa know everything? I prayed to the good Lord. Show me a sign. Show me what to do. Give me a reason to hope.

As Papa settled hisself into bed, I turned away. Now I knowed why he'd not been sparing of his moonshine. He planned to make more. Lots more. And he had plans for me, too. To stay here under his thumb forever and a day. His loud snores soon rose and fell all around me.

I looked for Widow Baker who was staying the night. But she was dead to the world in Granny's bed. She commenced sucking in deep breaths and blowing out whistles. Giggles come from Loe and Jewel. Mama hushed 'em and threatened 'em with a switching iffen they weren't asleep when she returned from the privy.

She passed me and Willie sitting at the kitchen table and looked back at me. "I'll be back directly."

I followed Willie to the front porch. He was going home to check on his Ma. "I'll be back tomorrow. And I plan to stay 'til things is settled."

"What things? Don't you get caught up in no killin'."

"Ahh, Hattie. There ain't gonna be no killin'. Plans to scare him so bad he'll leave this place is all. Don't you worry none."

"I'll worry iffen I want to." I stomped my foot and glared at him. "Seems I got good reason to and most everybody but me knows what that is. Most everybody includes you. Am I right?"

He twisted his hat like a wash rag and dropped his eyes. "I . . . I wanted to tell you 'bout Mr. Harper's plans he's cooked up. Honest."

"Why didn't ya then?" I threw my hands up in the air.

"Shhh. Keep your voice down." He dropped his hat, grabbed my hands and pulled me to him. His damp shirt smelled of the woods and his unwashed body, but it was a comfort just the same. "I need to know," I whispered.

"Yes, but me and your Ma agreed it weren't my place to do such. Your Ma's gonna lay everything out for you. Then you'll understand some men is just plain evil and need to be stopped."

I pushed away from Willie's chest and raised my eyes to his. At that moment I knew I'd go anywhere with him, over the next ridge or to some faraway place.

"Never give up hope," he whispered before he took my face in his hands and softly kissed my lips. Then he disappeared into the swirling fog. Off in the woods a whippoorwill called. Somebody was gonna die before first light. "Lord," I whispered, "that ain't the kind of sign I was lookin' for."

CHAPTER THIRTY-THREE

Clara's Secret

After everyone slept, Mama brung a quilt into the front room. We huddled together on a bench in front of the fireplace. I took her hands in mine as she looked into my eyes. "You recollect seeing them fancy shoes in the commissary a while back?" she said in a whisper.

Here was the matter of them shoes comin' up again. Why was she askin' such a thing now? "For certain. I knowed I could never have 'em. I refused Mr. Emmett's offer to try 'em on. But what does . . .?"

"I had no business keepin' you ignorant of men's wickedness, but you growed up before I seen it happening. Them shoes was a way to take a girl upstairs to find the right size shoes for her feet. Or so she would be told. She was also told she could pay for them shoes a little bit at a time." Mama hugged herself and shivered. I pulled the quilt tighter around us.

"There was some new shoes in a small room," she continued. But there was also a bed and no chairs to sit upon. If a girl didn't suspect anythin' amiss, she'd sit on that bed to try on some shoes. She'd never leave that room without being violated." The night sounds turned as quiet as death.

"There's more you need to know, and I reckon now is the time." She leaned closer. "I was one of them girls years ago with a hankerin' for new shoes."

"I hadn't ever heard of . . . You didn't . . ."

"You hadn't heard because no one talked about it and they never tried such a thing again. Until now. Mr. Emmett figured enough time had passed since then."

"How did you learn he was wanting to . . ."

"Willie." Mama smiled. "Seems he was in the commissary one day when Mr. Emmett bragged about his plan to satisfy some of them young miners. Especially the ones belly-aching about their meager pay or their dangerous jobs. That's when Mr. Harper said 'no.' He had a *better* plan. Then they spotted Willie and he had to leave in a hurry."

"What about you . . . Did you?" I swallowed hard and wished I could close my ears.

"No, I refused to go upstairs. Something about the whole thing didn't set right with me. But it seems them men didn't cotton to my saying no."

I sucked in my breath and blowed it out. "What happened?"

"On my way home, one of them liquored-up men stepped out of the woods. I'd seen him in the commissary before, always lookin' at me with a crooked grin on his face. I ran, but he caught up with me. I fought him, biting and scratching and kicking, but he was stronger. Finally, he had his way with me and tossed me aside. I was hurt and ashamed and didn't want your Pa to find out who done this to me. He would've killed him and then be hung for his deed, but the man left these hollers and was never seen again. I drug myself, including you, to Widow Baker's. Your Pa had gone huntin' and I had a few days to heal. Months later your brother was borned."

"Jim. His red hair . . ."

Mama nodded. "That's why he don't look like you and your sisters."

"Does Papa . . ."

"He knows, but the anger about what happened has kept him from lovin' Jim the same as our other children. And I reckon I've always tried to protect Jim from your Pa's anger and from becoming a miner or a moonshiner. I sent him away even though it grieved my heart to do so."

I took Mama's hands in mine. "It's time I left, too."

She nodded as her tears burst forth. We sat in silence for a moment. Then she reached for her dress tail, dried her face and sighed. "There's more I got to tell you. Mr. Harper has plans for setting up some young women in a house behind the commissary, to keep the miners happy. Iffen you agree to his terms, he would leave our family alone. He wants you as well as some other young women to head it up. A whorehouse. It's why your Pa is set on killin' him."

I held my breath. My stomach twisted like a snake wound up inside me.

"Mr. Harper says a woman ready and willing would keep the men agreeable and less likely to complain about their working conditions in the mines. That's his plans, and he's comin' back for our answer."

A screech owl cried out in the woods. "Iffen he should live that long," Mama added.

She stood and pulled her toward me as she quietly sobbed. I tried to comfort her as a mother would her child. I had never felt such love and sorrow bound up together at the same time.

"Where will you go?" Mama said in a whisper. "And when?"

"Got it figured out, but if you don't know where I've gone, you won't have to tell no story to nobody, especially Papa. Once I'm gone there ain't gonna be no need for any killin'."

"I'll try my best to help him see things that way, but . . ."

"I'll keep praying, too, Mama."

Morning came with sunlight sparklin' on the windows. I threw back my cover, stood and looked outside. Dripping pine trees moved in the wind throwing showers of rain against the house. Biscuits was browning, fatback sizzled, coffee perked. My heart ached for the pleasures of an ordinary day. Such a day might never come to pass again.

Mama and Widow Baker talked low in the kitchen. Jewel and Loe slept all wrapped up in their arms and legs and I laid our quilt over 'em. There was no sign of Papa.

When I stepped inside the kitchen, Mama pressed a cup of coffee into my hands.

"Where is he?" I whispered.

"Big Jim Camp. They sent word last night to come. He and two other moonshiners. They're banding together to set up a still where Big Jim declares it'll never be found. He's obliged to us since Willie warned 'em before them revenuers swarmed in here."

"Is Papa fit enough for all this?"

"He says he is. Had a right spry step when he left."

"Why didn't you wake me?"

"Thought about it, but my heart wouldn't let me. Besides, you needed some sleep before striking out and your Pa'll be gone neigh on two days."

I threw my arms around Mama and kissed her wet cheek. "Willie's been here since before daybreak. He's on the porch," she said close to my ear.

Excitement bubbled up inside me as I ran outside and pulled Willie out of the swing.

He looked like he'd just been to a funeralizing. Mine. He scrubbed his fists over his eyes.

"You're leaving, ain't ya, Hattie?"

I nodded. "Ain't no other way."

"Where will you go?" He pulled me close and squeezed me tight.

"Red Bird Mission School. They'll take me in, and I can work for my keep and for my learning. Widow Baker's done told me all about it. Will you keep an eye on Mama and my sisters?"

"For certain. I'm gonna be keepin' an eye on you, too. I've been hired as a lookout man for Big Jim as well as a runner for them moonshiners around there. Red Bird'll be only a stones' throw from my travels."

"But iffen you was to stop by to see me, nobody can know. Papa can't find out where I am."

"Maybe Widow Baker'll swear she seen you headed to Foggy Mountain. Maybe to meet up with the gypsy man."

"What about you?"

"I didn't see nothin'. All of a sudden you up and disappeared." He snapped his fingers and his face took on a powerful sadness. "No need to play like I'm grieving, 'cause that part's real. I'll sorely miss you, Hattie. I'll mope around like you was as good as dead."

"I ain't got much choice. Do you think it'll work?"

"Shorely as yearning to hold you in my arms for the rest of my days, but for now I got to let you go."

His words warmed my heart while they laid a powerful sadness over me.

I held him at arm's length. We both tried to smile as he pulled free of my grasp and dried his face on his shirt sleeve. Then he pulled a dirty, wrinkled handkerchief from a shirt pocket and patted my wet face.

"Thank you for knowing I got to go. I can't become who I was meant to be if I stay here. I got to become Hattie Mae, whatever that might be."

He sniffed as he nodded. "You won't forget me?"

"Never. We'll hold each other in our hearts for the rest of our days. Remember what you told me? We got to have hope."

Before the sun reached into our holler, Willie left to check on his Ma. "See ya soon, Hattie," he said with a wave from the yard gate. "I'll see ya before the sun rises again. I promise."

"But I won't be here." He never answered.

CHAPTER THIRTY-FOUR

The Right Time

Me and Loe spent the rest of the day setting our house in order. Then we toted water from the creek and even laid a fire in the warm morning stove. Mama could light it whenever it was needed. We worked together without a squabble. Truly a wonder.

Along about twilight, my sisters run off to play in the front yard. I trudged up the back porch steps. My feet and my heart felt as heavy as a bucket of coal. Scrapper met me beggin' to be fed. I slipped into the kitchen. Mama looked up from washing dishes. She sucked in her breath all quivery like as she turned back to scrubbing a pot.

I filled Scrappers dish with leftovers and carried 'em to the porch. A loud purring rose up and his stub tail twitched. I ached for such an everyday pleasure that might not come again. Here. In this place.

Once inside the kitchen again, I picked up a flour-sack towel and commenced drying our ironstone plates. Even though full of spidery cracks and chipped edges, I handled each one like fine china. I thought of Mama's chicken and dumplings or green beans, corn and tomatoes from our garden served on these very plates. Remembering good times at home squeezed my heart. I stepped over to Mama. I slipped my arms around her waist and rested my head on her back.

"It's time, Mama. I got to go. Tonight. Before Mr. Harper shows up expecting me to do his bidding. Before Papa returns from settin' up his still at Big Jim's."

Mama turned, dried her hands on her apron and pulled me close. She felt warm and smelled of lye soap. Loetta and Jewel run inside with a jarful of lightning bugs. They blinked on and off lookin' like a play pretty. "Whatcha talkin' about? Huh?," Loetta said in a loud voice. Not waiting for an answer, she held up the jar. "Can ya fetch me a nail so I can poke holes in the lid? Else they gonna die 'fore morning."

Mama opened a cabinet drawer, found a nail and give it to Loe. She runned outside with Jewel on her heels. The screen door slammed behind them.

Mama sucked in a deep breath and blowed it out. "His whiskey was stolen from him," she continued. "Plain and simple. Then Mr. Harper threatened to force us out of our home, but there ain't no coal underneath us like he claimed. Nothin' but lies. I overheard him talkin' to his thugs and they was havin' a good laugh 'bout fooling us. But the worst of it all? He was trying to take you and some other girls from camp to keep the young miners satisfied. Took the moonshine and he was trying to take you. Yes, your Pa knowed all of it. You can't fault him for being angry."

Mama looked spent. She sank into a chair at the table. I brung her a dipper of water and she gulped it down.

"Such evil like this has never been done in Ashworth before.," she continued as she handed me the dipper. "It's a new scheme Mr. Harper's come up with. Miners are threatening a strike. Wages and hours cut, besides them tunnels has become more and more dangerous. We got to pray his plans'll fall apart."

"Iffen they don't, send Willie to talk to Rachel Elizabeth's Pa. He might only be a foreman, but he's an upstanding man. Even

Papa says so. He'll put a stop to the whole thing. I would bet on it."

Mama stood. "Appears to me you got everything figured out." She held me out in front of her and broke into a smile. "What else you got worked out in that head of yours?"

"Big Jim's gonna help Papa make a good size run of whiskey. They'll ship it off to somewhere in Ohio. The Sizemore family can get by without him returning to the mines. And our Jim'll show up soon. For certain. He'll bring ya some of his wages he's saved from his store clerking. Didn't he promise he would? Wait. I disremembered. There's a fifty-cent piece hidden underneath my bed. Jim give it to me last time he was here."

I was back in no time with the money. "Thank you, Lord," Mama said. She hugged the little pouch to herself and tucked it inside her dress. "This'll be a mighty help," she said. She smiled and cried at the same time.

"I ain't gonna be around for Mr. Harper to use me as he sees fit," I continued as soon as Mama settled down. "A killin' ain't the answer. No need for it. Not now."

"I'll talk to your Pa. Maybe he'll listen to me. He does love you, you know. Always trying to protect ya." Mama leaned against the kitchen table and eased down on a bench. She looked up, her eyes full. I fell to my knees and laid my head in her lap. She stroked my head.

At last, I pulled away and stood. "His kind of love smothers the life out of me. I'd be leaving even if it weren't for Mr. Harper. He pushed me to going sooner is all."

"Reckon we can thank the good Lord for that. You needed a mighty reason not to stay. You was dragging your feet on going."

Mama patted a folded flour sack laying on the table. "Willie's gonna be a runner between you and me whenever he gets a chance. I'll send ya some cornbread or biscuits along."

I chuckled at the thought of Willie carrying food to me. "If he don't eat ever bite soon as he's outta your sight."

We both had a good laugh over Willie's love for Mama's cooking.

She stood and wrapped me in her arms. "Long as Willie knows where you are, and how you're fairin', that'll have to satisfy me, but that won't keep my heart from pining for you."

Mama looked into my eyes. Her lips trembled as she tried to smile.

"Willie's a good man," I said. "He's a man of his word. You know that don'tcha?"

Mama nodded, pulled a hanky from her bosom and blowed her nose. "He's givin' me a world of comfort."

My heart swelled with pride for my kindhearted Willie. I reached for Mama's hands and held 'em in mine. "Soon as you can, send Loe for Widow Baker's tonic. It'll be a powerful help to ya."

Mama nodded. "Not only her tonic. She's coming to stay with us awhile 'til things ain't so stirred up around here. She'll put a world of fear into Mr. Harper. He calls her a witch who can cast spells, like your Pa used to do. He'll not mess with us Sizemores again."

Loetta and Jewel run back inside with their lightning bugs and set the blinking jar on an apple crate beside our bed. Mama made certain they scrubbed their feet before changing into their night clothes.

Everything was settled, as far as possible. I had to go, but I had some time yet. Mr. Harper wouldn't return until sunlight fell upon our shadowy holler two days from now. Only he weren't a man of his word. We feared he might return sooner if he took a notion.

I slipped my book out from my tow sack as my sisters jumped into bed. I sat on the edge and they gathered close with squeals and giggles. I read two stories of their choosing, but my voice come out weak with the thoughts of leaving 'em. When would I lay eyes on these two again?

I closed my book and hugged Jewel and Loe. Then I hugged Jewel again and held my arms out for Loe. She pushed me away. "You're running away, ain't ya?"

Mama rushed into the room and scooped up Jewel. "We're makin' a trip to the privy 'fore bedtime." Sometimes Jewel was dry come morning, sometimes not. My baby sister was stubborn, but Mama was determined she would learn.

I stood and Loe faced me. "Tell me!" she demanded as she stomped her foot.

"Been considering leavin' for a long time. Seems ever way I thought possible slammed shut in my face. Then after Mr. Harper paid us a visit, I had no choice. Reckon we can thank the Lord for bringing good outta a bad thing."

Loe crossed her arms across her scrawny chest. "Tell me everything. I'm old enough."

We sat back down on our bed and I laid out Mr. Harper's evil plans. I didn't hold nothing back. Her eyes growed wide and then she throwed her arms around me near about knockin' me over.

She placed herself in front of me, hands on her hips. "Don't you worry about nothing here while you're gone. I'll help take care of things and especially Mama. Just wish I could go with you."

I stood up from the bed and placed my hands on her shoulders. "Maybe one day . . . Don't give up on hope. And I ain't gone for good. I'll appear back home when you least expect it. I promise."

•　　•　　•

I waited until my sisters' breaths come deep and regular. I slipped out of bed, picked up my sack and tiptoed into the kitchen. Mama sat at the kitchen table with our family Bible open in front of her. She raised her head. "This here book says you ain't got no cause to be afraid. The good Lord promises to be with you wherever you go. Ain't that something?"

She opened her arms and I fell into them. "Yes, Mama, it's a promise to take hold of."

She patted my back and after a bit we both straightened ourselves. I swallowed the lump in my throat and willed myself not to cry.

Along with my book, the dancing ballerina dress and Granny's box of lavender dusting powder, we added one of Mama's hankies, a pouch of dried 'sang, a change of clothes and undergarments and finally leftover biscuits and sweet potatoes. Mama was keepin' the double wedding ring quilt for the day when I'd marry and have my own place. Willie hadn't asked me yet. If he took much longer, I'd have to take matters into my own hands. I had no doubts of our love for each other, but why hadn't he come to tell me goodbye like he'd promised?

Fear of another unknown growed inside me. Not of walking up to Red Bird Mission, but of the people there who might turn me away. If they did, I had no other place to go.

Mama followed me to the back porch. "You gonna say good-bye to Granny 'fore you head out?"

"For shore. I'm gonna make her proud of me one day. And you too."

"You already done that. For both of us." She reached out, smoothed my hair, touched my face. Then she pulled me to her softness. "Lord, go with this girl of mine who's become a woman 'fore I knowed what was happening."

I rushed out the back door, not looking back, or I'd lose my nerve.

•   •   •

Underneath a rising moon her grave sparkled like a queen's jewels. Soon after Granny passed, I'd dug blue, green, clear, and brown bottles from the commissary's sinkhole. I'd toted 'em up the mountain, smashed 'em against a rock outcropping, decorated her resting place even though she'd done flown to Glory Land. Sometimes I'd come to pull weeds or lay flowers at her wooden cross, but always to unburden my troubles. It seemed I shouldered a gracious plenty.

I could linger no longer. As I turned from her grave, a laurel bush rattled its leaves. My hair lifted off my neck. Was someone there? The wind sighed. It rose in the air like a living breath, skipped amongst the tall pines, tossed their heads. Seemed like they whispered secrets not of this world. Clouds snuffed out the moonlight. My shirt, once worn by my brother, fluttered in a sudden breeze. Unnatural mutterings whirled around me in the thick darkness. Had they swooped down from the trees? I sucked in my breath while them mummers, as light as a bird's feather, spun into words.

Dreams . . . torn asunder . . . never mend . . . never mend . . . never . . . mend.

Scrapper hissed as his fur stood straight up on his back. Then he shot off into the woods. Had he heard same as me? An owl hooted close by. The words disappeared. They had been as real as the damp earth beneath my feet.

"The wind playing tricks on us, Granny? Reckon you knowed it already, but I ain't giving up on my dreams. I ain't letting 'em be torn to pieces. I'm gonna read and learn from all kinds of books, maybe even how to help sick or hurt people. Iffen I got the stomach for it. Widow Baker says I do."

I hugged myself and shivered, though it was a warm night for October. Heat lightning flickered against fast-moving clouds. If Granny could hear me, see me, she'd give her blessing. Because of her, I never followed after them gypsies, but waited for the right time to come. And it did.

My body ached to touch her crippled up hands, to see the twinkle or even the testiness in her cloudy blue eyes. I missed her something fierce.

The air stopped moving, turned as still as an empty church house. The dozens of crows slept without a flutter. Nary a leaf stirred. Even the nighttime birds hushed. A faint glow throbbed deep in the woods. Not yellow or green or blue. Always changing, no eye could fix the color. Foxfire, some folks would declare, but I knowed better. A sign the little people were astirrin'. I'd never seen 'em, but I'd heard enough tales of their mischievous ways to stay clear of 'em. For certain my feet wouldn't take me near. Best let 'em be.

Scrapper brushed against my legs, and I reached down to love on him. Whatever had spooked him earlier was no matter now. He meowed and scampered off towards the footpath. The same one I'd hastened up the mountain on this night. The one that trailed back home. I picked up my sack and hefted it over my shoulder.

"Come, Scrapper. We ain't going home tonight. Maybe one day."

I turned away. Turned my back on the little people in the deep woods. On the footpath leading home. On Mama and her soothing touch, on looking after my sisters, on sleeping amongst their arms and legs throwed over me. On Willie who had become more than a friend. My heart ached for him, for the smell of the outdoors on him, for his lips soft upon mine. Even so, I would be shed of Papa whose mind was as crippled up as his gimpy leg.

I hurried toward a foreign mountain ridge where Red Bird Mission waited beyond giant hemlocks and pine. No one-room school house like in Ashworth or Arjay's camp, but a big log building with stairs to climb and long hallways inside with classrooms lined up one after another. Another building just for sleeping and yet another for eating meals together.

Widow Baker had told me all this and more, such as the words carved above their front door: *Enter to Learn. Leave to Serve.* I could hardly imagine the wonder of it all. And books?

She declared a big room at Red Bird had shelves filled with books. A whole room of 'em called a library. A library. I loved the sound of that word. A library of books.

Yet . . . Like the devil hisself whispering *impossible* in my ear, them wispy words I'd heard earlier nagged me. Dreams. Torn to bits won't never mend.

"My dreams is alive! They is livin' and breathin' dreams as certain as . . . as . . ."

"As certain as Willie watchin' over you?"

I dropped my sack, turned, ran to him and pulled him close. "You heard me? You kept your word. I knowed you would."

"Didn't I say I'd see ya before first light?" He laughed. "Heard ya? This whole mountain heard ya, maybe clear to Red Bird." He pulled away and took my hands in his.

"How far can you go with me?"

"Until I'm certain you're there safe, but rest assure I'm fixin' to show up as regular as the sun rises over these here mountains. You can count on me. I'll be there."

He hugged me to his chest. I sighed and sank into him. All my fears of the unknown lifted into the night sky and drifted away. I looked up at his face and kissed his cheek. Then he planted a kiss on my lips, not holdin' anything back. Finally, we pulled away. The clouds uncovered the moon. It was full and yellow and lighted the pathway before us.

Willie laughed. "Looky there, Hattie. Reckon your Granny'd say we've been given a good sign?"

"For shore she would." My heart had never been so full.

He picked up my sack, and we headed towards Red Bird Mission. We hastened our steps and Scrapper, his eyes like golden jewels, padded along behind us.

THE END

GLOSSARY

Bloodroot — Wildflower.org
A low growing woodland plant with fragile white flowers. Used for a traditional medicine by many American Indian tribes to treat fever and rheumatism as well as for an insect repellent. Other traditional uses were for treatment of ulcers, ringworm, and skin infections. It was, and still is, used to produce natural red, orange, and pink dyes.

Breaker Boy — Onelook.com
The coal breaking occupation was very dangerous and difficult for these young kids. The function of a coal breaker is to break coal into pieces and sort them into categories of nearly uniform size. The second function is to remove as many impurities as economically desirable and feasible. The coal was then graded based on the percent of remaining impurities. The breaker boys would work a labor intensive 10 hours a day, 6 days a week.

Breaker boys sat on wooden benches perched over chutes and conveyor belts. Some of the boys would work on top of the chutes. These boys would stop the coal by pushing their boots into the stream of coal flowing beneath them and try to pick out the impurities. Others would divert the coal into a horizontal chute where they sat to pick out the unwanted material before the coal would go to the clean coal bins.

They were forced to work without gloves so they could better handle slick materials and for better agility. The slate they were trying to remove was very sharp, so the boys would often leave with their fingers cut and bleeding. If they were caught wearing gloves, the boss would beat them.

The breaker boys would sometimes have their fingers amputated by the fast-moving belts. New breaker boys would develop blood finger tips, which could be described as red fingertips. These new workers would develop this condition because of their soft finger tips scraping over the top of coal and rock. The condition would persist until their fingers toughened enough that they wouldn't bleed anymore. The only thing that would help the problem was to urinate on the finger tips to toughen them up.

Chicory — Growappalachia.berea.edu

A blue-flowered Mediterranean plant of the daisy family, cultivated for its edible salad leaves and carrot-shaped root. • the root of the chicory plant can be roasted and ground for use as an additive to or substitute for coffee

Drift mouth

the opening to an underground mine.

Eejit — Onelook.com

Irish and Scottish slang word for stupid

Eye Winker game — Playsongs.co.uk

On "Eye winker": Point to eye.
On "Tom Tinker": Point to other eye.
On "Nose dropper": Point to nose.
On "Mouth eater": Point to mouth.
On 1st "Chin chopper": Gently move chin up and down.
On 2nd "Chin chopper": Tickle chin.

Fatback

Fatback is a cut of meat from the back of a pig that's primarily made up of fat and has a firm, white texture. It can be used in many ways to add flavor, moisture, and richness to dishes.

"Fire In the Hole" — Song by Hazel Dickens

Refers to the term used by coal miners blasting-away rock. The cry was a way to warn other miners that a dynamite triggered explosion was about to take place. Coal miners led the labor movement for workers' rights. In 1933, the efforts of a group of organized and committed miners led to the National Industrial Recovery Act which granted workers the right to form unions and bargain collectively. A folk song inspired by the movement, called *Fire In The Hole* was written by Hazel Dickens in the 1950's. Dickens grew up in the coal mining villages of West Virginia during the Depression.

You can tell them in the country, tell them in the town
Miners down in Mingo laid their shovels down we won't pull another
pillar, load another ton or lift another finger until the union we have
won
Stand up boys, let the bosses know
Turn your buckets over, turn your lanterns low
There's fire in our hearts and fire in our soul but there ain't gonna be
no fire in the hole

Gypsy Queen — National Geographic by Aric S. Queen
"If you're looking for something interesting," the security guard said, "you should go visit the Queen Gypsy's grave."
I asked who this was and he began to tell me a story that's too long to go into here. In short, when Kelly Mitchell, "Queen of the Gypsy Nation," died in 1915 while giving birth, <u>as many as 20,000 Romanis showed up for her funeral</u> in <u>Meridian, Mississippi</u>, flooding the small town to pay their last respects. My interest piqued, I drove to the <u>Rose Hill Cemetery</u>, where she is buried, and wondered how I was going to find her grave among the thousands there.

Turns out, it'd be pretty easy. The headstone festooned with beads and trinkets — the one with a faded photo of Kelly leaning against it, and strewn with loose change, flowers, a tube of mascara, pens, costume jewelry, and other offerings meant to entice the Queen to provide answers to their problems from beyond the grave — kind of stood out from the crowd.

Hoe cakes

Hoe cakes are like pancakes only made with cornmeal, and usually fried in bacon grease in an iron skillet.

Kettle bottoms
Uky.edu

A term used by miners to describe isolated rock masses in mine roofs, which tend to be semicircular when viewed from below and have a rounded or flat bottom like a kettle. Most kettlebottoms are in-place fossil tree stumps. More precisely, they are fossilized, hollowed-out tree stumps filled with sediment. Kettlebottoms are tubular, conical, or bell-shaped.

Melungeons —
Tennessee Encyclopedia

A major phenomenon in the Melungeon lore of the 1990s and early 2000s was a revival of interest in the possible Portuguese lineage of the group, spurred in large part by college administrator Brent Kennedy's 1994 book *The Melungeons: The Resurrection of a Proud People*. In this work, Kennedy gleans from his own family's history a theory that the Melungeons originated as Islamic Moors from Iberia, Turkey, and North Africa, refugees from Spanish and English activities on the Atlantic coast in the 1500s. Masking themselves as Christian Portuguese to avoid possible ethnic cleansing, he asserts, the men made their way inland, intermarried to a limited degree with Native Americans, and created the people called Melungeons. Research into this theory is centered at the University of Virginia branch campus at Wise, and the Muslim-Portuguese account can be found at several Web sites devoted to Melungeons.

Mumblety-peg — En.wikipedia.org

Generally played between two people, with a pocketknife.
In one common version of the game, two opponents stand opposite one another with their feet shoulder-width apart. The first player then takes the knife and throws it to "stick" in the

ground as near his own foot as possible. The second player then repeats the process. Whichever player "sticks" the knife closest to his own foot wins the game.

If a player "sticks" the knife in his own foot, he wins the game by default, although few players find this option appealing because of the possibility of bodily harm.

Nippers

(sometimes called "trappers") had to open and close the heavy wooden door that sealed the mine. This was usually a boy's first job inside the mine itself and it was a difficult and dangerous one. The mine door had to remain tightly closed, except when coal cars came in and out.

Pack Horse Librarians — The Smithsonian Magazine

Women (and, some men), who were paid $28. per month, rode up into the Kentucky mountains, their saddlebags stuffed with books, doling out reading material to isolated rural people. The Great Depression had plunged the nation into poverty, and Kentucky—a poor state made even poorer by a paralyzed national economy—was among the hardest hit.

The Pack Horse Library initiative, which sent books deep into Appalachia, was one of the New Deal's most unique plans. The project, as implemented by the Works Progress Administration (WPA), distributed reading material to the people who lived in the craggy, 10,000-square-mile portion of eastern Kentucky. The state already trailed its neighbors in electricity and highways. And during the Depression, food, education and economic opportunity were even scarcer for Appalachians.

Paw-Paw — Appalachianhistory.net

Call it the American Custard Apple or the West Virginia Banana, but it's neither apple nor banana. It's the Paw-paw (*Asimina* **trilob**), the largest native fruit of North America, and it grows throughout Appalachia. Mature pawpaw trees produce fruits 2" wide by 10" long, which turn from green, to yellow, and then black as they ripen in the fall.

Where, oh where is pretty little Susie?
Where, oh where is pretty little Susie?
Where, oh where is pretty little Susie?
Way down yonder in the paw-paw patch.
Come on, boys [or girls, or kids], let's go find her,
Come on, boys, let's go find her,
Come on, boys, let's go find her,
Way down yonder in the paw-paw patch.
Pickin' up paw-paws, puttin' 'em in her pockets,
Pickin' up paw-paws, puttin' 'em in her pockets,
Pickin' up paw-paws, puttin' 'em in her pockets,
Way down yonder in the paw-paw patch.
—The Paw Paw Patch, Traditional folk song

Paw-paw fruits are rich in minerals such as magnesium, copper, zinc, iron, manganese, potassium, and phosphorus. The fruit also contains abundant concentrations of Vitamin C, proteins, and their derivative amino acids. The Peterson Field Guide mentions that the seeds, along with being an emetic, have narcotic properties

Red Bird Mission school—
***The Story of Red Bird Mission* by Roberta Schaeffer**
Bell County, KY, established in 1921. "**Enter to learn, leave to serve**" by the Evangelical Church at the head-waters of the Red Bird River. The river was named for Chief Red Bird of the Cherokee Indian Tribe. The land was made available by the Knuckles family of Beverly, Kentucky in Bell County. Timber and labor for building were contributed by local citizens.

Beginning with teachers eager to educate unschooled children, Red Bird Mission has continued to respond to the needs of the community with resources, aid, and love.

Scrip

From the National Park Service — nps.gov

Scrip filled an important need in a place during a time when cash was scarce. In the early 1900s, the strange little coins became a symbol of coal companies' control over miners.

Privately issued currency, usually in the form of metal tokens, redeemable only at the company store. Miners could "draw scrip" from the company in the form of tokens, essentially receiving credit against future wages.

Coal companies did not risk much by offering credit to its miners. There was no need for extensive credit checks on the miners as in today's world, since the company had the power to withhold any money due it. Any credit it issued thorough scrip was recorded through the store sales or redemption of the scrip for goods. It is this dark side of scrip, which Tennessee Ernie Ford sang about in "Sixteen Tons"- "I owe my soul to the company store." It is a widely held belief that all coal miners had to draw their pay in this artificial money, and then turn it in for overpriced goods at the company store which made them have to borrow more from their next payday to cover their present living expenses. Companies ordered the brass or nickel tokens by the thousands. They usually had the company's name embossed around the edge and a value, from 1 cent to 1 dollar, in the center. The companies sometimes ordered tokens with a little flair. It could be scalloped edges or a hexagonal coin instead of a round one. Some scrip had a hole punched in the center that might be the shape of a star or triangle or even the first letter of the company name.

Tag Board

Miners marked their entrance to the mine by placing a numbered tag over a hook. By doing this everyone knew which miners where down in the mine.

Tippey Toes Golightly — A moonshiner known for evading the government revenuers

Tow Sack — Al overview

A "tow sack" in Appalachia refers to a large burlap sack, essentially the same as a "gunny sack," used for carrying various items; it's a common term in the region's dialect, where "tow" signifies the rough fabric typically used to make such sacks.

Vinegar Pie*

Much like a chess pie, this recipe calls for vinegar instead of lemon juice, since lemons were hard to come by in Appalachia.

Whippoorwill — Blindpigandtheacorn.com

When a single woman heard her first whippoorwill in springtime, she must have felt her heart lurch in panic, for if the bird did not call again, she would remain single for a year. If the birdsong continued, she was fated to remain single unless she had been quick-thinking and made a wish upon hearing the first call. If she kept that wish secret, she ultimately would be married.

Whippoorwills singing near a house were an omen of death, or at least of bad luck.

***Vinegar Pie Recipe**

Shape pie crust in a 9" pie pan, edges crimped. Prick bottom & sides with fork. Prebake 7 minutes at 425 degrees

4 large eggs

1& ½ cups sugar

¼ cup butter, melted

1 & ½ tablespoons white vinegar

1 tsp vanilla

In large bowl, combine eggs, sugar, vinegar & vanilla. Whisk well to combine. Pour into prebaked pie shell. Bake 30-40 minutes. Cool to room temperature & refrigerate.

Modern day options: Serve with Whipped cream on top sprinkled with nutmeg.

ABOUT THE AUTHOR

Photo courtesy of Peter Finger

Carol Guthrie Heilman, a coal-miner's daughter from Eastern Kentucky, married a farmer's son, her high school sweetheart, over sixty years ago. They enjoy playing cards, taking long walks, and eating Southern food with friends in Charleston, South Carolina. They are blessed with a son and a daughter, as well as with their spouses and three grandsons.

Carol, an accomplished author, began writing family stories for newspapers and magazines. Her mother once said, "We don't have any secrets anymore." Her daddy carried her first published stories around in his pockets. He shared them with anyone who would listen.

Carol is a recipient of two Carrie McCray Awards for writing excellence.

NOTE FROM CAROL GUTHRIE HEILMAN

Word-of-mouth is crucial for any author to succeed. If you enjoyed *Becoming Hattie Mae,* please leave a review online—anywhere you are able. Even if it's just a sentence or two. It would make all the difference and would be very much appreciated.

Thanks!
Carol Guthrie Heilman

www.ingramcontent.com/pod-product-compliance
Lightning Source LLC
Chambersburg PA
CBHW030608170726
48283CB00002B/515